JUSTIN RISHEL

Every Dying Hour

Book 1 of the Martin Aubrey Series

First published by Rowdy Dog Press 2020

First edition

ISBN: 978-1-7344133-1-1

This book was professionally typeset on Reedsy.
Find out more at reedsy.com

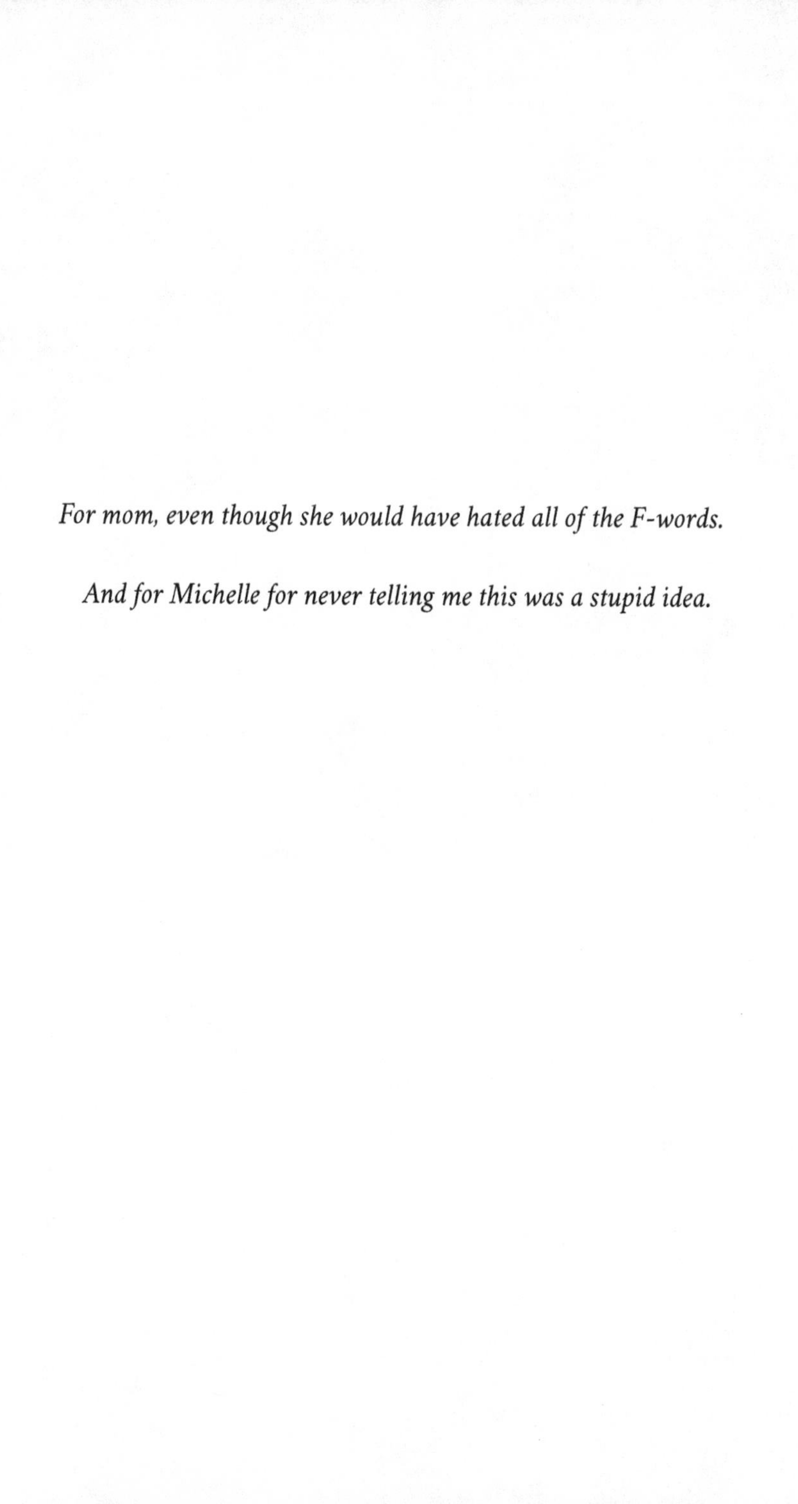

For mom, even though she would have hated all of the F-words.

And for Michelle for never telling me this was a stupid idea.

Contents

Prologue—The Speech

"We are not special, you and I. None of us here are. We may think so, looking back on our accomplishments and our contributions, but truly there is nothing special about us. We're all just animals.

"Let's take a closer look at that. No matter how advanced we as a species become, there are four things that should serve as constant reminders to you that we are essentially *animals.* Animals beholden to four biological forces beyond our control. We must do these four things if we as individuals and if we as a species want to survive. We have to eat, we have to drink, we have to procreate, and... we have to sleep.

"We can enhance ourselves, sure. Or manipulate our environment, certainly, to curtail or to minimize the need to do these four fundamental, animal tasks. We can create foodstuffs from biological materials without the aid of plant or animal. But we must *eat.* We can pull drinkable water from the air or the ocean, but we must *drink.* We can fertilize eggs in a tube, but to live on as a species we must *reproduce.* And we can medicate ourselves to prolong our waking hours, but eventually *sleep* will come to claim us. Or death will.

"Simply put, no matter how far we've come in our evolutionary process, no matter how high we ascend in our technological superiority over other animals, no matter what else we've managed to shed that connects us to the animal world, those four forces remain fundamental to our species: *eat, drink, mate, sleep.*

"At least, that's the way it used to be. Today, we place a massive layer between us and the animals. Between us in this room and the savage beasts out there. Today, I announce a scientific breakthrough. Today, you'll leave here a more advanced species. Today, you'll leave here with one of your most basic needs eliminated. Gone for good. Your lives are about to change forever.

"Ladies and gentlemen, we call it Zentransa. Our new drug, one small pill a day, is going to eliminate the need for… *sleep…* forever. A third of our existence, once lost to sleep, has been clawed back. Forever. Now, just begin imagining the possibilities of what you could do with that time. One third of your life safely back in your possession.

"Welcome to the new world, everyone."

—James Sarazin, Chairman and CEO of Ventana, Inc. (excerpt from a speech to shareholders announcing the release of Zentransa, December 2023)

1

The Martyr

April 2, 2043

Ralph Jacobsen knew he'd be famous in a few hours. Or, rather, he'd be infamous. But, famous or infamous, he'd be in jail. And he was fine with that.

He sat in the front seat of a white sedan listening to the rain come down in buckets outside, pounding on the windshield and roof of the car. In spite of the unseasonable chill in the springtime air, he sweated through his clothes. He tried to focus on his breathing, tried to calm himself, but his chest was constricted by the heavy, explosives-laden vest under his suit.

The longer he sat waiting, the worse he felt.

The explosives in the vest were fake. He knew that the blocks and wiring were made to look authentic, but they were heavy and tight. His sweating intensified; his heart rate quickened. Feeling the first signs of panic, he closed his eyes and forced himself to think about why he was doing all this.

He spoke the mantra his friends had taught him. "I am change. I am change. I am the mechanism with which change begins. I am not a cog in a wheel. I am a wrench thrown headlong into the wheel, forcing change. I am change. I am change."

Repeating the mantra helped calm his nerves and strengthen his resolve. Thinking clearer now, he allowed himself a moment to think back to how this pivotal phase in his life began.

Nineteen months ago, he had a desk on the megatrend trading floor of LRN Capital Management as a middling analyst. He was grossly overpaid and his future looked bright.

The beginning of the end came one morning when federal agents stormed his office. They burst through the double doors in front of the lobby and made a beeline for the C-suite. They sped past Ralph's desk in their cheap suits. They'd come to arrest the top brass of LRN for defrauding shareholders and customers of billions of dollars.

He'd deflated that day, feeling betrayed. The leaders he had trusted for so long were corrupt.

The next day, it got worse.

That board of directors gathered LRN's three hundred and fifty employees near the wall of windows on the fortieth floor. An old white man introduced himself as the chairman of the board and stood on a banker's box to address everyone. The end was the only part of the man's speech that Ralph remembered.

"In short, ladies and gentlemen, this company is insolvent. You are no longer employed here. There will be no severance. The paycheck you received two weeks ago was your last one. I'm sorry to have to tell you this, but you have an hour to clear out your desks and vacate the property."

Silence first, then murmurs of disbelief traveled around the room.

"Are we at least getting our bonuses?" asked a man behind Ralph. His name was Charlie something, late fifties. He was on the verge of sobbing.

Ralph, still shell-shocked from the news, would never forget the response from the chairman.

"Look, I'll be surprised if the lights stay on long enough for you to pack your shit."

Ralph wasted no time getting on the job hunt. At his first interview, he waited in the well-appointed contemporary lobby of a company called Gracie Partners Financial. After watching four of his former coworkers walk out of their own interviews, his heart sank. There were over three hundred megatrend traders pounding the pavement all over the city and they were looking for work in all the same places. Soon after he started his job search, Ralph learned that the best and brightest from LRN had found jobs within a few days. Ralph was not one of the best or the brightest.

At home, things turned from bad to ugly. As Ralph's job search went from days to weeks, his wife, Holly, grew impatient. Her firm was going as strong as ever. Her leaders weren't thieves.

Holly demanded they keep up appearances, so they still spent money as if nothing had changed. The money ran out faster than either one of them thought it would.

With no money and no employment benefits, Ralph had no way to get Zentransa. No Z pill meant he had to start sleeping. It took several days for sleep to come back to him in full force once he was off Z, but once it did, once sleep was part of his life again, it was as if it had never left.

He slept hard those first few nights. He would rise every

morning from their sparsely used four-poster bed wondering if hibernating bears had as much trouble waking. Every morning, his body felt like stone and his mind was a fog.

Then there were the nightmares. Quitting Zentransa cold turkey came with risks, chief among them were terribly vivid, violent, frightening dreams during those first few weeks of sleep. His body and brain seemed to be in a race to catch up on thirteen years of no sleep.

Soon, he slept six to eight hours a night while the rest of his social class was working, playing, and living. Once he became a sleeper, his friends completely abandoned him. His wife barely acknowledged his presence at home. He had become an untouchable, an outcast, a pariah.

Weeks after he started sleeping, Holly tired of him completely. He had to move out. He found low rent housing on the south side of the city, found a part-time job as a barista for twelve hours a day and a second job as a security guard for a total of fourteen to sixteen hours a day—about the most sleepers could work—and lived hand to mouth. He tried to keep his spirits up, but he knew deep down there was no way he could catch back up to the 'zoners' of the world—those who could afford to live a sleepless life.

In the front seat of the car, he closed his eyes and listened to the rain. The vest under his clothes was so tight he thought he might lose circulation in his extremities. The sharp-edged blocks and the wires and cabling felt like some kind of geometric octopus trying to strangle the life out of him. He wiggled his toes inside the brown shoes he was given and touched each thumb to the tips of his fingers just to make sure he still could.

Ralph was no expert on bombs, but the fake one he wore

felt real as hell.

"It is very important that it looks real," the man had said in his strangely accented voice. "For the cameras. They need to know vee mean beezness. That's the only vay they vill listen."

About a year ago, this phase of his life, of which he was very proud, began. During a casual night of internet surfing, he stumbled onto a forum called Plebianiacs, where the unofficial motto was "Sleep is human, sleep is freedom." Here he found a group of individuals not unlike himself with whom he could share his frustrations. This was a place where people listened and comforted each other, letting others like Ralph know they weren't alone.

An entire world suffered, a world with which he had been completely out of touch until he was catapulted into it.

He'd stay on the Plebianiacs forum for hours at a time chatting, commenting, and posting. His specialty was lewd doctored photos of the super-rich. He would fall asleep on his keyboard almost every night, rushing out the door on his way to work the next morning.

It was on Plebianiacs where he met Oscar. Like Ralph, he was another wayward sleeper serving the world of zoners. After their initial meeting online, Oscar would direct chat with Ralph regularly. His situation was almost identical to Ralph's—good job, good pay, lay-offs, no Z, then destitution. They hit it off immediately.

Ralph and Oscar started meeting in person after a few weeks of online chatting. First, beers. Then, they'd meet some of Oscar's friends. It wasn't long before Oscar was bringing Ralph to parties. Or they seemed like parties at first. Beers, booze, music. But every party ended up with the group just sitting around talking. The music would get turned off and someone would just start talking to the group. Usually, it was one of a handful of people, who Ralph assumed were like the elders of the group. They'd talk about things that made very real, visceral sense to Ralph.

"There is a wedge in our society," one of the elders said one night. Ralph and about twelve other men and women had met in a cramped dingy apartment that belonged to one of the elders. "A wedge that is being hammered into the cracks of our social classes and civilization itself. We can call it greed, that would be simple. But, we're all greedy. Greed is natural. Greed by itself is manageable in the natural world. The wedge I'm talking about is unnatural."

After a few parties, Ralph raised his hand and asked a question. The room was filled with smoke. Yellow light from single bulb lamps cut through the haze. Ralph sat on a futon next to three others and the woman leading the talk, Samantha, in a green flannel shirt and khaki pants, leaned against a window sill.

"Many years ago," Ralph said, "it was the communists that talked about these sorts of things. Are we communists?"

This got some nods and murmurs from around the room. It appeared others had similar thoughts.

Samantha, one of the more charismatic of the elders, gave a swift answer. "No, no, no." She waved her hands as if deflecting the notion out of her space. "The communists were fighting against the idea of capitalism in general. They were opposed to the idea of earning money, they were opposed to the idea of material possession. They wanted everyone to have the same stuff, at the same time, in the same way. Nice on paper," Samantha shrugged, "but you can't deny that part of the human spirit always wants a little more than they have right now."

"So… what are we, then?" Ralph asked.

"We're warriors of balance. The natural balance." She pounded her fist in her hand for emphasis. Every eye and every ear were tuned in to her message. "You think I don't want a beautiful house? You think I don't want a villa in the south of France and fly there in my private jet? Of course, I do. If you deny that, you're a liar… or you're stupid." Ralph leaned forward on the futon and nodded along with the rest of the group. "We're not communists. We seek natural order. We want to be able to fight the good fight and come out on the other side bloodied and battered, having earned what's earnable. We can't even do that. We can't do that in a world where Z exists."

All the talks came back to this—the Z pill.

Samantha went on. "It's pretty simple. Z removed sleep, one of the most natural parts of our existence. Before it was taken away, sleep was an equalizer—everyone had to do it. Zentransa allowed people to work longer hours, earn more money, buy more things, live better lives. Everything sounds great, right? Except that the demand for Z was so high from the outset that most people couldn't afford it. The divide between us and them grew and grew until our sole purpose became serving them and their sole purpose became being served."

"Doctors on Z cured cancer," he posited. It was true, it was almost impossible to die from cancer in 2043, even if you were poor. But Samantha looked at him like he just made a bad joke.

"I'm talking about a disease that affects ninety-five percent of the population. A disease delivered by a pill. And we're rotting from it."

Pretty soon Ralph attended sessions every night. After a few months, he led the talks himself. One night after a session, Oscar pulled him aside.

"Good session tonight."

"Thanks. I really felt inspired," Ralph said.

"That's good. Really good," said Oscar. "Listen, do you want to do more?"

Ralph squinted, puzzled.

"I mean more. Do you want to be part of real change?"

"I thought I was. Isn't that what this is about?" asked Ralph.

"This is important. No doubt about it," said Oscar. "You're supporting people and letting them know it's okay to be who they are and… yeah. It's very good."

"So…"

"So, do you want to do more? I can't say much else, but if I get your commitment now, you can be a part of something special."

Ralph didn't hesitate. "Yes, absolutely."

Oscar smiled. "Good. I'll be in touch. And look… don't mention this to anyone."

Nothing happened for a few days. Almost a week had gone by and Ralph began to assume that whatever this real change was, it either wasn't going to happen or it wasn't going to include him.

Finally, after a week of attending his usual sessions, Oscar pulled him aside. He was told to go to an apartment across town. There he met with Oscar, Samantha, and a few of the more vocal members from their evening sessions. It was here that he learned about One Front for the People and the real cause: work to subvert the popularity, manufacture, and distribution of the Z pill. The way they explained it to him, the only way to effect change in this world was to hit society over the head and make them pay attention. One Front for the People had been operating in the shadows for years, largely unknown by the general public. That was all about to change.

In the car, heart pounding against his ribs, Ralph checked the time on the watch the man with the accent had given him. 3:56 a.m. Four minutes to go. At precisely 4:00 a.m. he was to get out of his car and walk into a specific building. He was to walk inside and pass security, ignoring their questions or demands to stop. Once past security, he was to stand in the short hallway with the elevators.

"Just stand in the hallvay," the man with the accent told him. "Face the front of the building. For ven the cameras come."

Ralph inhaled as deep as the vest would allow. He closed his eyes and did his best to be mindful of the moment and his purpose.

He continued his mantra aloud. "I am change. I am change. I am the mechanism with which change begins."

His missions for One Front for the People started with defacing Zentransa ads and billboards. Once the others saw that he was committed and passionate for the cause, he graduated to sabotage. Ralph slashed tires on shipping trucks, used butyric acid to contaminate shipping containers of raw materials, disabled landing gear on cargo planes—anything to disrupt the flow of Z.

One night after an intense mission where millions of dollars' worth of Z was set ablaze, Ralph went home to his tiny apartment. With an aching body from the night's work and on the precipice of sleep, he received a call.

A man with a strange accent told Ralph he had been selected

for a special mission.

"Are Oscar and Samantha involved? Do they know about this?" he asked. Ralph sat in the dark, perched on the edge of his mattress. His stomach turned with excitement, pride, and fear all mixed into an impossible emotional cocktail.

The man explained they knew there was a mission but didn't know the details. Ralph was forbidden to discuss it with them.

"The only way to protect them is to keep them in the dark," the strange voice said. "You are special. Not like the others. Soon, you vill prove it to everyone.

"Are you ready?" the man asked. "Are you ready to really do something? Not just run around in the dark like a wandal, but actually make a deefference?"

"I am ready," Ralph said into the phone. "What do I need to do?"

He was given an address, told to come alone. To speak to no one on the way. Ralph did as he was told. It was in a dirty apartment that looked like it hadn't been properly lived in for ages that he was presented with the phony bomb vest, a brown suit, an analog watch, and keys to a car. He was also given detailed instructions.

That was twenty-four hours ago. Now, Ralph sat in a car that wasn't his, wearing a suit that didn't fit, fighting to breathe against the suffocating tightness of a fake bomb vest strapped to him.

He would end up in prison and it was likely he'd never get out. But he was committed to the cause. He was committed to change. If this was the only way, so be it.

Ralph checked the watch again—white hands ticking around a black face. 4:00 a.m.

The rain continued.

He reached with a trembling hand and opened the car door. He made his way into the crowded sidewalk. It was busy. Morning rush. He pushed his way into the flow of foot traffic, avoiding eye contact with the other pedestrians. He walked fast and stared at the ground, thinking it would make him stay focused. He was so focused that he barely noticed as he bumped into people on his way to the doors at the front of the building.

Cries of, "What the hell, pal!" and "Watch yourself!" followed him. He ignored their shouts. They had no idea of the profound changes he was about to jumpstart. They wouldn't understand even if he tried to explain it to them.

He pushed through the front door and heard the guard say something as soon as he cleared the door. Facial recognition sensors must have pinged on him as an unknown person.

"Good morning, sir. How can I..." the security guard started to say.

The guards' station was to Ralph's right—a circular desk with a high counter. Two guards sat behind it. A bank of turnstiles stood directly ahead of him. It looked to Ralph like a dozen turnstiles, each waist-high, requiring biometric scans to access entry.

"Sir, you have to check in. Sir?" the guard shouted at Ralph. "Sir, I'm going to have to ask you to stop."

He ignored the guard's plea but hearing it only made Ralph more purposeful. He ran, awkwardly climbing over the clear glass gates of the turnstile where others were queueing for entry. The vest was heavy and stiff, sticking to his sweaty skin. He made a beeline for the short hallway. With no gun, the security guard could do little more than shout.

Ralph turned as he entered the hallway with the elevators.

He walked backward a few paces then tore open his shirt to reveal the vest and fake bomb.

"Shit." The guard stopped dead. "Jones, call the cops. Now. Do it."

Ralph stopped and started repeating the mantra.

"I am change. I am change. I am the mechanism with which change begins. I am not a cog in a wheel. I am a wrench thrown headlong into the wheel, forcing change. I am change. I am change."

He was supposed to repeat the mantra until the news cameras arrived on site. Then, he could deliver the real message—the one he carefully crafted while being fitted with the vest. The man with the accent told him the message was perfect; Ralph agreed.

As he reached the end of the mantra, he felt reassured and emboldened. Like he had reached the end of a long race. So far, he had done what he was supposed to do and now he just had to keep repeating the lines. He started again.

"I am change. I am change. I am the mechanism with which…"

He looked down when he noticed the fake cellphone in the middle of his fake bomb buzz to life. It flashed and vibrated. He raised his head, felt his eyes go wide.

Ralph reached out a hand toward the guard. "Hel…"

The blast tore through the lower third of the building and out into the busy street. It cut down scores of pedestrians on the sidewalk, tossing bodies like winnowed chaff. Smoke, dust, and flying debris filled the air.

Ralph Jacobsen's body was instantly vaporized by the explosion.

Less than twenty-four hours later, One Front for the

People claimed credit for the bombing and with Ralph's help, OFP experienced a rebirth as a legitimate domestic terror organization.

2

Martin Aubrey

April 2, 2043

Martin Aubrey sat in the front seat of his car staring at the door of a three-story brownstone townhouse. From half a block away, he watched the door as if it were about to make a run for it—bursting out of the frame, ripping from its hinges, and wobbling down the well-lit street leaving a wake of splinters and paint behind. The door's escape typified the way Aubrey felt at the moment.

He was at the tail end of an investigation into insurance fraud. This was his life now. Hunting down rich people who were stealing from other rich people. Helping people who had mountains of money make the pile a little higher. Higher and higher. Not that he advocated theft. Aubrey had always prided himself on doing the right thing. As with most things, however, time and context changed the shape of right and wrong.

The situation that brought him to this point in his life was not so dissimilar. The end of a career he'd loved, one that gave him meaning, over a decision made in the heat of the moment; one that cost lives. His dream was to serve out his career as an officer in the Metropolitan Police Department and it was shattered in a few seconds, eighteen months ago. He understood it could have been worse. He understood very well that he was lucky to leave the police department with his freedom intact.

Aubrey glared at the door for a while longer even though he knew exactly where the alleged fraudster was inside. Weeks ago, he had hidden long-range biologics sensors and short range cerebral-signature trackers to watch the house from nearby street lights, bushes, and trees. They were all very small—only a trained eye would notice the small plastic discs and cubes as anything other than random objects to be ignored.

Aubrey's company, OWG Insurance Incorporated, made sure he had the best equipment available.

With one quick glance down at his tablet, he could see exactly where his man was in the house. The screen showed a transparent, blackish gray 3D rendering of the house. Moving around inside it were four human shapes, glowing red. Floating beside each were small numbers displaying vitals: pulse rate, blood pressure, body temp, and respiration rate. The biologics sensors were useful but limited. They could show him where humans were from very far off, but they could not identify an individual as anything other than a warm-blooded human being. He needed the short range cerebral-signature trackers to make sure he had his man.

On the third floor of the brownstone, a faint green-yellow halo flickered around the head and neck of a bright red human shape. It was too far for the tracker to get a crisp reading, but Aubrey knew who he was looking at.

Cerebral-signatures had been used for years for personal identity security. An individual's brain activity had been understood to be more unique than fingerprints since the early 2020s. The brain was a collection of a hundred billion neurons linked by a hundred billion connections through which hundreds of billions of electrical signals traveled. These signals bounce around the brain from one neuron to another controlling everything from fight and flight to basic bodily functions. Which specific neurons fired, in which specific order, and down which specific connection was totally unique from person to person.

Naturally, brain activity varied based on stimuli, but the aggregate of that activity created readable, predictable patterns. Powerful computers could take those patterns and create a profile for an individual called a cerebral-signature. A person's cerebral-signature, or CS, could be uploaded to a device programmed to detect it and cleanly identify them.

Aubrey had done just that. His company had provided him with the CS he needed and he uploaded it to the devices now hidden in the bushes. OWG required all prospective customers to have their brains scanned and their CSs were saved to a secure company database. Most companies did this. It was an easy and secure way to do business, but it also provided people like Aubrey an easy way to track and catch those that need to be tracked and caught.

Aubrey caught his reflection in the car's visor mirror. His brown hair had started developing streaks of gray since he left the police. He guessed it was from stress of starting a new career, but he was also pushing forty. Under a two-day beard, his pale complexion told him it had been too long since he'd had a vacation to somewhere warm and sunny. How long had it been? Years, was as close he could come to an accurate guess.

He rolled his shoulders inside his suit. It wasn't his preferred outfit, but he needed to look the part if he found himself entering an office building that morning.

Aubrey checked the time—3:00 a.m.

"Better hurry, Tim. Going to be late for work," Aubrey muttered to no one, still staring at the door.

Three to four in the morning had been rush hour for most of the corporate world since the invention of the Z pill. With no need for employees to go home and sleep, companies quickly figured out that they could start demanding more and more time from their employees. Eventually, the pill became another perk similar to health insurance or stock options. Much like health insurance, the pill was difficult for most to afford without an employer subsidizing it.

With what amounted to a twenty-four-hour work day, local businesses in and around the city center had to stay open all day, every day to survive. Most hourly employees were not paid enough to afford the pill and did not have benefits. So, business owners hired shift workers, ensuring round the clock staffing.

A few moments after 3:00 a.m., Tim's bright red, haloed figure moved downstairs. He made a brief stop near where the other three red bodies were gathered then quickly headed toward the door.

Tim Frass came out of the front door of the brownstone just as it began raining. He quickened his pace, ducked under a raised briefcase and slid into his car parked on the curb. As Tim began to drive off, Aubrey tapped an icon on the console to start his car. After a few more taps on more icons the car jolted forward. On the console, the icons dropped to the lower half of the screen and the top half turned into a live video feed of the back of Tim's car. Yellow circles highlighted the license plate and other unique features of Tim's car.

"Maintain a minimum following distance of fifty meters. Do not exceed a following distance of one hundred meters," Aubrey said.

"Understood. Following distance threshold set to between fifty and one hundred meters," a female voice replied from the car's speakers. Aubrey's company granted him a significant budget for upgrades to his company car and he spent all of it.

Tim's case was pretty straightforward in Aubrey's opinion. One night, four thieves broke into Tim's house while he and his family were on vacation and removed eight valuable paintings. The Frass family arrived home, found their home violated, and called the police. The next day, Tim filed an insurance claim with OWG for the stolen art.

When the case came to Aubrey's attention, OWG had raised a red flag and placed all payments to Mr. Frass on hold. OWG had been notified by a local art broker that prior to the robbery, Tim was trying to sell his eight paintings, hence the red flag. When Aubrey began investigating, he found two more reasons to be suspicious: the Frass vacation, it turned out, was planned at the last minute and Tim had recently come under significant financial strain due to some unwise investing. All Aubrey needed was something to connect Tim to the thieves and the case could be turned over to the police.

They made their way through the light traffic of the residential streets. As he turned onto a highway leading into the city, another voice came over the car's speakers.

"You are approaching city limits. All vehicles are required

to relinquish control to the Metropolitan Traffic System. To proceed, enter your destination. You are approaching city limits. All vehicles..."

A soft male voice repeated the command until Aubrey keyed in the address of Tim's office building.

"Destination confirmed. Estimated time to arrival is twelve minutes."

Exiting the suburbs north of the city, New Aberdeen rose like a gleaming plateau of glass and metal. It jutted out of the hectares of luxury apartment buildings and carefully manicured parks. Aubrey was impressed every time he entered from this side of the city. He was impressed by its size, but also what it represented: efficiency, opulence, and commercial prowess.

New Aberdeen rested between Baltimore and Philadelphia, tucked in behind Interstate 95 at the head of the Chesapeake. Rising from the ashes of the chaos that erupted after the 2020 elections, the city was a product of the flight of wealth from neighboring metropolises—Baltimore, Philadelphia, Washington D.C. Riots, widespread violence, and panic left the old cities in ruins. Corporations fled first and the populous followed soon after.

The city was the brainchild of a wealthy industrialist from Philadelphia who brought together the smartest, richest, and most ambitious people in the northeast United States. Together, they planned and built the now sprawling and prosperous city with the intent of making it the most advanced and efficient cities in the world. Although always in a state of growth and development, New Aberdeen grew to two-thirds its current size in just ten years using cutting-edge building technologies and astronomical influxes of cash from its investors.

New Aberdeen boasted the only fully artificially intelligent traffic system in the country, round the clock simulated daylight hours, surveillance and security measures everywhere, and one of the best equipped first-responder services in the world.

Fully incorporated as a city of Maryland in 2032, New Aberdeen was a haven for the rich and a beacon of hope for the under classes. That beacon, however, was just that, a moving guidepost showing what could be, but likely never would be.

Had Aubrey entered the city from the south, up from the old suburbs of Baltimore, he would have felt much different. He knew that side of the city well from his former life as a cop. Most of his work, back then, involved the south side where the poorest of the poor lived in the most basic housing allowable by law; housing erected in great haste as the flood of people flocked to New Aberdeen from the burnt-out husks of once great cities.

Entering from the south side gave a different feeling altogether. The city didn't appear as a symbol of wealth and power or an architectural marvel complementing its surroundings. It appeared as a joke, mocking those for whom the city meant toil and served as a constant reminder of their unbreakable status.

"Thirty seconds before we're put under MTS control move in to a following distance of twenty-five meters," Aubrey said. He wanted to make sure they were close when they switched over to the Metro Traffic System.

The car confirmed the commands and they drifted on past the last exit before entering the city. As instructed, Aubrey's car sped up to get closer to Tim's. They passed into city limits and as they did a small light on Aubrey's dash went from green to orange and the car's operating system said, "Autonomous control deactivated. You are now in the Metropolitan Traffic System."

Instantly, cars converged to within inches of each other. Eight lanes of traffic moved like a solid mass, a noiseless river of color and reflected sunlight. The river flowed into the city and diverged into branches which broke from the main stream at perfectly timed moments. Intersections did not really exist in the city because there was no stopping and starting. Everyone just flowed in and around. One moment the cars were packed in tight with no room for light between them, the next a space would open up and a car would be pushed up and aside to its destination. All of this occurred with no accidents, not even dings or scratches. The river of traffic never stopped. There was no need for traffic lights. The MTS knew where everyone was going and preplanned the best, most efficient possible way to get them there, positioning each car precisely based on its plan.

Aubrey watched Tim's car on the console screen and was surprised when it took a right turn two blocks sooner than expected. The MTS was too efficient to deviate like this, he thought. Tim was making a detour.

Aubrey looked at his tablet and pulled up a log of Tim's daily activities over the last few days. Nothing stood out until he noticed a stop Tim made one morning seven days ago.

"Add a stop to our route. Jabil's Coffee. Second Avenue, between 28th and 29th street, request parking on the far side of the street," Aubrey told the car.

"I have confirmed our route adjustment with the Metropolitan Traffic System," the car replied.

Across the street from Jabil's, Aubrey flipped a switch on a micro drone and held it out the window. The rain was coming down heavier now, pelting his hand with large drops. The drone was a risk in such a downpour, but Aubrey had to take the chance. After a second, its tiny rotors began to spin, slicing through the heavy rain as it took flight to a height of around twelve feet above the car.

Aubrey manipulated a digital joystick on the tablet and spun the drone so its camera pointed at Jabil's. He tapped a few more buttons to feed the camera's video through the bio-sensor readouts on the tablet. With two frames side-by-side, he could see the live feed on the left and the bio-readout on the right.

Aubrey scanned the coffee shop until he found Tim at a small table in the back. Jabil's was busy, but Aubrey had clear line of sight on Tim. By the looks of the bio-readout, Tim was stressed—heart rate, blood pressure, and respirations were all elevated. They peaked as a man in a gray suit took a seat across from Tim.

Other than the fact that they both wore a suit, their appearances could not have been more different. The man in gray had salt-and-pepper close-cropped hair and a well-groomed beard. His head was rectangular and his skin well-tanned. He had the bearing of someone who rarely laughed or smiled. Tim on the other hand, looked sloppy with unkempt, shaggy hair. He was thin, but not on purpose. He looked as if he'd never lifted anything heavier than his mobile phone.

They spoke for two and a half minutes, according to the timer on the live feed. On video, their conversation was mundane and pleasant, but the bio-sensors told a different story. Toward the end of the conversation, Tim's vitals were elevated. He was anxious, stressed, and probably frightened.

On more than just a hunch, Aubrey began a physical profile matching sequence. He ran a section of the live video through a program that read physical characteristics like height and weight in addition to nonverbal communication like posture, gait, and head and hand gestures. The technology was bleeding edge and, as far as he knew, his company was one of the first to use it. He then ran a section of the security footage from Tim's house the night it was robbed. He told the program to find a match for the man in gray with one of the four people in the security footage. The program worked for a minute and then told Aubrey that the profile of the man in gray was a 79.8 percent match for one of the men in the security footage. In comparison, the man in gray was less than a ten percent match to the other three people in the security footage. It was not definitive, but close enough to fill the gaps in Frass's case.

Tim hired this man and his crew to steal his art. Then, he would pay them a portion of the insurance payout. Finally, after some time had passed, the hired thieves could sell the paintings and collect the money again. It would be a double payday versus Tim just selling the artwork legitimately, which he had tried and failed to do anyway. Based on his reaction during the conversation with the man in gray, Tim had broken the news that payment was on hold. The man in gray did not appear to be happy.

After the man in gray left, Tim remained seated. Aubrey guessed he was trying to calm himself. It seemed to have worked. His vitals began to normalize.

Tim walked out of Jabil's and got into his car, which seamlessly entered the flow of traffic and continued downstream toward his office. Aubrey followed close behind.

Tim made it to his office without taking any more detours. At the curb, near the front entrance of his company's building, he got out of his car which dutifully pulled away toward the parking structure where it would wait until summoned at close to midnight when Tim was ready to leave work.

Aubrey instructed his car to pull ahead a half block and park on the same side of the street as Tim's building. In the car, Aubrey began preparing his report on Tim Frass. In it, he included his observations from that morning, emphasizing the meeting with the man in gray and a recommendation that OWG's fraud artificial intelligence program perform a search for the man in gray. The search would take some time. The AI system would search every law enforcement database it had access to, which was basically all of them; every social media site on the web and dark web; and every public photo on the internet. The AI could work fast, scanning a few million photos a second, but it still took time.

In addition to the report, Aubrey elevated Tim Frass's case from yellow to orange. OWG's fraud investigation department color-coded cases: green, yellow, orange, and red. Green meant you were not on their radar, red meant you were going to prison. The meeting with the man in gray convinced Aubrey that Tim was basically guilty, but not completely guilty. Not yet at least. Orange status would simply amp up the already abundant resources they gave Aubrey and dedicate more AI time to the case.

After hitting send on the tablet and confirming the Frass case's new orange status, Aubrey looked out his car window at the busy throng of pedestrians making their way to work. The rain continued to pour, and it was now the height of rush hour, 4:00 a.m. The city's lights made it feel like a bright dusk.

As he watched the people rushing around, his eyes caught a man who looked out of place. He had on a rumpled, brown, over-sized suit, which wasn't so odd in itself, but he looked both nervous and steadfast as if he were walking into a life or death job interview. His head was bent low against the rain and with a determined face, he pushed his way through the crowd. It didn't seem to Aubrey that he noticed anyone else on the sidewalk at all, even though many were bumping into him.

Aubrey watched the stranger go by then stared ahead, letting his mind wander, as it often did these days. He couldn't help but look back on the last eighteen months and wonder where he would be if he had done things different. He pondered the impact of his choices. Choices that would alter everything. Choices that took an innocent life and a guilty one, forcing him to leave the job that gave his life purpose.

He had wanted to be in law enforcement as long as he could remember. Protecting kids from bullies, then beating up those bullies had been a hobby of his since he was a small child. That had been the common thread in Aubrey's life—keep bad people from hurting good people. Every major decision in his life—joining the Marines straight out of high school, studying criminal law in college, becoming a cop—had been influenced by one powerful objective: protect the good people from the bad people. Naturally, the line between good and bad would blur eventually. Now, sitting in his car contemplating his current state, he wasn't sure on which side of the line he belonged.

Did one short series of choices made in the heat of a stressful moment determine good or bad, he thought. Shouldn't good or bad be decided on many more decisions than that? This question made him think of how many people he, himself, had arrested who were first-time offenders. How many of those had ended up in prison after one bad choice?

The prison, also known as the Keep—owing to its castle-like appearance—and its system of justice could, at the very least, be fair on some level, he thought. There, that mysterious group of executioners would decide on behalf of the rest of humanity who was good or bad; who deserved freedom, life, or death. People could, and often did, argue the morality of the prison system, but they could not argue with its efficiency.

Aubrey's problem, and what would bring his world crashing down, was his decision to deliver his own form of efficient justice.

He wrestled with these ideas and was about to instruct his car to take him home when he felt the world rock violently forward.

Airbags deployed, slamming into his face and chest. His seatbelt strained against his shoulder and waist as his body flew forward. His lungs emptied. His head was dazed, and for a moment his body hung limply against the taut seat belt. Pinging and pounding sounds came as his car was pelted by thousands of pieces of something from outside.

While he tried to right himself and get his bearings, he managed a glance outside and saw the air filled with smoke and dust. Through the thick plume surrounding his car, he saw the crowds of people lying limp on the ground.

3

The Blast

His vision blurred. Aubrey fumbled with the buckle of the seatbelt. The ballistic glass windows on his company car had kept him relatively unharmed as concrete, glass, and steel debris had flown through the air at many times the speed of sound. But the force of being propelled forward against the seat belts and the impact of the airbags against his skull left him dazed for several moments. The pressure in his ears was so great, he could have been under a hundred feet of water. His neck and shoulders were battered and twisted. He squeezed his eyes shut and shook his head while clutching his forehead with one hand and tried to manipulate the seatbelt latch with the other. He coughed and gagged on the gas released by the deployed airbags until he finally heard the click of his seatbelt unbuckling.

He pushed the deflated airbags out of his face and opened the car door and stepped out.

Coughing and squinting through the dusty, smoky air he surveyed the scene. The people on the sidewalk had been blown down like weeds in a stiff wind. Then, almost in unison, the hundreds of rush hour pedestrians around him rose and bolted away from the source of the blast, somewhere to his left.

Hands and arms scrambled and clawed to move toward safety. Aubrey's door was nearly taken off its hinges by the rushing crowd and he had to lean back against his car to avoid being swept away in the human current rolling by. The tide of fleeing men and women spilled into the street, filtering through parked cars.

He coughed into his tie, which he held up like a makeshift respirator, half choking on the residual gas from the airbags and half choking on the dusty particulates in the air outside. Still gathering himself and making up his mind about what to do next, he waited for the bulk of the panic-stricken to pass. The flow of people thinned but still numbered in the dozens. Cries, wails, and shouts now reached his ears from the direction of the explosion.

In that moment, he felt he had been transported to a scene on another world. The rain had stopped suddenly as if the blast had disrupted the mechanism producing the downpour. Smoke plumes poured from the epicenter.

His senses were assaulted by the aftermath. His nose filled with the acrid scent of burning plastic mixed with the earthy smell of pulverized concrete. Dust lay on his tongue—sharp and coppery. Car horns and security alarms mixed with screams of pain and cries for help to create a blur of sound swirling around him. The wind blew in his direction and he felt the heat from the fires. Hunks of concrete littered the tops of vehicles and the ground.

He watched the survivors rush past him with ashen faces. Their expressions were frozen in looks of shock and fear.

Tears and blood blazed dark trails through layers of filth on their cheeks. At their feet, dust, blood, and rain mixed on the sidewalk to create a reddish-brown slurry. Many of them slipped and slid in their haste to flee.

Out of nowhere, a woman stumbled face first into his chest. He caught her by the shoulders and helped her steady herself, but she didn't seem to notice him—she ran as soon as she got her feet back under her.

Through the bouncing heads of the fleeing crowd, he caught glimpses of the epicenter of the blast. The building Tim Frass had entered moments ago had been torn apart. At least the bottom dozen floors had been ripped from the front of the building like a giant ice cream spoon had scooped them away. What was left were ragged cross-sections of the inner floors. Sparks flew from the edges of floors and ceilings, water spurted from pipes, rebar and pieces of the skeletal substructure jutted out into open air. Fires burned in random spots on the upper floors.

And people. People were lying everywhere inside the building.

If possible, the area just outside the front of Frass's building looked worse than the inside. No one fled. Precious little moved at all. Amidst vast amounts of rubble, several figures writhed and flailed. Their moans filled the air with the animalistic cries of the mortally wounded.

Without thinking, Aubrey moved toward the blast center.

He made his way, fighting the tide of people. Eventually, the retreating crowd thinned, revealing the unlucky ones lying here and there.

The carnage was like a bell curve of death—concentrated in the middle at the blast's epicenter and gradually dissipating further out.

Hunched and coughing, he walked on. The first victim he passed was a woman. The back of her red pant suit was covered in a thin layer of gray dust. Fresh blood poured from a head wound, matting her short brown hair. He knelt beside her head and extended two fingers to the side of her neck.

No pulse.

He moved ten feet further down the sidewalk to another body curled into the fetal position against a car parked on the curb.

It was a man in a suit like Aubrey's. His bald head was slick with sweat and grime. A porkpie hat lay next to him.

Again, Aubrey felt for a pulse. Present, but weak. The man shuddered. Aubrey rolled him onto his back and saw it—a piece of rebar, two-feet long, protruding from the man's abdomen. Blood pooled under him, mixing and congealing in the dust. The pool spread rapidly. There would be no saving this man, but there could be others not so far gone.

With gut-wrenching guilt, Aubrey moved to the next victim.

A woman lay a few feet away on the other side of the sidewalk. Her black and blue face screwed up in agony and she wailed. Her hands clutched her right thigh which bled profusely from under black medical scrubs, the blood running in a wide rivulet across the concrete toward Aubrey.

"I'm bleeding out," she cried as he knelt beside her.

Aubrey gently padded around her upper thigh until he felt the tear in the fabric. He pulled it away to reveal the wound. A gaping slice in the back of her upper thigh, a few inches below her buttocks. It belched blood. Whatever had cut her, metal or glass, it had done so rather cleanly. The cut was straight and smooth on its edges.

He loosened his tie, careful to keep the half-Windsor intact, and removed it. Sliding it over the foot of the woman's injured leg, he looked at her and said, "This is going to hurt."

She closed her eyes tight and nodded gravely.

He worked the loop up her calf, over the knee, and past the wound. He maneuvered the tie above the gash, then cinched the knot down until it was an inch away from her leg. He gave the knot of the tie a single twist. The woman moaned.

From his pocket, Aubrey removed a pen. He pushed the end of the pen through the twist. He rotated the pen several times, watching the tourniquet bite deeper into the woman's leg. She cried desperately, then went quiet.

When the blood flow had been staunched to his satisfaction, he looked back at the woman's face again.

Her eyes were closed and her face placid. A quick check of her pulse told Aubrey she was still alive. She'd merely fainted.

He folded the elastic waistband of her pants over several times until it securely held the end of the pen in place. Then, he dipped a finger in the blood that had collected under her leg. With his bloody finger, he wrote a crimson T on her forehead to alert the medical-drones and paramedics she'd been fitted with a tourniquet. He looked at his watch and, with the same bloody finger, wrote 0407 next to the T.

The time didn't register until Aubrey was at the head of the next victim, a twenty-something male in gym shorts and a t-shirt. The blast had gone off around 4:03 or 4:04 a.m. Four minutes had passed since his car jolted and the world outside it fell apart.

Time had a bad habit of slowing to a crawl in moments like these.

A quick examination of the young man in gym clothes told

Aubrey there was little hope. A third of the poor man's skull had been caved in by falling debris and his pulse was barely perceptible under Aubrey's fingertips.

Over the next fifteen minutes, Aubrey repeated this pattern. A short glance around at one point told him other concerned citizens were doing the same. In the stretch of sidewalk in front of him, he continued, stopping to assess each of the wounded he passed. If he could do anything to help, he helped. If he could not help, if they were too far gone or dead already, he moved on and found someone he could help.

The dust was still thick, nowhere close to settling. It stung his eyes and lungs in equal measure like millions of tiny glass shards. Each breath brought pain. He'd give anything for a real respirator. Several times, feeling near asphyxiation, he stopped to breathe through the lapel of his blazer.

As he stumbled through the chaos, he heard the whoosh and flutter of the medical-drones overhead. As a former cop, he had plenty of experience with them and knew that right now they were scanning the area, assessing damage. The refrigerator-sized drones would report back to the hospital with recommended personnel dispatches and equipment.

Additionally, the Metropolitan Traffic System would shuffle every car on the city's roads so first responders would have two lanes to themselves from their point of origin to the scene.

He glanced to his left and watched a large open space begin to form in the road. It grew as cars were moved off this block and new cars prevented from entering.

Aubrey moved closer to the front of the target building. As he neared the epicenter, the severity of wounds and the number of dead grew steadily. Aubrey's limbs worked robotically—years served in warzones around the globe created deep-seated muscle memory and now it bubbled to the surface.

He applied more tourniquets, compressed free bleeders, and administered CPR. For those that couldn't be helped, he'd instruct an able bystander to hold a hand for comfort. The drones had already triaged the crowd to some extent, and he knew the EMTs would come prepared. He also knew that the first few minutes of a trauma victim's treatment could decide their fate, so he tried to work fast.

Twenty minutes after the blast buzz-sawed through the building and sidewalk, Aubrey reached the section of sidewalk nearest the epicenter. The haze here was thick. Barely penetrable. Just as the air cleared for a second or two, the building burped a cloud of the ash- and powder-laden atmosphere. Black and white smoke streamed constantly from inside. The noise of the chaos had settled. Cries for help and wails of pain remained, but the cacophony of the screaming, panicked pedestrians fleeing for their lives had disappeared. The new silence sent a chill across his skin.

Aubrey stood for a moment trying to make sense of what he was looking at. In front of the wounded building, he stared at what he took for a pile of debris laying in a long, rounded berm. It had been pushed up against the cars on the curb and crested them in places, spilling onto their roofs and beyond into the street.

The debris pile was covered in the same gray dust as everything else. As he examined it, sounds emitted from it. Muffled moans. The pile moved in spots, undulating like an enormous pupa ready to emerge from its pupal case.

What he had taken for debris was actually people. People mixed in with dust, rock, concrete, and metal to form a grotesque aggregate. Pedestrians were swept into the wall of cars by the force of the blast—piled atop one another like grains of sand in a desert's ocean of dunes.

Aubrey ran to the end of the pile nearest him. He started high up, thinking bodies at the top would be easiest to remove first. So much dust and debris were mixed with the bodies and all painted with the same gray tone that flesh was indistinguishable from stone and steel.

He shouted for help while reaching into the pile. He swept dust off something at eye level that looked near human-like. A limb. Soft under his fingers. He traced it to its end and found fingers. The nails had been painted a dark color, visible through the dust. He reached up for what he assumed was the shoulder, gripped it and the wrist and pulled.

The body began falling from the pile. With one hand he carefully cradled her neck, while letting the rest of her slide to the ground. With her came chunks of concrete and a plume of dust. He dragged the woman ten feet away from the pile and went back. At least a dozen more survivors appeared around him to assist. A routine began. Aubrey or another nameless survivor would remove a body from the pile and drag it away, where other survivors would apply what first-aid they could.

He had no idea how long it lasted. After what felt like hours, but must have only been minutes, the pile was shortened by more than half. Victims lay in a neat line, shoulder to shoulder, down the filthy, detritus-covered sidewalk.

His arms ached. His lungs burned with irritation. His hands were cracked, bloodied, and caked in filth. After three more trips to the pile, Aubrey and the other survivors made it disappear. He doubled over in exhaustion, breathing long and slow through his lapel. His breaths rattled in his chest and his throat was on fire.

Sirens blared from the street to signal the first responders arriving at the scene. Aubrey stood and counted a dozen emergency vehicles of all types near him. He could hear what must be another dozen in the distance on their way. The new arrivals jumped from their vehicles in clean blue, black, and red uniforms carrying a variety of bags, tools, and equipment. Stretchers shot from the back of the open ambulances. Soon, the scene was crowded with paramedics, firemen, and police. Large box drones touched down in open areas on the street, opening their rear doors to accept patients for quick flights back to the hospital.

Aubrey assisted for a short time, but soon realized he was getting in the way more than he was helping. He found the hood of a nearby car and sat for several minutes.

He sat there, thinking and breathing, pondering how quickly someone's life could permanently change. About how all these people who survived would think about their lives as two halves: one before the blast, one after the blast.

He thought about how fragile the human psyche was and what a few seconds of terror would do to some people and the chain reaction it would have. Survivor today, alcoholic abusive husband tomorrow creating junkie kids, perpetuating more crime. Or survivor today, religious faithful tomorrow, motivational speaker, faith healer, up-lifter of souls…

"Aubrey?"

He looked up.

"Shit, yeah it is you. You were here for this? This close?"

The uniformed cop was immediately recognizable as someone Aubrey knew from his time on the police force.

Mentally searching for the man's name, Aubrey said, "I was

in a car down the block. Came to lend a hand. How're you doing, Davenport?"

Aubrey recalled his name easily once he remembered that he and some others on the force used to tease the officer about being named after a couch.

"Yeah, well good on you, man. I'm sure you helped a lot." Davenport looked closer at Aubrey. A shocked expression crossed the young man's face. "Listen, you need anything?"

Aubrey shook his head and after looking at his hands, at the grime and blood all over them, he guessed his face was just as bad.

"OK. Look, the medics and drones have the survivors pretty well in hand," Davenport said. "Just sit and rest as long as you need to, but pretty soon we'll need…"

At that moment, he remembered the man in the oversize suit. Aubrey saw him moments before the blast. The man was distracted and anxious. He hadn't noticed the other pedestrians bumping into him.

Aubrey sprang to his feet. "I saw him, Davenport. I saw the guy who did this."

4

Ralph's Surprise

Martin Aubrey sat on the edge of a desk belonging to Detective Aaron Lewis. The detective was off getting coffee. He and Lewis were old friends, going way back to their rookie year on the force. Where Aubrey took life and work too seriously at times, Lewis seemed to never take it seriously enough. His was an easy-going, blasé style, but he was smart enough to stay out of trouble and always did right by his team.

Not much had changed in the eighteen months since Aubrey had his own desk at the Metropolitan Police Headquarters. Around thirty desks sat crammed into a space with barely room enough to walk between them. Phones buzzed and chimed constantly and desktops were covered in tablets, monitors, and files. The décor had not changed at all; everything was still old, faded, and peeling. Seeing it all again—the fake tile floors, chipped laminated desks, and squeaky faux leather chairs with covers slowly curling away from their cushions—made him wish to be back more than ever. This was, after all, the first time he'd been back to the police station since his abrupt departure a year and a half ago.

Like most jobs these days, the officers and detectives here worked nearly twenty hours a day. Snack wrappers and fast food containers littered every available space with garbage bins overflowing as all of their daily meals were taken there.

Zentransa had long been supplied as a perk of wearing the badge. The Metropolitan Police Department was not unique in offering this benefit, but it was one of the few jobs where the perk itself was worth almost as much as the salary each employee was paid. In justification of the expense, the mayor and Chief of Police would often say, "Crime doesn't sleep, neither will we."

Most of the faces around him were still familiar to Aubrey. Some weren't so happy to see him, but most, like the two he was waiting for, were friendly and welcoming. Being back was comforting to some degree, despite the mixed reception. The surroundings, the noise, even the smell in the air of coffee mixed with aftershave mixed with body odor was familiar and comforting to him.

That morning's blast was the first of its kind in the city and as a result, the entire station was buzzing in a whirlwind of activity. Everyone in the building was occupied with some aspect of the blast's aftermath. Around Aubrey, every desk was taken up with a detective or uniformed officer interviewing a survivor or a witness. Many of the survivors were hospitalized and, if able, would give statements there. Others had given statements at the scene and sent home after field medical evaluations. Those survivors who had actionable information and could walk were brought to the station for further questioning. Looking around, Aubrey could see that most of those giving statements were in various states of hysteria as they relived their tales. The din was nearly impenetrable.

A tablet on Lewis's desk flashed with an incoming message. Aubrey glanced at it as the screen lit up with the notification "(1) Cloud File Shared With You" and he saw the time—6:03 am. It had been roughly three hours since he started his day by following Tim Frass. Two hours since the blast.

Aubrey was certain Tim no longer existed. Now that he had a chance to think about it, Aubrey had never had a subject die while investigating them. He began to wonder what type of report he would have to file when Aaron Lewis returned with someone he knew—Detective Julian Winger. He gave a weak smile as a greeting to Aubrey. Even when they worked together, Winger had never been too personable with Aubrey. The expression he now wore on his small round face with thick horn-rimmed glasses and balding pate proved his feelings hadn't changed much.

"Here you go, Marty." Lewis passed him a paper cup of coffee. He spoke over the noise. "Coffee still tastes like shit, I'm afraid. You know Winger, I think."

Aubrey nodded.

"Thanks, Aaron." Aubrey sipped his coffee while Lewis sifted through some files on his desk. "Feds involved yet?" Aubrey asked.

Lewis held up several file folders and read the labels on each. He looked to be searching for something but hadn't found it. "Shit. You kidding?" Lewis threw the files back onto his desk and shook his head. "The Mayor and the Chief are keeping those morons as far away from this as humanly possible. The FBI hasn't been worth a damn for twenty years. And this happened in our city, so it's our case."

"Sounds about right," Aubrey said.

Lewis and Winger sat on battered swivel chairs and sipped their coffee. They stared at Aubrey with expectant looks.

"Should I start from the beginning?" Aubrey said.

"Sure," Winger replied.

Aubrey walked them through the last three hours spending most of the time explaining what happened after he watched Tim Frass walk into the building. He described the out-of-place man in the ill-fitting suit. He told them how he looked too nervous and afraid for someone just going to work.

"How do you know," asked Winger, "that he didn't just have a big meeting or something?"

"No." Aubrey shook his head. "This was different. His fear was more profound than that. He also looked purposeful, like he had something to do."

"And you got all that in a few seconds. As he walked past?" Winger crossed his arms.

Aubrey stared at him for a moment stone-faced, then said in as level a tone as he could muster, "No. But, I've been thinking about it and seeing as how the building exploded right after he entered..."

A chime rang out from the desk and they all looked over to see the tablet on Lewis's desk. It flashed a reminder for the message that Aubrey saw a few minutes ago.

"Good timing." Lewis picked up his tablet. He tapped the screen a few times and nodded toward the large monitor on his desk. It came to life, displaying a mosaic of twelve images arranged in three rows. "This should be all the video footage from around the time of the blast. Metro Surveillance sent street views and building management sent over the footage from inside the lobby."

Aubrey saw that the bottom row of images were views from

outside the building while the top two rows were various angles from inside the front lobby. Aubrey recognized the views from inside and outside the building from the many times he had followed Tim Frass.

Watching the bottom row, Aubrey saw the sea of foot traffic flowing along on the edges of the river of self-driving cars. Glancing at the top row, he saw a tributary of people leaving the sidewalk to enter the building.

"That's my car right there." Aubrey pointed at the screen as it went by. He watched as a gap opened in the traffic allowing his car to drift to the side of the road, parking somewhere off screen.

"How long had you been parked before seeing our guy?" asked Lewis.

"Not long. Couple of minutes maybe."

"Look, there's Tim Frass," Aubrey pointed at the screen. "And there he goes into the building. Now, our guy should be along shortly."

Moments passed and Aubrey grew nervous. Was he imagining the nervous man on the sidewalk? Aubrey was distracted with his own thoughts at the time. He could have made a mistake. He shook his head and with it his doubt vanished as he watched a man wearing a brown, bulky, and poorly-fitted suit enter the bottom right corner of the widest shot of the street.

"There," shouted Aubrey, jabbing a finger at the screen. "There he is. Mark him."

Lewis tapped his screen and a green halo appeared around the frumpy man in a brown suit on the screen. Aubrey's hunch from the street that morning was confirmed as every exterior shot zoomed in tight on the subject. Seeing him from different angles highlighted how different he looked from all the other people that morning. Head down in the ill-fitting suit, muttering to himself, and bumping into people with no awareness of his surroundings. He looked uncomfortable not just in his suit, but in his own skin.

In the video footage, the building seemed to catch the man by surprise. He almost passed the doorway when he stopped and, being on the street side of the sidewalk, had to fight his way across the flow of foot traffic to reach the front doors.

Winger held up a hand. "Pause it there, Aaron."

Lewis stopped the footage and looked at Winger with a questioning look. On the screen, the man Aubrey suspected to be the bomber stood frozen just outside the entrance of the building, hand outstretched.

"Can I talk to you about something?" Winger said, jerking his head to the side. Lewis stood and the two men walked twenty feet away.

Aubrey didn't need to hear them speak to know what they were discussing. Winger was clearly concerned about showing Aubrey the rest of the footage. Aubrey had identified the man, which was all they needed him for at this point. Lewis was likely arguing that Aubrey used to be a cop and it wouldn't hurt to have an extra set of eyes. After all, Aubrey had been a good detective—he still was, albeit in the private sector.

Aubrey watched the men talk for a moment longer. Finally, Winger nodded and the men returned to the desk where Aubrey sat.

"OK," Winger said as he and Lewis took their seats. "Let's keep going."

Lewis tapped the tablet and the video resumed. The man

in the brown suit entered the building, Aubrey and the two detectives shifted their eyes to the top two rows of small screens. With a tap on his tablet, Lewis removed the bottom row, enlarging the remaining six screens.

The man emerged into the building's main lobby. Two of the views, both facing the doors, flashed a red circle around the man's head while text appeared at the bottom of each screen—*Facial Recognition Unconfirmed Identity Not Verified.* The man walked with purpose. He leapfrogged a turnstile. The audio from each screen was synced; Aubrey and the detectives could hear the security guards ordering the man to halt.

Near the elevators, he turned. From every one of the six angles, they could clearly see the man in the ill-fitting suit tear open his jacket and shirt to reveal the device within. It was some sort of utility vest bulging with narrow, rectangular blocks, cables, and wires. In the center of the vest was a small cellphone. Its screen was blank.

The guard cursed and yelled for the other to call the police. Then, the bomber started to talk.

"I am change. I am change," chanted the man as he walked backwards. "I am the mechanism with which change begins. I am not a cog in a wheel. I am a wrench thrown headlong into the wheel, forcing change. I am change. I am change."

The bomber continued to back up, chanting all the way. He made it well into the short hallway and continued to chant.

"I am change. I am change. I am the mechanism with which…" The bomber paused and looked down. The detectives saw it too. The phone in the center of his chest, hitherto blank and lifeless, had begun to flash. The bomber looked up and began to say something. All four small screens went white.

Lewis pulled up the exterior shots again and the three of them watched the blast tear through the bottom floors of the building and the street outside. Aubrey wasn't paying much attention. Something about what they just saw bothered him.

"Go back. No, go back to the inside shots," said Aubrey.

Lewis pulled the interior surveillance up again and reversed the footage.

"Not that far," Aubrey instructed. "Go to the second before his phone rings. And get rid of all the shots except for this one." He pointed to a screen with the most direct shot of the man's face.

"Let's watch it again and isolate the audio on the bomber," said Aubrey. What he was looking for, he did not know. Something about the last few seconds on that tape seemed off.

They watched it again and Aubrey saw it right away.

"Play it again," demanded Aubrey. Lewis did so. "See? See his face? What does that look like to you?"

"Fear."

"Regret, maybe."

"No." Aubrey was adamant. "He isn't afraid. He's surprised. He didn't know it would go off. I even think he was about to say 'help' when it went off."

"Nah," said Winger. "I think he just lost his nerve and freaked."

"I don't think so," argued Aubrey. "He's resolute a second before and shocked and panicked when the phone lights up."

Detective Winger frowned, looking doubtful, and shook his head before turning toward Detective Lewis. Lewis stared ahead and replayed the last few seconds again and again as if trying to make up his mind.

With no indication which theory Lewis agreed with, Winger continued, "So, even if he is surprised or shocked, why does that really matter?"

Aubrey spread his hands and cocked his head.

"What does it mean?" asked Aubrey, who looked at Winger as if the answer to this question was painfully obvious. "It means..."

"It means," interrupted Lewis, "that someone else detonated the device. It means someone was watching him. It means someone else likely made the bomb and this was all carefully planned by more than just our dead friend here. It means, in short, that this was not a one-man show. There is a new terror network operating in the city, and I suspect this is not the last we'll hear from them."

Winger looked from Lewis to the frozen image on the monitor. The bomber's face covered it. His eyes were wide and his mouth was agape in obvious horror.

Aubrey crossed his arms and let out a heavy sigh as he too stared at the image on the monitor.

"What he said." Aubrey cocked his head toward Lewis.

"Well... shit," said Winger.

The three men sat for a few moments and contemplated the implications of what they had just concluded. Lewis stood and grabbed his phone. Aubrey watched him walk away, send a message to someone and come back. As he did, a uniformed major approached with his hand outstretched.

"Goddamn, Aubrey," said the major. "How'd you get mixed up in this? Wrong place at the wrong time?"

"Good to see you, Major Corser. That's what it looks like, sir." They shook hands. The major placed a firm hand on

Aubrey's shoulder.

"Terrible, terrible stuff," said Major Corser. "Hate it... just hate it. But I'm glad you're alright." The major jerked a thumb toward the two detectives now standing. "Helping them solve the case already?"

"Actually, yes he is, sir," said Winger. "He just saved us a lot of time and probably gave us a few hours' jump on the people responsible."

"Damn. Don't miss a beat, do you, Aubrey? Once a cop, always a cop."

"Thank you, sir. But it's just a guess right now and..." began Aubrey.

"Your guesses were always better than most." The major kept his hand on Aubrey's shoulder for a moment then glanced at his watch. "Damn. I have to run. But listen, it's damn good to see you back in this building even if it's under these circumstances."

Major Corser stared at Aubrey for another second, nodded, then walked away toward a row of offices down the hallway behind them.

Detective Lewis looked at Winger and said, "The Unit will be meeting in five minutes in the war room." Lewis was referring to the Domestic Terror Unit, of which Aubrey used to be a senior officer and detective. Lewis looked hard at Aubrey as Winger walked off toward his desk to prep for the meeting.

"Listen, you're free to go. But your help was... *is* invaluable." Lewis raised his eyebrows and sighed as if he had forgotten what to say next.

Aubrey was caught off-guard by the sudden dismissal. He felt silly, as if he half expected them to let him stay at the station, maybe attend the meeting and share some theories and ideas on what to do next. He knew, in his logical mind, that this was impossible.

For a few short moments, while reviewing the footage and discovering Ralph's surprise, he felt useful once again. It was a feeling he hadn't known for eighteen months. For a fleeting moment, it was there again. Now, he was thrust back into his role as civilian. Useless, in his mind. Useless and unable to do anything that really mattered.

"Oh, yeah." Aubrey nodded and straightened. "Sure. Thanks, man." Lewis nodded and turned to go, but Aubrey called out.

"Hey, Aaron."

"Yeah?" Lewis turned.

"If you need anything…" Aubrey's gut cringed. Pathetic.

"I'll reach out. Don't worry." Lewis gave Aubrey a half-smile before turning toward a hallway with which Aubrey was only too familiar.

5

Moment Zero

Aubrey sank back onto the edge of Lewis's desk, watching his old friend disappear down the adjacent hallway. More detectives filed into the hallway after Lewis. These cops were members of the city's Domestic Terror Task Force; Aubrey used to be one of them.

After a moment, Aubrey looked around the room at the other officers, in and out of uniform, going about their business. He was, simultaneously, out of place and right where he belonged. An invader and a native all at once.

On his way to leave police headquarters, he stopped to use the restroom. He stood at a urinal against the wall farthest from the door when he heard two men enter.

"... got their hands full with this shit. DTTF is gonna need all hands on deck pretty soon. No way they can do this on their own."

Their voices bounced off the white subway tiles covering the walls. Their dress shoes clacked on the hard, smooth floors.

"Oh, yeah, you can bet they'll be pulling us in pretty soon."

Two stall doors creaked open behind Aubrey.

"Better tell the wife and kids daddy won't be around for a while," echoed a voice from within a stall.

Aubrey finished and made his way to the sink to wash up.

"Speaking of, they're already pulling in outside help," said one of the voices. In the mirror, Aubrey could see the backs of both men through the half-open stall doors. "Did you see that guy Lewis and Winger were talking to?"

Aubrey's hand stopped above the faucet handle.

"Which guy?"

"That dude in the dirty ass suit. He was holding court over there while they were watching something on Lewis's screens. And they were listening to him, too. Like, really listening to him. Then, the major came over and spoke to the guy. You must have seen him. About six-foot, brown hair. Filthy as hell. Must have come straight from the blast site."

A short pause.

"Oh, yeah," said the other voice. "That wasn't just some dude, Simmons. That was Martin Aubrey. Yeah, he had just come from the scene. I think he was there when it happened. Plus, I know I'd listen to whatever he had to say because he used to be a solid detective."

Aubrey knew where this was going. He hurried to finish washing his hands. He wanted nothing more than to avoid an awkward encounter if he could help it.

The sound of two near simultaneous flushes went off behind him. A quick glance up and he could see the men in the mirror begin to turn.

"What do you mean used to be?" the other officer asked.

Aubrey shut off the water and turned to leave. He was two feet from the door when the two men reached the bank of sinks.

"Blue on blue."

Aubrey pushed the door open.

"He killed a cop."

* * *

October 15, 2041

Thirteen police officers, dressed in civilian clothes and protective vests, stood near the rear of an unmarked police car. With badges hanging on chains around their necks and assault rifles slung in a cross-body fashion, twelve of them stood in a half circle listening to one man in the center. They were on a lightly trafficked street at the edge of the city in the heart of the industrial center. Predominant in this part of town were long, low buildings housing large, automated machines or vast warehouses. Most of the vehicles that passed were driverless delivery trucks, and foot traffic was almost non-existent.

Lieutenant Robert Banden briefed the men on the morning's raid. "We have good intel that the recent string of missing girls is somehow linked to this location. As you know, girls get into what they believe is a Metropolitan Traffic System taxi and are never seen again."

Nods from the group as he continued. "MTS has tracked at least one of the counterfeit cabs back to this location—a derelict warehouse, out of use for a couple of years." On a large tablet, he pointed to a 3-D image of a long rectangular building two blocks from their position. "Initially..."

"Fast forward, Lieutenant," said one of the men.

"Shut the hell up, Richardson," the Lieutenant replied in

his same robotic tone. "Initially, it was thought that this was just another drop site: a cab picks up a girl, she's alone, she's probably drunk or high from a night out, and the cab brings her here where she's snatched up. But drones and bio-sensors show activity inside—six individuals."

He continued describing the situation as they knew it and the plan for that morning's raid. Having heard it once the night before, they nodded along automatically. The lieutenant explained that they suspected the people inside the abandoned warehouse would, at the very least, have information on the missing girls, the false taxi, or both. There were three exits, but only one in use. Two officers would cover the rear and side exits. Two would remain behind as a quick reaction force. The rest would divide into two entry teams.

Across the street from the target's main entrance, the entry teams, Lieutenant Banden, and the quick reaction force would stage beside an abandoned factory building out of eyeshot of the target warehouse.

Outside the target's main entrance, a small courtyard was surrounded by a block wall about two meters high. The entry teams would stack on either side of the main entrance. Four to a side. The first team would enter through an iron gate, traverse the courtyard, then gain entry to the building. After making entry, the second team would join and the two teams would sweep the one-story building from front to rear. The six people inside were concentrated in the front three rooms of the building.

"I don't expect resistance," the lieutenant concluded. "There doesn't seem to be any advanced tech inside and our surveillance leads us to believe there are no weapons. They are all definitely Z'd up though, which means they're well paid and they keep to themselves. Basically, we know they're up to something, we just don't know what. So... let's go find out."

The group of thirteen made their way down the street, splitting off into their assigned groups, readying their weapons as they walked. The empty streets were an echo chamber capturing and amplifying the click and clatter of gear and firearms being jostled, loaded, and positioned. Lieutenant Banden did not expect any resistance, but the Special Crimes Unit always erred on the side of over-preparation.

Aubrey was assigned to the quick reaction force along with Sergeant Julia Chambers. From the corner of the cover building, he peered around to view the target. It stood between two towering, out of use factory buildings. From his point of view at a caddy-corner from the main entrance, Aubrey saw the walled courtyard the lieutenant had referred to. Looming just beyond it was the high curve of the skylighted roof over the broken-down warehouse.

Behind Aubrey, the entry teams lined up in two separate, well-armed stacks of bodies pressed against the wall of the cover building.

Lieutenant Banden tapped Aubrey and soundlessly motioned for him to move back. The lieutenant took up the position Aubrey had just held and peeked around the corner of the factory toward the target. The lieutenant touched his earpiece.

"Whiskey, Yankee, are your exits covered?" he asked in a near whisper.

"Yankee, roger," came one reply over the radio.

"Whiskey, roger," came the next.

The lieutenant turned to the two entry teams behind him. He raised a flat hand and waved it stiffly forward. With that, the teams silently broke from cover and half-ran, in two lines, toward the target building's front wall.

The second team, designated Fox team, passed nearest to Aubrey. The last officer glanced at Aubrey as they passed. Matt Hughes was the newest member on the team. Seeing his fresh face in tactical gear struck Aubrey as a juxtaposition of youth and energy and old-world violence. Hughes's bulbous nose, which protruded from under his ballistic goggles, was a common target of the team's good-natured ridicule.

Aubrey watched the two teams jog across the street. The two lines of cops stretched as the spaces between them grew, resembling a deadly caterpillar bristling with weapons like vicious spikes. The teams moved as one unit. Each armored section acted as a part of the whole.

Martin Aubrey would always remember the next eleven minutes and twelve seconds as the point by which all other events in his life would be said to have occurred before or after. It would become what he referred to as *Moment Zero.* After *Moment Zero,* he would consider his life to be in a state of falling action.

Moment Zero plus zero seconds:
The two entry teams reached the target building and stacked against the block wall on either side of the iron gate. The two four-man teams faced inboard toward the gate. When the last officer of each team reached the wall, Aubrey watched them reach forward and squeeze the arm of the officer in front of them. The signal was passed forward until it reached the first officer in each team, the breecher.

The breecher on the team to the right of the gate reached forward and turned the handle on the metal gate. It opened.

His team followed as he entered the courtyard. They traversed the small courtyard without haste.

As the breecher neared the main entry door, gunfire erupted from the building.

A staccato of sustained fire spilled out toward the entry team. More gunfire poured from the large window next to the front door, shattering the glass in a pyrotechnic display of glimmering debris.

The firing swept the entry team down with a cruel storm of metal, bending and twisting their bodies like weeds.

Moment Zero plus ten seconds:

From his vantage point, Aubrey could see the entire four-person entry team. The third and fourth officers lay on their backs, writhing. The first two officers were not moving.

"Aubrey, Chambers, move up to support," the lieutenant said aloud. In his earpiece, Aubrey heard the lieutenant again. "Fox team provide suppressive fire and pull the wounded out of there."

Running full-speed toward the chaos, Aubrey saw the members of the second entry team turn their weapons on the front of the building. Two fired through the gate over the head of one officer attempting to drag out the casualties. The last team member held his weapon high over the block wall, firing blindly at the building.

"Don't spray and pray, Hughes. Controlled fire only," came the lieutenant's voice in Aubrey's ear.

The building continued to spew gunfire onto the entry teams. Light arms—semi and full-auto, Aubrey thought. As far as fire power went, they were evenly matched… for the moment.

Moment Zero plus thirty seconds:
Crouching low, Aubrey flung himself against the block wall shoulder first. Ten feet from the iron gate, he watched the last wounded officer pulled abreast of the gate, dragged by the shoulder straps of his vest.

The scene went quiet. The lieutenant could be heard over the radio ordering in medical assistance and armored backup from a nearby station. Suddenly, a low *DOONK DOONK DOONK DOONK DOONK* sound blasted from the building. Large holes punched through the concrete block walls. Dust and bits of cinderblock fell on Aubrey's shoulders.

On instinct, Aubrey fell to his side. The sound continued. *DOONK DOONK DOONK.* Cracks in the air directly over his head as the rounds flew by. Whatever weapon they had inside it was powerful, busting through the cinder block wall like it was paper.

Something close to .50 caliber, Aubrey thought.

Craning his neck to look behind him along the wall, he saw Chambers lying on her back. She lay motionless. Careful to stay low, he pulled himself across the ground toward her. He looked and felt for a wound across her front and, after several seconds, he found it. A hole in her chest plate, near center-mass. The high caliber round had punched through the wall and her body armor.

He tapped the communicator in his ear and relayed her status to the lieutenant, who was still back at the corner.

Rolling onto his chest, Aubrey crawled on his elbows toward the gate. He and Chambers had been the only officers on his side of the gate. All the wounded waited for help on the other side, but the steady gunfire kept the able-bodied officers from getting to them. If something wasn't done about the combatants inside, the wounded and those trying to save them would get eaten up.

Moment Zero plus sixty seconds:
Hugging the ground, Aubrey looked up and saw Richardson on his belly staring at him from the opposite side of the iron gate. Rounds continued pouring out of the building, the loud and steady *DOONK DOONK DOONK* interspersed with the much more rapid crack of small arms fire. Richardson's eyes were steady, conveying a foregone conclusion—he and Aubrey would have to put an end to this chaos, just the two of them.

Aubrey reached down to his waist, pulled an object the size of a soda can from his belt and showed it to Richardson. Richardson looked at it, then reached down and pulled an identical object from his belt. They nodded at one another. The pulse grenades were non-lethal but could stun anyone within a radius of fifteen feet. Finely tuned to the human brain, the grenades sent an electromagnetic pulse that would drop anyone in range for a period of a few seconds to a full minute.

Aubrey peeked around the edge of the block wall and saw the large window next to the door. The glass had been shattered out of its frame along with most of the mullions and transoms.

"Window," shouted Aubrey. Richardson nodded his understanding. Aubrey rolled onto his back and shimmied his body so he was feet first against the wall. Richardson did the same on his side of the gate.

The two men pulled the pins from their grenades and locked

eyes. Aubrey held up his left hand and began counting off with his fingers—one, two, three. On three, both men did a full sit-up and hurled their stun grenades at the window. The white canisters flipped end over end and so true was their aim that they threatened to bounce off each other before they sailed through the open window. In the 2-3 seconds it took for the grenades to detonate, the two men gripped their rifles and moved into crouching positions.

A bright white flash inside was followed by the sudden silence of the guns. The grenades had had their intended effect.

Moment Zero plus one minute, thirty seconds:

"Let's go," Aubrey said to Richardson. They sprung to their feet. Rifles up. They ran toward the bullet-mangled front door. Just short of the door, Aubrey spun and put his back against the wall. Waiting only briefly for Richardson to do the same, Aubrey lifted his left leg and slammed it in a donkey-style kick against the lower half of the door. What was left of it burst inward.

The men spun around, rifles leading the way inside. They scanned the room from the middle out, each man taking his respective half of the room. The scene was what Aubrey expected: four men scattered on the floor, unconscious. Two of them appeared to have pistols, a third held a modern semi-automatic rifle, and the fourth man lay behind the weapon responsible for most of the casualties outside and the ominous *DOONK DOONK DOONK* noise. The long black weapon was an antique, from the early 21st century. A nearly four-foot-long barrel protruded from a boxy receiver fed by a belt of six-inch long rounds.

"Jesus, Aubrey," said Richardson. "What is that behemoth? And look at the size of those casings." He picked up an empty one and dropped it quickly. "Still hot."

".50 cal. Old one too. Probably a Ma Deuce." Aubrey surveyed the rest of the room. It was a mess of papers, ancient furniture, and computer equipment, some kind of office. Wood paneling covered every wall. Above them ceiling tiles hung here and there, but most of them were missing leaving wires and sundry pipes exposed. "Let's cuff these assholes and find the other two. But first..." He tapped his ear piece. "First room clear. Four suspects down." Then, he and Richardson zip-tied the four unconscious men.

Moment Zero plus two minutes, five seconds:

Aubrey and Richardson tore methodically through the second and third rooms with no contact. Each was a smaller version of the first: desks, chairs, papers everywhere. Wood paneling on the walls. These rooms, however, had been made into makeshift sleeping quarters with small, dirty mattresses in random places. There was one room left to search and then the vast warehouse.

There was no door to the fourth room, just a short hallway. With Aubrey in the lead, they began creeping toward the last room. As they approached the end, Aubrey did a quick sweep of the area in his eye line without breaching the opening into the room. Gesturing for Richardson to join him on his right side, they pushed forward into the room. As their rifle barrels entered the room, they began to sweep in the same manner as the first three rooms. Their bodies did not enter until all sections aside from the corners had been swept.

Finishing his sweep, he saw an overturned heavy steel desk. The instant he saw it, he knew what it was and sprang back behind the corner of the hallway, pulling Richardson with him. He moved just in time to see a spindly arm lift a large, unwieldy pistol over the edge of the table and fire wildly in their direction.

Holes burst through the corner of the hallway and the ceiling, but the shooter fired blindly. Aubrey flipped down a small lens from his headset. In it he could see the view from the small lipstick camera mounted just under the flash suppressor at the end of his rifle. Still in the relative safety of the hallway, he went to one knee and stuck his rifle out beyond the corner. Through his eyepiece, he could see the skinny appendage start to shake as it took intermittent shots toward their general vicinity. With his thumb, Aubrey pressed the small button on the side of his rifle and let the magazine fall into his open hand. He stowed the magazine in a pocket on his left thigh. From the other leg he pulled a magazine with the letters 'A.P.' stenciled on it. His rifle was now using tungsten tipped armor-piercing ammunition. Aubrey sling-shotted the charging handle back to eject the old bullet and chamber the new 'A.P.' round.

"Good idea," Richardson said, seeing Aubrey's switch to the more powerful and better penetrating ammunition. "That desk looks like thick gauge stuff. Probably why he decided to hunker down behind it. OK, let's put this guy out of our misery."

Aubrey aimed at a spot on the desk where he guessed the shooter's torso would be and squeezed the trigger three times. He heard a groan and the arm drooped over the edge of the upturned desk. The pistol clattered to the floor. An instant later, two more arms sprouted from behind the desk next to the lifeless one. They were empty and shaking. The sixth man was surrendering.

Moment Zero plus five minutes, fifty-three seconds:
"OK. OK. That's it. I'm done."

They ordered the man to come out, hands up.

"I want your body cameras to show that I came out willingly and gave myself up," he said, holding his hands high in the air.

The man was scraggly, with an almost purposeful haggard look juxtaposed by large diamond earrings and a large gold necklace. Aubrey spun him around and made him go to his knees. Together he and Richardson zip-tied the man's hands and feet together then called back their status to the lieutenant.

"Wait here, Scraggles," Aubrey said to the man now hog-tied.

"Scraggles is kind of fitting. Nice work." Richardson looked over the suspect once more then looked at Aubrey. "Speaking of body cams…" Richardson pointed at Aubrey's chest. A large black mark crossed his armored chest plate. In its path were the plastic and wiry remains of Aubrey's body camera, totally destroyed. Tattered and singed nylon lay in the wake of the bullet's near miss. "Jesus. Looks like one of those .50 cal rounds. You must have a rabbit's foot up your ass, buddy. How much good luck you got left?"

Aubrey stared down at his chest. He'd had close calls before, but this was different. He had no idea when it had happened. The long dark mark crossed his chest, almost horizontal, squarely in line with his heart.

A squelch from his ear piece interrupted his thoughts.

"Move into the warehouse." The lieutenant was calmer now that the firing had stopped. "Looks like there is a room in the center we hadn't noticed on the scans. No bios on the sensors, but something unusual in there. Clear it. Report anything you find."

"Roger that," they responded in unison.

Moment Zero plus seven minutes, twenty-five seconds:
A single metal fire-door separated their room from the warehouse. Taking no chances, they opened it with caution and verified there were no threats in the visible parts of the vast space in front of them. The room in the middle of the huge, empty warehouse was like an island. It had a large metal door with a large chrome handle.

"Not a safe," Aubrey said.

"More like a freezer," Richardson replied. The two men looked at each other with growing dread.

Richardson grasped the handle and opened the door while Aubrey raised his rifle to inspect the room. He was hit by a blast of cold, musty air. Inside, lights flickered to life. Strips of plastic curtain hung in his way and he pushed them aside with the end of his rifle.

He saw a gut-wrenching scene. On the floor were four young women, naked and unconscious. Tubes ran from each arm to clear bags of yellow liquid hanging from hooks in the wall. They lay on towels or mats of cardboard. Some of the mats looked fresh, others were soiled through. Train track needle marks littered their arms and legs. The points of entry for the IV tubes were bruised and crusty with old pus. Glancing around, Aubrey saw a large pile of crumpled clothing in one corner of the room. The pile of clothes looked too large for just these four women.

Aubrey and Richardson quickly ran around the room checking each girl for a pulse. Satisfied that they were all still alive, Aubrey surveyed the room more thoroughly.

By the door he had just walked through, a small metal table held several baggies of brownish powder, dirty pans caked with resin, and a small camping stove. Filthy intravenous needles lay in a pile next to the stove. In a box next to the table were full, fresh bags of the kind hanging from the walls. Aubrey recognized half of them as simple saline solution, the rest held a golden liquid and had an odd combination of substances printed on them.

Having seen enough, he tapped his ear piece relaying their discovery to the lieutenant. "Tell the medics to hurry."

Moment Zero plus nine minutes, forty seconds:
Aubrey left the freezer and ran back to the fourth room.

Officer Matt Hughes was already there securing Scraggles's wrists in carbon-fiber restraints, readying him for transportation. The plastic zip-ties were cut away and lying on the floor. The suspect was kneeling, hands behind his back. Aubrey stood in the doorway seething. His rage couldn't be contained. He lunged at the kneeling Scraggles.

Aubrey seized him by the top of the head and pulled it back hard. Scraggles gagged and coughed. He swung the partially handcuffed suspect around and threw him into the front wall of the room. Just as he did, Richardson rushed in from the warehouse.

"Whoa, what's going on in there?" Richardson yelled and pointed, but he wasn't pointing at Aubrey. He pointed down the other hallway back toward the third room. As he did, the rookie turned to look. "The next room, what's going on? Check it out, rookie." Richardson ushered Hughes back down the hallway into the third room and stood with his body, and body camera, facing in that direction.

Aubrey hurled the bedraggled suspect against the wall again. Scraggles crumpled to the floor, his spindly arms limp at his side.

"Kept those girls alive so you could have your own personal rape den?" Aubrey kicked a steel-toed boot into his stomach.

Scraggles coughed and moaned. "Rape den? Come on, man. I run a business to make money, not to get off."

"Tell me, then. What the fuck is going on back there?"

"This is a warehouse ain't it? Warehouses are for storage. We store inventory." Between coughs Scraggles spoke in a wry, sing-song mocking tone.

"Inventory?" Aubrey picked Scraggles up and jammed an elbow into his throat. "Are you telling me you sell them? You keep them alive so you can sell them?"

"I want a lawyer," Scraggles wheezed through a half-crushed windpipe.

"Fuck you. Why are they naked? I know you've been… sampling the product."

Scraggles looked at Aubrey with a look that one would give a naïve child. "Quality assurance, man." He coughed again. "I have to vouch for my product."

Aubrey took a step back. With both hands, he raised the butt of his rifle, ready to bash in Scraggles's skull. As he was about to lean into a blow sure to knock the man out cold, Scraggles's hand whipped from behind his back holding a short blade.

Scraggles lunged. The knife shot toward Aubrey's exposed neck. In one movement, Aubrey jumped backward and brought his rifle down to his hip. He pulled the trigger and Scraggles fell back into the wall with the sound of wet meat hitting something cold and hard. He slid down the wall like a wet slug, his dead body slumping to the side as it hit the floor.

Aubrey was numb. For a few seconds, he was deaf, blind, and dumb.

Richardson entered the room and, with wide eyes, he took in the scene. Aubrey standing there with his weapon raised. Scraggles, knife still in hand, dead on the floor.

"He came at you with that blade?" Richardson asked.

Aubrey nodded, still staring at the body on the floor.

A deep low moan brought Aubrey back. Looking away from the body he noticed a spot on the wall in front of him. At the top of the bloody trail left by Scraggles's body there was a small hole in the solid brick wall. Tiny wisps of smoke issued from it. He reached out and touched the hole. It was hot.

On the other side of the wall, he heard it again. A low moan, more sustained this time. Then, a shout. "Hughes?"

Aubrey looked down at his rifle. Across the magazine, in bold black ink appeared the letters A.P. He had forgotten to change back to his standard ammunition. Like a hot poker, the tungsten tipped round had torn through Scraggles's body and the brick wall, then through to the next room.

More moaning came from the other side of the wall. The sound made Aubrey think of an animal dying. He knew it wasn't an animal.

Moment Zero plus eleven minutes, twelve seconds:

A second passed and a shout came that Aubrey would never be able to scrub from his memory.

"Officer down."

6

The Day's Dirt

April 2, 2043

Martin Aubrey stood on the sidewalk outside Police Headquarters waiting for his car. It was late morning and the street was still busy with silent cars moving along to their destinations. Several uniformed officers were making their way into the station. Some nodded a greeting; most took no notice of him. One officer looked Aubrey up and down then gave a knowing look.

Aubrey looked down for the first time that day and saw that he was filthy. His clothes were covered in a thick layer of gray dust and his shoes were coated with brownish-red muck. He slapped at his trousers and the sleeves of his coat, dusting himself off the best he could.

It was then he noticed his hands. Dried blood, a crimson so dark it was almost black, embedded in the cuticles of his nails, the cracks and wrinkles of his skin, in the webs of his fingers. The hems of his shirtsleeves were stained with mud, blood, and dust.

He was desperate for a shower. He needed to wash the day's

dirt away and watch it flow down the drain in a brown watery swirl.

The ride home did not take long, but in that short time Aubrey managed to relive the last eighteen months—that disastrous day when his mistakes and his temper led to the death of an innocent cop, the resulting cycles of debilitating depression, the constant dense cloud of guilt hanging over him, the day he met the officer's family and the memory of their overwhelming generosity and forgiveness, the decision to turn in his badge.

Over the months since then, he had come to accept his new life and his new role in society. He had come to accept that he would never be a cop again. Today, coming so close to his old world, reliving it for just a few moments, and now being pulled away was almost too much to bear. He felt the darkness descending like a cold blanket. He had medicine to keep the darkness at bay, but he always ended up deciding not to take it. He had decided a long time ago that he deserved to feel this way. He deserved to feel something close to what the family of that rookie felt after they discovered that their husband, father, son, brother had been killed in action by a fellow cop.

7

Home

ZENTRANSA®
(azolpidem extartrate)

Manufactured by:
Ventana, Inc.
New Aberdeen, MD 21000

FULL PRESCRIBING INFORMATION
(1) INDICATIONS AND USAGE

ZENTRANSA (azolpidem extartrate) is indicated for the indefinite elimination of the need for sleep for physical restoration and rejuvenation in adults. [see Clinical Studies (14)].

WARNING: ABNORMAL AND VIVID DREAMS OR NIGHTMARES

Sudden discontinued use of **ZENTRANSA** can result in abnormal dreams, vivid dreams, and/or nightmares. Consult a doctor before discontinuing the use of **ZENTRANSA**. [see Contraindications (4) and Warnings and Precautions (5.1)].

Martin Aubrey left the police station and went home. That night, he would sleep for the first time in months. He knew the risks of combining a stressed mind with coming off Z cold turkey.

He slept anyway. He needed it.

* * *

He opened his eyes to a street packed with cars, but none moved. It was as if they had powered down in mid-transit and their passengers had vanished. Martin Aubrey was alone, standing in the street between his own car and the strange, unmoving river of traffic. Looking around, he realized he was outside the same building Tim Frass had walked into earlier that day. The same building that had its lower third ravaged by the blast of a suicide bomber. Now, it was intact.

"What..." he said aloud as he tried to figure out how he was here and how the building had righted itself so quickly. His voice echoed in the empty street, bouncing off every surface again and again.

Suddenly, down the street, an explosion ripped through the silence. The origin of the detonation was out of sight. Plumes of smoke rose high in the air as a car burned. Seconds later, glass and metal debris rained down on him. Although he shielded his head and face with his arms, the shrapnel found its mark, leaving small wounds on his arms and back.

The air settled. Aubrey straightened up. Just as he did, another car exploded a bit nearer to him than the last. And then another, off to his left. They were coming every few seconds, closer and closer. Each time, more debris pelted him.

"Need to move." Aubrey spoke aloud to the empty street between explosions. He was answered with echoes of his own voice. He made to flee and only then did he realize his legs would not obey. He could feel them. He could feel his pants rubbing against his skin. He could even wiggle his toes, but his legs were planted firm. They would not take a step.

"Run," he screamed at his legs. Nothing happened. He was rooted to the pavement by an invisible, unbreakable force.

Staring down at his legs, concentrating with all his power in an attempt to force them to move, he noticed his clothes. He wore his standard civilian attire: suit and tie, but on his feet were black combat boots, weathered and well-worn. Running diagonally across his torso was a wide black strap. After a quick glance over his shoulder, he saw that the strap was connected to an assault rifle slung across his back. Aubrey whipped the weapon around to examine it. It was exactly like the one he had while he was enlisted in the Marine Corps so many years ago. Short and light. Comfortable in his hands. He knew it was his. There were many like it, but this one was his.

CRACK

A shot rang out down the street and a window near him burst. As a reflex, Aubrey brought the rifle to his shoulder and sighted down the barrel for a target. Dark shapes bobbed in and out of view a hundred meters to his right. Black shapes. Shadows maybe. They darted between cars, moving too quickly for a decent, well-aimed shot.

CRACK CRACK CRACK

More shots from the enemy to his right. He ducked. Keeping low but trying to maintain a visual on his enemy.

CRACK CRACK CRACK

Shots from his left.

CRACK CRACK

More shots from the building across the street. Glass shattered all around him. Rounds ricocheted off the pavement near his feet. Air hissed from punctured tires.

One more time, he tried to force his legs to move, to let

him run. He was a dead man standing here like this. His legs refused to move. They would not take even a single step.

Cars continued to explode around him at random, but it felt like they were getting closer, more frequent. They were bracketing his position. Red flames, glass, and metal flew in all directions as they detonated. His enemy on the ground was undeterred by the explosions. The dark shapes kept coming, bouncing from shadow to light; they bobbed in and out of sight, moving ever closer.

Aubrey's ears rang from the blasts and his head swam from the frequent concussive blows. He could hear the shapes shouting at him from the shadows. They were screaming in an unrecognizable language, but their anger was clear. They were coming for him. They fired steadily at him, stopping only to scream in their strange tongue.

The shapes came closer still. His breath was steady but deep. He stared through his rifle's sights trying to get a clean shot at them. He saw his chance. A dark blur moved between cars fifty meters away to his left. As it cleared the rear fender, he had a clear shot at its center mass. He squeezed the trigger and... nothing. The metal under his finger turned into a rubbery glob. He released the trigger and examined the rifle. The trigger had reformed into hard, cold metal. Panicking, he put the rifle back to his shoulder and found another clear shot. He squeezed. Nothing. Again, the trigger was mush as he depressed it. He tried again. Nothing. He tried again. Nothing.

Aubrey's faceless enemy was getting ever closer. His legs would not move and his rifle would not fire. Alarm and hysteria rose in him to an uncontrollable degree when the car next to him let out a low, crunching groan. Hot wind blew across his face and neck just before red and orange flame engulfed him. As the heat consumed him, a shadowy figure materialized inches from his face. Unlike the others, this one had a face. Soft young eyes and a large nose. It was instantly recognizable as the face of a cop Aubrey once knew. Matt Hughes. A rookie that was now dead. Dead by Aubrey's hand.

Hughes raised a pistol to Aubrey's forehead.

He jolted upright in bed. Out of breath and his heart pounding like a jackhammer in his chest, he forced himself to inhale deep and slow several times. Managing to calm himself down, he glanced at his watch on the nightstand—2:36 a.m. He swung his legs over the edge of the bed and sat with his head in his hands trying to collect himself.

In spite of the nightmare he knew would come, Aubrey had needed real sleep. In general, he liked sleeping over not sleeping. He likened it to a brain vacation. And he liked dreaming. He always felt more creative and sharper after a few nights' actual sleep. He made it a rule to abandon the Z pill for a week every three or four months for that reason. The nightmares always came, but he felt they were a worthy trade-off for the benefits he gained.

Tonight, Aubrey slept to give his brain the time it needed to work through the trauma of the day before. He believed that there were some things the brain could not do while you were awake, stimulated by a world that was always on.

Ironically, he had to take a sleeping pill to go to sleep tonight. Abstaining from Zentransa for one day would only give you a couple of hours on the first night. You had to be off for two to three days, or more, to get back to the normal human sleep cycle and he needed some solid sack time tonight. There were mental wounds that needed healing.

The day's events had not been any worse than what he had experienced while serving in combat theaters while he was enlisted in the Marine Corps or while he carried a badge. In fact, he would say today was rather benign compared to most days in either of his past lives. But the combination of the blast, its aftermath, and his coming so close to his former life as a cop, the life he had loved, with its reminders of his mistakes, brought a great many emotional stressors to the surface. His self-hatred for pulling the trigger on that day eighteen months ago, the last time he pulled a trigger, and the guilt that came with it, all bubbled up in the short time since leaving the station earlier that day.

Hours after returning home, he had raged once more against decisions of the past. When his self-loathing became unbearable, he knew he had to escape. Sleep. He had to actually sleep.

The nightmare had been like others he'd had in the past after firefights abroad and violent exchanges working for the police.

Flashes of fire, faceless enemies, the inability to fight back or escape. These things he'd expected so he wasn't surprised. But all the same, he had hoped this time would be different. The Z pill itself contributed to the nightmares' intensity. Scientists were unsure why, but dreams seemed to stockpile while a person was on Z. The first night of real sleep always brought with it vivid, visceral dreams and often nightmares. It was as if, in one night, the brain opened the floodgates of stored thoughts, fears, and anxieties that would normally come as a slow trickle, night by night. The longer one took Z, the longer one abstained from real sleep, the more intense, lifelike, and disturbing the dreams became.

Aubrey thought about having a drink. He could call into the office and make his excuses, but something told him that getting back to work would help more than alcohol.

"This too shall pass." He stood and left the bedroom.

Entering the living room of his austere, tidy apartment, he picked up his work tablet from a small wooden end table near the sofa. The polished concrete floor was cold underfoot and artificial light from the street outside shot through gaps between thick blackout curtains.

He sat on a stool at one end of the kitchen island and scrolled through OWG's internal messaging system to see if there had been any replies to his earlier message about the blast and the likely death of Tim Frass. There were only a few. Most came from his boss and one from his boss's boss. Other than that, the rest were junk.

He hardly knew anyone on his team or in the company on the whole. This was due to the nature of being a field investigator, but also because he chose not to befriend anyone. Relationships would make this job feel more permanent and his old job further away.

The messages were encouraging. A lot of concern for his health and well-being, urging him to get some rest and not rush back to work. The last message was from several hours ago.

Frass's death confirmed, his boss had written. *Silver lining: we think your conclusions for potential wrongdoing were spot on. Now we have enough evidence to hand over to federal authorities to start criminal investigation targeting Frass's accomplices. They'll take it from here. Let us know when you're ready for work and we'll send you a good one.*

"A good one," Aubrey said aloud. He wasn't sure their idea

of a *good one* was the same as his, but nonetheless he replied to the last message almost immediately.

Ready to go. Please send. He set the tablet back down and walked to the window, pulling back the curtain. The full might of daylight assaulted him. He squinted and turned for a moment to allow his eyes to adjust. Even though it was not quite 3:00 a.m., the city was lit in near-daylight brightness. He knew that down on the street, had there been no clocks available, one would have no idea it was the dead of night.

The light from the street stung his eyes and brought to mind one of the quiet, yet profound side-effects of Zentransa on the human body—blindness. Without sleep, the eyes did not experience eight to ten hours of darkness each night. With the absence of darkness, the eyes essentially worked overtime. In the early days, when people did not expect this side effect or heed warnings when it was theorized, there were an alarming number of cases of near or total blindness among middle-aged adults. According to scientists, the eyes simply wore out early.

The Z pill did an excellent job of tricking the brain into thinking it was asleep, causing it to release the chemicals necessary to repair and restore the body. The eyes, however, were like a tool that only had so much life in it. They wore out with use.

The solution was quite simple: darkness. People began wearing dark sunglasses for a third of their day, in and out of doors. Workplaces began scheduling "twilight time" where the lights would dim to near darkness for long stretches. Some companies had dark rooms with dimmed computers and tablet screens.

The city lights, however, blazed twenty-four hours a day

necessitating Aubrey's use of blackout curtains. It turned out that reducing the time a person was exposed to simulated sunlight abated the rate of "Early Onset Age-related Macular Degeneration."

A corrupted circadian rhythm was another matter non-sleepers, or zoners, had to contend with. Human beings are meant to sleep and the natural twenty-four-hour cycle is disrupted by the subtraction of that crucial part of a person's day. Since the release of Zentransa, those who could afford usual doses of the pill struggled with circadian rhythm disruption—losing track of the time and the days of the week.

The taking of the tiny pink pill was the only break between days; hence, the days ran together. In severe cases, the inability to grasp time caused certain mental health problems—temporary insanity, paranoia, and schizophrenia. In mild cases, it caused confusion and constant tardiness.

The solution to the circadian rhythm problem was quite simple. In the early years after the pill's introduction to society, the city installed giant clocks almost everywhere. The objective was to never have a spot in the city where one could not view a clock.

City officials accomplished their goal and then some. One could stand in any spot in the city's enormous footprint and see multiple clocks. The clocks, in an effort to convey not just the time but also time-periods of the day, were equipped with color displays showing the sun, moon and stars, or a twilit sky. Workplaces were also encouraged to ensure people actually left their jobs at some point in the twenty-four-hour cycle to go home. Some companies complied, but many did not. The Police Department, for instance, would never send anyone home with a crisis like the current one brewing.

Aubrey stared down at the street a while longer. This was an unofficial hobby of his. He liked to watch the people. In a strange way, he envied them. Not that he wanted to be them. No, he wondered how many of them were still doing the thing they loved. How many of them had been tempted but failed to make the decision that would ruin their lives? How close had they come before turning away and choosing another path?

He allowed his self-loathing to last a few more minutes then he closed the curtains and turned back to his bare apartment. Aubrey had furnished it with the necessary things and little more.

With a restless mind and nothing to busy himself, Aubrey spent the next few hours browsing the various news sites and TV networks for updates on the bombing. The death toll had finally plateaued at fifty-two and the number of casualties had remained steady across all sources at one-hundred-thirty.

In his mind, he pictured the process of moving all that information behind the scenes. The volume of communications to and from the authorities and to and from the public must be something to behold. This was, unfortunately, one of those few things where science could not intervene. A person had to craft the communications. A person had to contact the families. A person had to break the bad news.

When Aubrey heard the same update for the fourth time, he decided to disconnect for a while. He walked to the bedroom, passed his bed with its white linens tucked tight, and to the dark wood dresser, one of only three pieces of furniture in his room. From a box atop the dresser he removed a pair of VR eye cups, about the size of swimming goggles, and two silky black haptic gloves as thin as latex.

He donned the gear and adjusted the eye cups while he waited for the workout program to boot up. After several seconds, the on-screen menu appeared before his eyes as floating white words hovering in front of a green background. He used his index finger and thumb to scroll down through the various options until he found his workout of choice. He selected it with a single tap of his thumb and fore finger.

The space around him materialized into a boxing ring—a blue mat and red and white ropes. He scanned the arena. It was empty, per his preferred setting. Holding up his hands he saw they were covered in black twelve-ounce boxing gloves.

A calm male voice said, "Your opponent is entering the ring, Martin."

From the floor near the opposite corner, a burly man with a shaved head and green trunks slid into the ring.

Standing upright, the man slammed his gloves together with a loud slap. "You're mine, meat."

Aubrey punched his own fists together and raised them into a basic boxing stance. "Let's go, big boy," he said and stepped forward.

"Round One. Begin," the voice said. A single ding sounded at ringside.

* * *

Stepping out of the shower ninety minutes later with a towel draped across his shoulders, Aubrey picked up his phone from the nightstand and saw a notification for an unread text message. It was from Detective Aaron Lewis.

Watching the news?

"Shit." Aubrey had turned off all his devices before working out. He raced to the living room and snatched up the remote from the coffee table. The television came to life.

"... a hitherto unknown domestic terror group." She was an attractive, young talking head standing in front of a graphic depiction of the city. "With us now is Charles Brunson, BNN's Senior Global Security Correspondent. Charles, what do you make of this claim by One Front for the People?"

The screen split to show a sharp looking, middle-aged man wearing a tweed jacket.

"Well, to go back to your first statement, they aren't totally unknown," Brunson said. "In the circles I associate with, we know them, but not for acts of terror. One Front for the People, or OFP, or One Front, has been, up until yesterday's bombing, a sort of glorified support group for the unemployed with a mildly radical leftist agenda. Their one, most fundamental belief is that the Zentransa pill has done irreversible damage to the socio-economic fabric of this city..."

"Charles, their past isn't completely peaceful though is it?" the reporter interrupted.

"Not completely, no," Brunson replied. "They're mostly vandals dabbling in light sabotage, but..."

"They seem to have graduated," the reporter interrupted again. "They've moved on to more deadly tactics. Tell me, what is their aim? What are they trying to achieve with this bombing?"

"Well... I think, probably what all terror groups want: fear," said Brunson with a degree of finality.

"Yes. Well, people are afraid aren't they," the reporter said, concluding the conversation.

The view on the TV changed, now showing the bombing

site. The reporter in the studio was now talking to a reporter on the scene. The scene looked quiet and was littered with bright red, orange, and green flags in addition to small square cards imprinted with unknown symbols on them.

Drones hummed above the street, scanning and logging the placement of every flag and card. Men and women in hazmat suits walked slowly and methodically around the scene, examining every square inch for evidence. Another reporter, an older male, appeared on screen.

"Thank you, Meredith," he said. "Investigators here at the site of this tragic bombing..."

He picked up his phone and replied to Lewis' text message.

OFP? The hippie vandals? Really? Aubrey typed.

Yep. No more comms from them except the one claiming responsibility, Lewis replied.

Aubrey shook his head and typed. *I ran into some of these guys way back. Didn't strike me as killers.*

They are now. Already rounded up a couple of them, Lewis replied.

Aubrey stared at his phone. He imagined his former colleagues detaining and questioning members of OFP. He could see the detectives questioning them, formulating theories, game planning the next arrest.

Aubrey felt an unmistakable pit forming in his stomach.

Good luck, he replied to Lewis. After waiting several minutes, he realized Lewis would not reply. He imagined his friend and everyone else at the police station was pretty busy at the moment.

On the television behind him, a man's voice boomed from the speakers.

"I think I speak for everyone in the Ventana family when I

say our hearts go out to the victims of this horrendous attack."

Aubrey turned to see a familiar face on the screen. He didn't know the man personally, but everyone in New Aberdeen would recognize one of its founders—James Sarazin. He stood on the white stone steps in front of Ventana Tower, company headquarters, reading from a thin tablet. Men and women in suits stood behind him, expressions of grief on each of their faces. Sarazin himself looked as serious as Aubrey had ever seen him. Usually, when he appeared on television, he was exuberant with a nauseating level of positive energy. Beneath swooping black hair, his tanned face was stiff.

"We've offered the police any help we can possibly give, whatever they need, all they have to do is ask. Additionally, we've started a fund to assist families who have suffered the loss or maiming of a loved one in this heartless..." Sarazin paused and looked down as if composing himself. "... this heartless attack that has left so many hurt. Anyone interested in taking advantage of the assistance fund should visit the website on your screen now." A web address appeared on the bottom of the screen—*ventanafund.ba*. "Once again, I'd just like to say..."

"How large a sum are you setting aside for the assistance fund?" A reporter off-screen interrupted.

Sarazin looked toward the camera. "I've personally seen to it that the funds will be substantial. And if we run out, I'll put more in." He looked back down at his tablet but was interrupted again.

"OFP is staunchly opposed to Zentransa. Can you comment on the rumors that they've attacked the city as a message to you and your company?" Another reporter spoke off screen.

Sarazin looked off to his right, into an unseen crowd of

reporters. "I don't comment on rumors."

"Would you stop the production of Zentransa if they demanded it?"

"Again, I... we don't comment on rumors."

"Can you say whether or not..."

It was Sarazin's turn to interrupt. "And we don't negotiate with psychopaths." On screen, Sarazin's eyes narrowed and his nostrils flared. "These people are sick. Whatever they demand, if they demand anything, it's coming from the mouths of sociopath killers. I wouldn't consider their demand any more than I would a rat's." He looked down again, shaking his head. After a moment, he looked up, visibly calmer now. "Once again, our support goes out to the families in their time of need and the police as they hunt down these murderers. Thank you."

With a wave of his hand, he turned to leave amid a cacophony of questions.

8

Boarding School Syndrome

April 16, 2043

Sunlight had barely begun to creep through the window of Preston Warbly's dorm room when his alarm clock began chiming. He stared up at a ceiling covered in superheroes and tried to force his eight-year-old mind to wake up. It was Friday which meant pancakes in the cafeteria and PE in the afternoon. His two favorite things in one day was why he loved Fridays at St. George's Academy. Across the room in a high loft-bed, his roommate Charlie Lattimore slept soundly on his back. Charlie was usually an early riser and it was rare for Preston not to be shaken awake by him already late for breakfast.

Preston forced himself to swing his legs out from under the superhero covers. He sat up on the edge of the bed rubbing his eyes with the heels of both hands.

"Charrr-leeee?" Preston sang to his roommate. "Oh, Charrrr-leeee? Wakey wakey, eggs and bakee."

Charlie did not stir in the slightest, so Preston hopped down and made his way to the closet-sized bathroom to brush his teeth. On his way, he passed the gaming corner with its stack of consoles under two fifty-five-inch monitors. A pile of controllers, VR headsets and gloves sat between the crown jewels of the boys' room—two fully immersive VR chairs. Just about every dorm room at St. George's had at least one VR chair, but Preston and Charlie were among the few with a pair. Technically, the boys had three if the busted one in Preston's closet counted.

Preston's temper could sometimes result in smashed consoles, broken tablets, and at least one irreparably damaged VR chair.

In the bathroom mirror, Preston caught sight of one gaming monitor—the one with a spider's web of cracks radiating from its center. Two nights ago, Preston had lost to Charlie at *Speed Krank 7* for the fourth time straight, so he punched the screen. Seeing it was a reminder that he needed to call his mom and dad about getting a replacement.

With a mouthful of foamy toothpaste and a drippy toothbrush in one hand, he said, "Charlie, come on. Don't think I won't leave without you."

Preston finished brushing his teeth and washed his face. He strode to a pile of clothes in the center of the room and picked up his uniform bottoms from the day before. He slid them on as he tried to wake Charlie again.

"Charlie," Preston said with a little more force. "Let's go. Get up. We'll get stuck with the crusty pancakes from the bottom of the serving thing if we don't hurry."

Amongst the pile of dirty clothes, he found a white collared shirt emblazoned with St. George's seal. He was pretty sure he had only worn it twice that week. He kicked aside dirty shirts, shorts, and socks looking for his shoes. His search brought him near Charlie's bed. He gave the entire thing a shove.

"Let's go," he shouted with his head down, still searching. "You know what my dad says, 'sleep is for poor people.'"

Seeing Charlie lying there reminded Preston of how much he couldn't wait to be sixteen years old. Then his dad would let him start taking Z. Legally, he was supposed to wait until he was eighteen, but his dad had said that, as a Warbly, Preston would be ahead of everyone else for the rest of his life. He might as well start Z early too.

Preston continued searching for a while longer before finding one shoe under Charlie's backpack and the other behind a dusty game console. He sat on the carpet to slide the shoes on and gave Charlie one more plea.

"Charlie, seriously. Get up, man."

Charlie didn't move. Preston marched over to Charlie's bed and shook him hard by the shoulders, bouncing him against the mattress, but he didn't budge.

"Let's go. Stop playin'. I'm starving," Preston shouted. He shook Charlie again. And again. And again. Charlie didn't open his eyes, didn't move a muscle.

"OK. Still playing this game? I know what will wake you up." Preston had no other options. He stomped over to the sink and filled a paper cup to the very brim with cold tap water.

"You leave me no choice, Charles Lattimore," said Preston. "Wake up or you're getting wet." Charlie made no reply to his threat.

"OK. One… two… three." Preston dumped the full cup of cold water on Charlie's face and bent over double, laughing himself silly.

"Oh my god, oh my god, I can't believe that just happened," Preston said, unable to catch his breath. "But for real, I'll help you get cleaned up. Come on, let's go. I am really hungry."

Charlie didn't move. Didn't make a sound. His face hadn't changed one bit. Not even half a smile. He didn't squint or furrow his brow. Nothing.

Preston's stomach fluttered.

Charlie was either the best actor on earth or something was very wrong.

* * *

Mr. Robards, Assistant Head of School at St. George's Academy, left the main office and was on his way to the cafeteria when the Warbly boy ran up in a state of panic.

"What... what do you mean he won't wake up?" Robards asked.

"I'm telling you," Preston shouted, "he... won't... wake... UP. I tried everything. Literally, everything and he just won't wake up."

Mr. Robards assumed it was a joke at first, but Charlie was not the type. Maybe Preston had talked him into it, but something felt off. Preston's insistence and concern seemed genuine.

"I mean, he won't wake up. Something is wrong, Mr. Robards." Preston looked more panicked by the minute.

"Preston, tell me what happened. What did you boys get into last night?" Drug and alcohol use among kids Preston's age was not uncommon.

"Nothing. I swear, Mr. Robards. Please hurry." Preston pulled at Mr. Robards's arm.

Mr. Robards could usually tell when a kid was lying and all his instincts told him Preston was telling the truth.

"OK. OK." Mr. Robards nodded. "Hang on a second."

Mr. Robards whipped around, poked his head in the door of the main office, and called out to the school secretary. "Call the nurse. Tell her to go up to Charlie Lattimore's room. I'm on my way up there right now."

Mr. Robards had gone twenty feet when he stopped abruptly and ran back to the open door to the main office.

"Actually, just go ahead and call an ambulance," he yelled at the secretary. She nodded her reply. "And tell them to send an actual doctor—not a drone."

Resuming his half-run to the boys' room, he pulled a tablet from his coat pocket and began searching the school's database. He found Charlie's parents' contact information and made ready to call them the instant he confirmed something was really wrong with the kid. There were several numbers for both parents and, this being a weekday, he thought work numbers would be best to try first. Glancing at their profiles he saw Charlie's mom worked at McBane Group. He had no idea what the McBane Group did, but he recognized the father's employer right away—Ventana Inc.

***

April 16, 2043

Metropolitan Tribune

Mysterious Illness Infects Child of Prominent Family, One Front for the People Claims Responsibility

Eight-year old Charles Lattimore III, son of powerful pharmaceutical executive Charles M. Lattimore Jr, was taken to

St. Mary's Children's Hospital this morning in what doctors say is a state of "un-wakeable sleep."

"We've never seen this before," said Doctor Hassan Uday in a press conference. "We're referring to it as acute hyper-somnolence or AHS. The patient is in a semi-permanent sleep. Unlike a coma, there are clear signs of brain and other physiological activity."

Even without a clear idea of what the disease is or what has caused it, doctors remain encouraged.

"We can keep him alive indefinitely, similar to comatose patients," says Uday. "But a cure or treatment is going to require more time and more research."

Hours after Lattimore's illness went public, the terror group One Front for the People claimed responsibility for the mysterious poisoning, but police are skeptical. "We think it's likely that the organization known as OFP is simply looking to cause more fear," said a police spokesperson. "But we consider every claim seriously until we can prove it otherwise."

Just weeks following the first in a series of bombings that have rocked the city to its core, an alleged representative for OFP released a recorded audio message to media outlets stating the terror group had poisoned Lattimore.

April 20, 2043

The Metro Sun News

Who is safe? Third "Boarding School Syndrome" Case Discovered

Following the third case of what people are calling Boarding School Syndrome, doctors are ramping up their work with police to stop its spread. This comes after One Front for the People, the domestic-terror group, yet again claimed they are behind the sickness.

In their statement, OFP parroted previous statements that they are targeting children of the wealthy to "bring to light the inequities that exist in our society brought on by the invention of the vile, unnatural pill that eliminates one of humankind's most basic needs in the name of the propagation of wealth for the already wealthy."

Some experts still remain skeptical OFP could pull off such an attack, but officials state that they continue to take their claims seriously.

"We just don't know what it is," states Dr. Joyceanne Luss, Chief of Internal Medicine at Metropolitan General Hospital. "And until we do, we can't claim to know anything about its origin or what vectors are spreading it. Three cases so close to each other are… worrisome."

April 21, 2043
The City Daily Post
OFP Claims Fifth Bombing
The fifth suicide bomber attack in One Front for the People's reign of terror struck Sundheim Plaza today, killing fourteen people and wounding at least thirty-seven. The recent string of bombings has rattled city and law enforcement officials. Dozens have been slain and hundreds wounded in what the mayor is calling "the darkest time our peaceful and prosperous city could ever imagine."

The usual claimant, the group calling themselves One Front for the People or OFP, has once again come forward to take credit for the grisly violence. One Front for the People, a domestic terror organization once thought to be a disorganized band of half-hearted vandals, has re-emerged with deadly force over the last several weeks…

9

Darkness

April 23, 2043

For Martin Aubrey, the three weeks following the first bombing passed in a haze. He received a new case from his boss at OWG Insurance. Had he been in a normal state of mind, Aubrey might have agreed with his boss that it was in fact, a "good one." A fifty-something commercial property owner with extremely bad luck—she had lost millions of dollars in inventory, buildings, and machinery in a series of fires at three of her properties. Over the course of five days. Usually he would have relished working on that kind of case, but he could only manage to do enough each day to placate his boss before he lost all motivation.

He sat on the sofa in the dark. The only light came from the monitor of the computer in his lap. He'd just sent a report on the status of the case to his boss—enough to put a checkmark in today's column for having done some work. He closed his company's intranet page, disregarding a round dozen unread messages in his email inbox. He opened a web browser and turned to the thing that he'd spent most of the last three weeks doing. He scoured headlines for information on One Front for the People and the recent attacks. News sites ranging from mainstream to the obscure, forums ranging from legit to borderline wackadoo—these were his new haunts. He did it mostly to stay abreast of the situation, but, if he were honest with himself, he really hoped to find something the cops may have missed—a pattern, a trend, anything.

Four more blasts had rocked the city—two within days of the first. Then, after ten days in which people thought the terror might have ended, it was renewed with two bombings in one week.

Almost as soon as the dust had settled after each blast, information on the bombers would rush like a tidal wave onto all the mainstream media outlets. As information dried up, the news outlets would start rehashing old bits of information—re-framing it, rethinking the possibilities. The public wouldn't let them talk about something else, therefore it wasn't long after each blast that the average citizen was an expert on the lives and habits of the five bombers.

Ralph Jacobsen was quickly identified as the first bomber. He was a high-flying finance guru who fell on hard times. Reports from friends stated that he gave up his pursuit of the sweet life once he became involved with OFP. At the same time, his contacts with old friends and family faded.

The second bomber, Royce Bayez, came from a part of the city well known to have a high crime rate and low income. Little was known about his life before joining OFP, but investigative journalists discovered a small art collective where he lived and worked. Bayez worked out of a studio in the collective's ramshackle building and sold his artwork on the streets. Bayez's contact with the outside world was limited prior to his joining OFP.

Soon after Bayez came Christina Jeffs, a religious fanatic who spent the bulk of her time on street corners wearing large sandwich board signs displaying messages like "God help us" and "the end is near." In the time period leading up to her involvement with OFP, she had long since disowned her family and was well known in her part of the city as a harmless annoyance. After Jeffs had been identified and her past excavated, public opinion was that the OFP message had turned religious in nature. Then came Leon Mills and Steven Van Weisen.

Leon Mills was a small-time crook who spent most of his life in and out of county lockup, but somehow managed to stay out of prison. As far as anyone knew, before joining One Front for the People, he spent his time bouncing from one trap house to the next committing petty crimes to keep his veins well supplied with euphoria-inducing drugs.

Steven Van Weisen, the most recent bomber, was a male prostitute who went by the street name Mongo Kattan. Mongo, like three bombers before him, had no connections with his family. He also had no employment or medical records for the last ten years. Authorities and the media alike could only guess at how he lived his life before giving it up for the OFP cause.

With the exception of Ralph Jacobsen, all of the bombers lived largely off the grid, had little or nothing to do with mainstream society, and left little behind in the way of any records of their lives. They were, in Aubrey's mind, perfect candidates for the job of suicide bombers: little to live for, little to leave behind, susceptible to being taken in by a cause like that of One Front for the People.

He set the computer on the coffee table and walked to the window, his bare feet shocked by the cold floor. He tied his robe and parted the curtains a hair, peering out into the world. The street below him was bright and busy. The silent, infinite stream of cars flowed between the shores of foot traffic, all contained within the canyons of glass and steel and concrete. The twenty-four-hour cycle was in full swing.

Martin Aubrey, like many people in the city, was on edge and kept indoors. His reasons for doing so, however, were much different than the rest of the city. He wasn't afraid of the bombs or OFP. What he feared was the crushing feeling of walking outside among the people he looked down on from the window. Facing a world where he was just one of them—the ordinary people, the citizenry hivemind.

Incarcerated in the world as a private citizen, he was exactly like all of them out there walking around in fear. He considered fear an addiction. You became bound to it like you would a chemical narcotic. It rotted your mind and ultimately, you let the fear tell you how to feel. You let it tell you how to act. You let it tell you where to go, who to talk to, what to say. Going outside would mean admitting to himself and to the world that he was just like them out there. With nothing better to offer aside from more fear. He wasn't ready for that just yet.

He flopped back down on the sofa. Nearly every flat surface of his apartment was covered in takeout boxes. Dirty laundry hung over the arms of chairs and collected in piles on the floor. A sour stench wafted from the kitchen.

It had been twenty-one days since Aubrey last saw Tim Frass. Twenty-one days since the first blast. Twenty-one days since his short meeting in the police station where he helped

Lewis and Winger make their first major breakthrough. Had he helped? Aubrey liked to think so. He liked to think that maybe he had saved them time, if nothing else. He was fairly sure that someone would have come to the same conclusion, but maybe Aubrey had bought them a day or two. Even if he bought them a few hours' worth of a head start that would be something. He couldn't help but question how much his help had mattered. Buildings were still blowing up. People were still dying. Had he done anything to stymie the flow of blood on the streets?

After the first bombing, the police began rounding up known members of One Front for the People. There weren't many. OFP, Aubrey remembered, was a highly secretive, underground group of activists who never made public appearances. They did their work in the shadows. And in spite of several highly publicized arrests, the bombings kept happening. After each blast, another member or two of OFP would be seen on the news being detained by police. Inevitably, some talking head would ask, "Are we safe now?" Almost in direct response, another building would be ripped apart by an explosion.

The sleeping sickness OFP claimed to be spreading got second billing to the bombs. People were calling it Boarding School Syndrome which, to Aubrey, sounded like a shitty way of saying "rich kids are the ones getting sick, so why should you worry?" OFP had gone from hippie vandals and protestors to terrorists practicing both conventional and chemical warfare. Something about that just did not compute with him.

In many ways, infecting the children seemed more dangerous to Aubrey than the bombs ever would. Explosives were destructive and devastating to be sure, but they were also mechanical. They made sense. For every blast, there were mechanisms that worked together to make it go boom. In his head he could see it working. You could touch, hold, defuse, possibly destroy a bomb. Moreover, when it went boom, pieces of the bomb were sent flying. Those pieces could be found and then they could be identified. Identify the pieces and you could find their source. Follow the source to a buyer. Follow the buyer to a maker.

Boarding School Syndrome was different. Inside BSS, the moving parts and pieces were naturally much smaller and much harder to find. If they were there at all. And the motive seemed different. Yes, Aubrey thought, both the bombs and BSS were meant to instill fear in the populace. That was basic terrorism. However, on one hand the bombs targeted people at random and killed or wounded en masse. On the other hand, Boarding School Syndrome was targeting individuals—the children of prominent people OFP saw as being responsible for the chief ill of society: the Z pill. And unlike the bombs, BSS wasn't killing anyone yet.

In addition to a disparity in purpose, the differences in simple logistics bothered Aubrey. BSS victims were spread out over a huge geographic area at locations inside and outside the city. The bombings, however, had all taken place inside city limits in congested areas to ensure the grisliest outcome each time. The change in target locations brought with it a change in scope for each type of attack. Growth in scope like this often required the organization itself to grow in its potential reach and sophistication.

To Aubrey, however, the most important question was not why OFP was poisoning kids or where they were being infected. It was *how* OFP was infecting the children. How did a domestic terror organization have it within their means to create and deploy a hitherto unknown disease or toxin?

Children of prominent families with ties to every important institution, political party, and financial center of the city had been infected. And OFP promised it would keep happening. They made no demands outside of a full stop to the manufacturing of the Zentransa pill.

Was it as simple as OFP's demand implied? Or was there more to it? Every terror group wanted to create fear and sow the seeds of mistrust, but usually their end game included something more material—money, territory, or power.

Aubrey closed his eyes in the dark living room as these thoughts and questions coalesced with intense feelings of helplessness. Uselessness rose once again to the surface of his mind. He slid from the couch to the floor, his knees hitting before he realized he was falling. His robe billowed around him. Before he knew it, his forehead touched the freezing concrete. He lay there in the fetal position attempting to control some part of him that still remained connected to the world.

His inclination at the moment was to raise his head and slam it on the unforgiving floor as hard as he could. He thought of how easy it would be to chalk up all his feelings of ineptitude and detachment to a head injury.

Not today, some part of him said—the part that still remembered his old self. His self before losing his badge. Before his carelessness killed a fellow cop. And his old self wouldn't allow such a pity party. His old self was of the stuff Marines were forged, of the stuff cops were made. It was his old self that prevented his downward spiral from continuing further.

Aubrey pulled his head from the floor and rose to a sitting position. He kept his eyes closed, rested his hands on his knees. He breathed slowly and deliberately, controlling his breath the way he used to on the rifle range at the five-hundred-meter line. He imagined himself in the prone position, on his belly with the buttstock of the rifle placed in the pocket of his shoulder and the sling wound tight around his left bicep. He could hear his old instructor's words, "If that arm ain't numb after ten well placed shots, it ain't tight enough."

At five-hundred meters, staring down open sights, the target appeared smaller than the front sight-post. Rather than centering the post on the target's center mass, like he would at closer ranges, he would have to do the opposite: center the tiny black blur of the target on the front sight-post which was no wider than the tip of a ballpoint pen. Calm and steady breaths made the front sight-post move in a predictable figure-eight pattern, enabling him to time his shot at the right second. This required intense focus and more importantly, control of one's mind.

This is what Aubrey attempted to regain while kneeling on the smooth concrete floor of his apartment—control. His breathing steadied after a few moments and his mind began to clear. He needed to plan his next moves. He needed clarity around his goals. New feelings of purpose began to flood his mind.

Just as it all came to him, just as he felt some return to normalcy, he heard the familiar buzz of his phone's polymer case vibrating against the wood top of his desk twenty feet away.

Aubrey rose to his feet. When he picked up the phone and

saw who was calling him, he was shocked. When he last spoke to Detective Aaron Lewis twenty-one days ago, he assumed it would be the last time. In spite of promises to stay in touch, he knew how these things went. Yet, here was Lewis's name on his phone, calling Aubrey.

Aubrey tapped his screen to accept the call.

"Hello, this is Aubrey."

"Hey, Marty. It's Aaron. Glad I caught you. You busy?" Lewis asked.

"Sure... I mean, not really. What's up? Whatcha need?" He regretted every syllable the second he uttered them.

"Look, would you be able to come down to the station again? Tomorrow, if you have time."

"Yeah, sure. Need another statement?"

"Umm, no. Not a statement. We were wondering if you could come down and take a look at some stuff. Maybe give us your take on a few things."

Aubrey's stomach tightened. His breath failed him.

"My take. On what? You mean... for the OFP thing?" Verbal communication seemed to be failing Aubrey.

"Let's talk in person," Lewis said. "Be here at 0400 and we'll talk more. Look, I gotta go. I'll see you in the morning. Thanks, bud."

Aubrey ended the call and stared at his phone. For a moment, he considered the possibility that he might have hallucinated the last thirty seconds and that he might actually still have his head on the floor. Then, his phone buzzed with an incoming text message.

It was Lewis again. *Make it 4:30. Bring coffee,* he wrote.

Still staring in disbelief at the small screen in his hand, Aubrey replied, *Got it. See you then.*

The tightness in his stomach was gone and his breathing steadied of its own accord. He had the sudden urge to clean his filthy apartment.

10

Called Up

"So, Chief Inspector Long shows the surveillance footage of the first bomber, the one you, Winger, and I looked at. Remember?" Detective Aaron Lewis signed for Martin Aubrey at the New Aberdeen Metropolitan Police Headquarters' security station. They'd met outside the station and Lewis had walked him through the green tiled lobby and past the long detectives' room where they'd met three weeks before, hours after the first bombing. The room was not as busy now, but the atmosphere was no less tense. The security station sat just beyond the lobby where it played gatekeeper to the inner bowels of the police station.

Lewis's blue Oxford shirt was only partially tucked into his pants and his tie hung loose around his neck. He looked burnt out, like he hadn't seen a razor, a shower, or a decent meal in weeks. His usual pudgy white face looked gray and his eyes had sunken into their sockets. He figured that the last three weeks were no better for Lewis than for Aubrey himself.

Lewis handed Aubrey an ID badge, printed from a small kiosk. The kiosk was one of several stationed in front of a glass booth where a uniformed officer sat with a watchful eye on those wishing to pass through his security gates. The officer behind the glass looked close to retirement but maintained a vigilant watch as he monitored all biological and cerebral scans of visitors to ensure identities were legitimate.

Aubrey looked down at the badge. It was a standard police ID badge made of thin plastic and contained an RFID chip. Aubrey's picture, name, and the city's seal adorned most of the front of the badge. What caught Aubrey's attention, however, was a thick red bar across the bottom. Inside it appeared the word CONTRACTOR.

"Contractor?"

"Yeah. I mean, we can't pay you." Lewis shrugged. "And we can't force you to do anything. And there's no expiration date at the moment. So, maybe contractor isn't the right word. More like a consultant, I guess."

"But you want me to work for you. On the OFP investigation."

"*With* us. We want you to work with us. But yes," Lewis said.

Aubrey nodded. At once, he felt elated at the opportunity and fearful of not living up to it. The three weeks of misery in his apartment faded away like a distant memory only to be replaced by newer, equally powerful feelings of dread. This was the dread one feels after finally being granted a thing they've longed for only to receive it with a feeling they don't deserve it and don't know what to do with it now that they have it.

The two men were still standing by the now vacant kiosk as would-be visitors trickled in to take up the kiosks around them. The gravelly voice of the officer behind the glass came from an unseen speaker. "Gentlemen, if you're finished, please move it along."

Lewis waved at the officer and ushered Aubrey out of the way. They started down a short corridor where they scanned their badges to get through a security station and then through a thick metal door off to one side. At each location their identities were verified through biologics and cerebral scans. As they entered the second, quieter, hallway, Aubrey stopped Lewis.

"Can you explain why I'm here? I mean I'm more than happy to help. More than happy, trust me. I just don't get why—out of the blue—you need help from me. Why would they want me back here?"

"Alright. I didn't finish my story earlier. You remember the footage we looked at? Of Ralph Jacobsen?" Lewis said.

"Ralph Ja... yeah, the first bomber. What about him?"

"A couple of hours after you left the station that day, Chief Inspector Long showed that footage to the entire task force as part of the first briefing. We're talking fifty people. She must have shown them the last few seconds of that clip a dozen times," Lewis said.

"Why so many times?" Aubrey pictured the Chief Inspector. Chevelle Long had been a lieutenant when Aubrey started on the force and soon worked her way up. Since Aubrey had left the force, she'd been promoted to Chief Inspector of the Domestic Terror Task Force. This placed her squarely in the second most senior position at the station. Only the Chief of Police outranked her.

In addition to being tall and well-built, Chief Inspector Long was also a force of will with the intelligence, ambition, and relentless nature fitting her rapid ascent in the force. She was not someone to be trifled with.

"We had talked to her before the briefing and shared the theory... your theory... about Ralph being surprised the bomb was going off, about how he probably went in as a volunteer thinking that the bomb was a fake. Then, we explained the implications—remote detonation, Ralph was not a lone wolf, it's maybe a new terror cell, etc."

Lewis checked the time on his phone, then continued.

"So, before she made the big reveal in the briefing, she wanted to see if anyone else could see what you saw. Do you know what happened? No one in there. No one in the entire task force had the same hunch you did. And so far, it looks like you were right. We think the first guy was definitely a volunteer, sort of. And maybe the next ones were, you know, inspired by him or something. But poor Ralph had to be blown to bits to set precedent." Lewis shrugged. "And look," Lewis looked around before continuing. "We haven't really gotten anywhere lately..."

"What about all the arrests? They haven't yielded anything?"

"No. Nothing substantial." Lewis shook his head. "What they're saying on the news about us not being any closer to stopping the bombings—it's not that far from the truth. We're arresting them when we can find them, but it doesn't seem to slow them down. Not one goddamn bit." Lewis was failing in his attempt to keep his frustration in check.

Aubrey waited for him to continue while noting the obvious strain the investigation was having on his friend. He knew Lewis to be an easy-going guy, often unflappable. For Lewis to lose his cool, even a little bit, was a sign the investigation and maybe the police force itself was struggling.

With a sigh, Lewis continued, "So, Chief Inspector Long

wants fresh eyes on things, and not just the bombings. On BSS, too. Especially BSS. We've stalled on both, but we haven't gotten anywhere on the sleeping syndrome. We have exactly zero leads and exactly zero ideas on how they're doing. Look," Lewis glanced around for the second time, "she's feeling the heat from the top brass and they're feeling the heat from the mayor and he's feeling it from his constituents. I think they're willing to pull out all the stops for this. You aren't the first outside resource and you probably won't be the last. I wouldn't be surprised if they call in a fucking psychic next."

"I have a crystal ball at home," Aubrey said with a wry smile. "If you had said something, I would have brought it."

Lewis smiled, chuckling to himself. "Hey, on top of all that you still have a pretty decent amount of good will down here. Shit man, you've kicked in doors with half the damn force. A lot of people will be happy to see you back."

Aubrey nodded and raised his head. "A lot, but not all. Still some bad blood here where I'm concerned. I know that."

Lewis stared back at Aubrey but said nothing in response.

Aubrey looked around the hallway, noticing fresh paint on almost every surface. The air smelled sterile. Again, he noticed Lewis's haggard appearance with thick stubble on his cheeks and stained rings under his armpits.

"When was the last time you went home?" Aubrey asked.

"Home? Shit. I wish. Come on, let's get down there and I'll introduce you to some people you'll be working with."

Aubrey and Lewis started down the hallway once more when Lewis stopped and turned.

"Hey, where's the coffee I told you to bring?"

Aubrey always marveled that humankind's addiction to caffeine in its many forms hadn't vanished with the advent of

Zentransa. With or without the Z pill, the human body still tired physically and the mind dulled as the day wore on. The pill was the great rejuvenator, but it didn't provide endless amounts of energy or mental acuity.

"Oh." Aubrey had forgotten about the request. "Sorry, it slipped my mind."

Lewis's faced dropped. "Fuck. The shit they have here is pure piss water. I swear it's actual piss." He sighed. "Come on, let's go."

11

The Command Center

Martin Aubrey and Detective Lewis entered the command center for the Domestic Terror Task Force. Aubrey was familiar with the long rectangular room—desks down the middle with offices and conference rooms on one side and tall windows lining the wall on the other. Artificial daylight spilled in from the street reflecting off tablet surfaces, monitor screens, and large white faces of old-fashioned dry-erase boards scattered all around the room.

Aubrey wondered if anyone in the room could tell him the time of day without looking at a device. He doubted they could, owing to the Z pill and round-the-clock working hours.

The mood in the room was as somber as a funeral. The entire task force looked to be present and all of them looked as bad as or worse than Lewis. A few stood around a large board at the far end of the room. Most huddled around desks poring over images and data. Several of the conference rooms were occupied with tired-looking men and women. Everywhere around the room, people spoke in low tones as if they were afraid to speak any louder lest they awaken a vengeful god who would lash out and destroy them all for their ineptitude.

Detective Julian Winger approached Aubrey and Lewis as though he'd been expecting them. He led Aubrey to a desk in the far corner of the war room.

"I'll catch up with you later," Lewis said, making for an office in the opposite direction.

Winger motioned to two more detectives sitting at a smallish desk hunched over files covering its surface. They both looked up as Winger and Aubrey approached. The nearest, a tall female with straight dark hair dressed in an equally dark suit, stretched out a hand to Aubrey.

"Deputy Inspector Liz Reynolds," she said. "And this is Detective Ryan Grant." She nodded across the desk to the still-seated Grant, who nodded his greeting. His buzz-cut blond hair and baby face made him seem younger than he probably was. Reynolds continued, "You and I worked a couple of cases together a few years ago when I was in narcotics."

"I remember," Aubrey said after returning Detective Grant's nod.

"Grant and Reynolds are working on BSS," Winger said. He went on to explain that the two officers would bring Aubrey up to speed on BSS, then later that morning there would be a briefing on the bombings. Lewis wanted Aubrey to attend and would come by later to get him.

Winger excused himself as Aubrey pulled up a chair from a neighboring desk. "Where is the rest of the BSS team?"

At this, Reynolds frowned and fell into her seat. She looked across at Grant, who sat leaning his chest against the desk with elbows splayed to the sides as if eager for dessert. "This is it," she said, spreading her hands.

Aubrey scanned the large room again. He looked back at Reynolds and Grant—the only two people working on Boarding School Syndrome. In Aubrey's mind, there could be many reasons for this, but only one made sense.

As the leader of the Task Force, the Chief Inspector was putting all her resources into figuring out how to stop the bombings because they were actually killing people, versus BSS which had not yet claimed a life. This was sure to be a calculated decision as she would want to be seen doing something about BSS without jeopardizing the investigation into the bombings and the capture of the bombers.

There was a great deal of politics involved in managing a task force. The Mayor, city council, and Chief of Police were more than likely breathing down the Chief Inspector's neck to stop the bloodshed. This disturbed Aubrey in more ways than one because it meant that she would never deviate more resources to BSS. It also meant that she was as much concerned about what they appeared to be doing as she was about what they were actually doing.

"So," Detective Grant said, "I heard you used to be a cop."

"Yeah," said Aubrey. "Used to be." He decided to leave it at that. The two officers appraised Aubrey for a moment and to his relief, did not pursue the story further.

After a long pause, Grant said, "I guess we should get started."

"I think that's a good idea," Aubrey replied.

Reynolds and Grant spent the next two hours walking Aubrey through everything they had on BSS. The status of the case was what Aubrey had guessed: the police were diving deep into poisons, bio-weapons, and their delivery methods. In the last several weeks, they had interviewed doctors, weapons experts, toxicologists, and even ex-spies. They were researching every possible way BSS could have been weaponized and deployed to infect the children. But at this point, they had neither an idea of what poison, chemical, or neurotoxin was being used nor how it had been administered to the children.

They had many theories, but no conclusive evidence. Making things more confusing and frustrating, no OFP detainee had given them any actionable intelligence on Boarding School Syndrome.

"Even confidential informants and snitches can't give us anything worth a shit," Grant said at one point in their rundown of the case.

In a moment of silence, it occurred to Aubrey that they were thinking the way everyone expected—like cops.

"I think we need to be more scientific about it," Aubrey said after a moment.

"You mean to say our approach in evidence gathering is not scientific? We're using the most advanced investigative tools available," Grant retorted. "And our methods are..."

"No," Aubrey interrupted. "Not that. I just meant, so far, you've investigated it like a crime. Let's look at it like an illness. Like doctors. Like scientists."

"The doctors and scientists are already doing that," Grant said. "You know, because they're doctors and scientists... and we're, you know, cops."

Aubrey nodded and let the sarcasm pass over him. "We need to be all three. Scientists, doctors, and cops. Doctors are looking at it from the perspective of a disease to be cured or treated. Scientists are trying to figure out what it is chemically. Cops are looking for who did it and how. We *have* to be all three if we want to crack this one."

There was a pause in which it appeared that Reynolds and Grant were wondering how serious to take Aubrey on his suggestion.

"How do we do that?" Reynolds asked with raised eyebrows.

Aubrey leaned back in his chair and clasped his hands in front of him, resting his chin on his thumbs. After a moment he said, "I don't know. But I think we need to start at the very basics."

"Which are?" Grant asked with his hands spread, palms up.

Aubrey stared out the bright window turning the question over in his mind. What were the basics? Where to start to understand the medical, scientific, and criminal aspects of the case? Start with the crime? Start with the medicine? Or start with the science? He decided the medical aspects—the affected victims now seeking a cure, the symptoms, etc., were the end result of a crime having been committed. The crime, of course, involved whatever means the perpetrators used to infect the children. Infecting the children required, first and foremost, the thing itself—Boarding School Syndrome. Whatever it was—poison, toxin, pathogen, or chemical weapon—creating and deploying the thing required science. They should start by focusing on the science first.

"What is BSS actually doing to these kids?" Aubrey asked. "Let's start there."

"It's putting them in a coma-like sleep state," Reynolds said. "From this state, they cannot be woken up."

"Coma-like, but not a coma," Aubrey said.

"Right," replied the two officers in unison.

"They're basically sleeping."

"Yes," the two officers responded again in unison.

"What do we even know about sleep? What do we even know about the state they're in? Have you spoken to any sleep experts?"

"No," Reynolds said. "I don't see how that will help."

"This case… BSS, it feels different than the bombings. Doesn't it? It feels like a fifty-thousand-piece puzzle and we only have a handful of pieces. Meanwhile, we're trying to figure out what the damn picture looks like without even the box top to look at. You know what I mean?" The two officers shook their heads. Aubrey continued, "Well, I'm just trying to give us more puzzle pieces to work with. I'm trying to see more of the whole picture."

"Well, Mr. Aubrey," Reynolds said after a long pause, "you're lucky they aren't paying you. So, good luck with that and," she nodded in the direction behind Aubrey, "it looks like your meeting is about to start."

Aubrey turned and saw Lewis gesturing for him from the threshold of a conference room. As he walked away from the two officers, he overheard Grant say, "Sleep experts? What the hell, Reynolds. I thought he was a good investigator."

"Used to be," Reynolds replied.

***

The conference room was small and set up more like a classroom than a meeting space. Team leaders from the task force sat in rows of aluminum chairs facing a large touchscreen monitor on the wall. A short stocky woman, who introduced herself as Technical Specialist Morgan Lee, began giving the morning's briefing to the group.

"Good morning, everyone," Lee said. "Further testing

confirms our suspicions on the type of explosive used in the most recent blast. Chemical analysis of the blast site shows markers for the industrial explosive polysemtex-D. The same explosive used in all previous blasts." The screen displayed the chemical symbol for polysemtex-D.

$C_{12}H7N_{14}O_{18}$

Lee pressed a button in her hand and the symbol was replaced by a three-dimensional molecule rotating on screen.

"Polysemtex-D, as I mentioned, is an industrial explosive," she continued. "Highly prized for terrorist applications, such as the ones we're currently dealing with. Therefore, it is highly regulated and traceable. However, due to surges in industrial developments around the globe in countries less scrupulous than our own, it is also highly available. As a result, it is a favorite for any budding terrorist."

Aubrey had heard of polysemtex-D both as a Marine and a detective. It was the gold-standard explosive for blowing up buildings and killing people en masse.

Lee pressed the button in her hand again. The screen now displayed a collage of images: cream colored bricks in a neat pile next to a loosely coiled loop of some type of thick wire, several small metal tubes with rings on one end, a collection of various types of batteries, and a random assortment of electronic equipment.

"As you can see in this image," Lee said, "PSD can be detonated easily by anything from detonating cord, or det cord," she pointed to the coil of thick wire, "traditional blasting caps," pointing now to the small metal tubes, "or simple wires and batteries. Pretty primitive, but that's what makes it so popular with the terrorist set."

At the sight of the detonating cord and blasting caps,

Aubrey's mind flashed back to a hot day in the desert many years ago. He was a Marine in the middle of a deployment to one of the armpits of the world. He stood watching the Explosive Ordinance Disposal team disable an improvised explosive device hidden in a pile of garbage at the edge of a ramshackle town. The IED was blocking Aubrey's team's intended path down the shoddily paved road.

The Gunnery Sergeant in charge of the EOD team was showing Corporal Aubrey the new det cord and blasting caps they had just been issued.

"This new det cord packs a wallop, Aubrey," the Gunny said, holding a tightly wound coil in one meaty hand. "Three times the punch of the old stuff. And this little dude is pretty badass too." He held up a small silver metal tube with a ring through one end. "New blasting caps. Give it a twist to adjust the timing." The Gunny twisted the metal tube to the right and red LEDs lit up one whole side. "Turn it all the way to right, get all the red lights, and you're all set. Turn back to the left to reduce the fuse time." He did so and Aubrey saw the lights die out one at a time until only one red LED lit the end of the tube. "Pull the ring and things go boom boom. Slicker than shit, huh?"

The Gunny plugged the end of the det cord into the silver blasting cap and twisted it back all the way to the right, relighting all the red LEDs. He then handed the whole bundle to a young Private First Class who had been busy nearby donning a bulbous blast suit.

"Don't forget to pull the pin," the Gunny yelled as the PFC lumbered away toward the IED.

Lee went on to explain that the traceability of PSD was easy due to chemical fingerprints. Around the world, the handful of manufacturing facilities each had distinct chemical identifiers found in the PSD made there. Although each batch of PSD would behave the same when detonated, they could use these fingerprints to identify where it was made. Chile's facility, for instance, would produce PSD with higher trace amounts of chlorine due to air pollution from an abundance of metal foundries there. India would produce PSD with higher trace amounts of iron resulting from the red clay in the soil.

"The problem is," she said as she clicked the button in her hand again. A map of the world appeared with six red dots on various locations. "There are chemical fingerprints from almost all the PSD manufacturing facilities in the world. There are six facilities on earth and our bombs come from four of them. This, obviously complicates the tracing of the buyers, makers, etc. As we attempt to pin down..."

The door swung open and a young uniformed officer burst in. "Chief Inspector?" he asked.

"Yes? We're in the middle of something." The reply came from the back of the room. Aubrey had not realized she was in the room until that moment. An ebony skinned, impressive figure with sharp cheekbones and chin, Chief Inspector Chevelle Long could intimidate the hardest of men.

"S-sorry, ma'am. We just had another one," he said, panting.

"Another what, officer?" She stood. Her full height forced the officer to angle his glare upward.

"Bomb, ma'am. Another bomb."

12

The Chechen

Anatoli Rubinski stood in a darkened room of an apartment in an area considered by many to be the wrong side of town. He faced the window and tucked the cell phone into his pocket.

The Chechen, as Rubinski was called by his men, knew where he was going from here. He knew where he was going to deliver the package, or the "volunteer". He knew when he was going to do it. His plans were well thought out and he had every contingency prepared. No one had to tell him to be careful. His mission was clear.

He stared out of the dirty window for a moment piecing together the night ahead, mentally checking off all the tasks needing completion and the loose ends that needed tying up. This would be the sixth time, so most of this was automatic by now. Volunteer, drugs, vest, suit, van, ear-piece, instructions, detonation. But with heightened awareness everywhere and police on every corner, things had become more complicated.

He ran his finger along the window sill and stared at the thick layer of dust now stuck to his fingertip. He grunted in his low, gravelly voice. He rubbed the dust between his index finger and thumb until it became so many tiny balls falling away to the filthy floor. These safe-houses were only temporary, of course, but each seemed grimier and more germ-ridden than the last.

Life in the field was nothing new to him, but urban combat was a different kind of dirty. He had thought nothing could be worse than bivouacking in triple canopy jungle where everything on four legs, six legs, or eight legs wanted to kill you. Where the mud swallowed people whole. Where disease took healthy, robust men at dusk and had them shitting in their shoes by dawn.

Urban warfare was somehow worse than any environ he'd waged war in; somehow it was filthier. He felt imprisoned by this putrid city and its massive walls of buildings everywhere.

He'd been involved in so many conflicts in so many shithole parts of the world that each new one eventually blended in with the rest. The particulars—why, when, where, who—faded in short order. This one, however, would stick with him like an indefatigable canker sore painfully residing on the roof of his mouth.

The Chechen walked toward an adjacent room where his men were awaiting their instructions. He was a short man but had always been what his father had called "cock strong." He had never known whether his father was referring to the phallus or the chicken, but felt the meaning was the same either way. He had always been able to take care of himself. Half a lifetime as a soldier and another half as soldier-for-hire had hardened him into cold rolled steel.

The Chechen entered the room where four of his men sat in a rough circle around a fifth. The men looked up as he entered, the nearest jolting to a stand so fast his chair toppled over backward.

No one spoke as the Chechen stared at the fifth man in the middle of the room. The fifth man slouched sideways. An IV tube ran from his left arm to a bag of foggy-white liquid hung from a hook on the wall. He sat open-mouthed, drooling, and staring at a spot on the wall.

Liquid restraints, the Chechen thought. He had no need for cuffs or zip ties when using his homemade concoction. He also had no need for leverage or hostages or bribes. All he needed was the right dose and a voice. The "volunteer" never developed cold feet. He had spent years perfecting the right mix to produce what he called *the voodoo.* He had spent many more years employing it in the field. This project was a perfect application.

"Is our volunteer ready?" the Chechen asked. He spoke in English to his men. He hated speaking English—it was clunky, disjointed, and inarticulate. He longed to speak his native tongue, but his men came from disparate, dark corners of the globe and they needed a universal language.

"Yes," the man next to him said. Nodding vigorously, he continued, "He has been on the proper dose for four hours, just like you said. He should be ready."

"Stand up," the Chechen ordered. The volunteer got clumsily to his feet. He stood hunched and swaying, but otherwise the volunteer looked sturdy. The Chechen watched a rope of drool fall from the man's open mouth, stretching down to the volunteer's knees before breaking off and falling to the dusty floor.

"Give me a five," the Chechen said and stuck out his hand in front of the fifth man. The man continued drooling and staring at the floor, but raised a hand and in slow motion, placed it in the Chechen's.

"Up high," the Chechen said, raising his hand high in the air. The volunteer complied with no change in his expression or glare.

"Down low," said the Chechen, lowering his hand. The drooling man lowered his hand but before he could connect, the Chechen pulled away. "Too slow, as your people say."

His men burst into laughter which lasted, according to the Chechen, a little too long. He stared at the volunteer a while longer, considering him.

"This one is more... drooling than the others," the Chechen said. "I may have been off on the mixture a bit." He looked again into the face of the volunteer.

The man beside the Chechen said nothing.

"He vill draw attention. Fix it," the Chechen said with finality, turning to leave.

His man cocked his head to the side. "F-feex it?"

The Chechen turned back and stared hard at his man. He gave the man a look of utter confusion. "FIX. IT. You have two hours. Then, we move. Maintain his dose until then."

The Chechen left the room and could almost feel the men behind him looking to one another in confusion. He heard one of the men whisper, "'Ow zee fuck do we keep heem from droolink?"

* * *

The Chechen and his men sat in a darkened van three blocks from the target building. The volunteer sat strapped into a jump seat against the bulkhead. He was dressed in a clean, dark suit, his hair stiff with gel and slicked back. Unseen in his ear was a wireless ear-piece. And his mouth was shut tight.

Under the volunteer's white shirt and tie, several pounds of high explosive were strapped to his torso.

The Chechen turned from the passenger seat to look at his volunteer one last time. Small, whitish spots stood out on the man's cheeks where drops of the cyanoacrylate glue had landed and dried. From here it looked like dried toothpaste. After all, who would ever think his lips were glued together, the Chechen thought.

Surveying the man further, the Chechen thought the volunteer looked like just another overstressed corporate finance dick. The Chechen loathed people like that—dedicating themselves to a life of working themselves to death only to make other people more money. It made his current project all the more bearable.

The Chechen spoke into a small one-way transmitter. "Touch your head." The volunteer's hand flew up and landed on the crown of his head. "Stand up." The man stood, his head clanging against the roof of the van. He made no sound at this; he stood hunched against the roof.

* * *

It was almost 4:00 a.m. and traffic swelled as the peak of rush hour hit. James Pitts leaned against an office building in the downtown area of the city. He looked relaxed to a passerby, but his head was on a swivel.

The bombings in the last few weeks had everyone in the city on edge, but none more than first responders, especially cops like him. Being a cop was not something he ever actively pursued; he more or less fell into it by accident. A college degree didn't get you very far these days without the right connections—of which he had precisely zero. The police force was desperate for warm bodies some years back, so he went with it.

Like most things he did in life, he found ways to make it easy and, most important to him, tolerable. His dad had always said he was a natural "skater" and not the kind on wheels or blades. His dad told him he skated through life, finding a way to glide along the easy path while others trudged and toiled to get by. Jimmy Pitts was born smart enough to do almost anything, but too lazy to do anything all the way. His philosophy was to do just enough to avoid negative attention, but not so much to garner any unwanted positive attention. Thus, trouble and responsibility were avoided. He pitied those not keen enough to figure out the game as he had. More so, he pitied those that felt they had to do so much to succeed.

Pitts's strict code of self-preservation aside, anyone finding themselves in his inner circle knew they could count on him when they really needed him. Like now, in the midst of the random blasts and the sick kids, he was on high alert for action. These life or death situations were momentary blips on the radar and didn't bother him—he always managed to dodge permanent damage. This, however, felt different to him. The relentlessness of the bombers, their ability to evade capture, and the randomness of the blasts all made him more uneasy than usual. As a result, he was more aggressive than usual when the drunk man ran into him.

"Hey, buddy," Pitts said to the drunk as he reached out to steady him. The man wore a nice suit and would have looked rather dapper with his slick hair and clean face if it wasn't for the fact that he was blind drunk. "Watch where you're going, alright. Why don't you go home and lay down? You hear me, pal?"

The man didn't say anything but tried to force himself forward past Officer Pitts, acting as if he had just run into a potted plant and not a full-grown man in a police officer's uniform. More than his behavior struck Pitts as strange, however. The man's ear-piece had a blinking green light, which Jim assumed meant a live call was taking place but the man wasn't talking and didn't appear to be listening. His face was blank. More than that, the guy's face looked... weird; his cheeks were puffy and distended.

Not swollen, Jim thought, more like... they're about to burst. His lips too.

The man struggled to move past him, but Pitts kept a firm grip on his shoulders. All he needed was this guy getting himself killed after he let him go. Pitts realized that while the man continued to struggle, he made no move to shove Pitts. The man simply would not stop trying to walk by.

"Hold still, pal," Pitts yelled. "Let me take a look at you, goddamn it. Hold still."

In one quick motion, Officer Pitts swung the man into the building, threw a forearm into his chest and with the other arm jammed an elbow under the man's chin, pinning him against the building. The man continued to squirm, trying desperately to make his way wherever he was trying to go.

"Pal. Pal. Take it easy, OK. Keep resisting me and things are going to turn very bad for you. You hear me?"

Pitts stared at the man for a moment more trying to get a closer look at his face. Again, Pitts was taken aback by the man's puffy cheeks. They were getting puffier by the second and looked to be putting some strain on his lips, which were pale and cracked, but holding tight together. It looked so unnatural. His entire face was tightened and strained. Then, Pitts noticed strange white stains on the man's cheeks and chin, as if spots of skin had been bleached. His crusty lips had the stains too.

Pitts continued to examine the man, turning his face left and right when suddenly, the man's body went rigid. His face began turning blue. Instinctively, Jim eased back on his restraining hold. It didn't seem to help. The blue turned a deeper shade, now almost purple. The man had stopped trying to walk away altogether and instead turned his head skyward. His chin bobbed up and down like a cork in rough water. He began swallowing convulsively—like he was trying to dislodge something from his throat. Pitts realized at once that the man was choking on something.

* * *

The van drove in the opposite direction the moment the volunteer was let out. The Chechen held the one-way transmitter, giving verbal instructions. They chose the drop off point because it had the straightest and easiest route to the target building. He was a practiced hand at this particular exercise, but he had to be careful. Things could go off the rails in a flash.

Turning to his men, he said, "Drone."

One of the men in the back removed a small black object from a bag and thrust his hand out of the window. The drone buzzed into the air. A live feed appeared on the van's oversized console touchscreen. The Chechen watched the bird's eye view as the volunteer, dutifully following orders, made his way to the target building. He thought about how convenient it would be if all of his men were so obedient.

The ear-piece acted as a tag as well as a receiver. Following the man in the suit, even in the dense crowd, was easy. They zoomed in tight on his figure boxed in a green outline, moving steadily toward the building.

A block and a half away from the target building the small green square around the volunteer stopped, then staggered. As the crowd around the man cleared a bit, the Chechen and his men saw the volunteer in the hands of a uniformed police officer. Everyone in the van was transfixed, watching as their volunteer was thrown against the building by the officer. No one made a sound. Seconds passed when finally, the Chechen spoke. "The switch," he said, holding out his hand. His eyes were still glued to the screen. "Hand me the…" He paused mid-sentence. The volunteer's neck bent backward; his face was looking straight up. "Zoom in tight. Vaat is he doing? Vaat is wrong with his face?"

"*Bid,*" one of the men cursed in his native tongue. Leaning over the Chechen's seat to get a closer look he said, "Ze drool… ze, ze glue, I think. Ee is not swallowing… you must tell him."

"Tell him…" The Chechen didn't understand, then in an instant he realized what was happening. He jerked his hand with the transmitter toward his mouth. His hand and the device crashed into the edge of the van's console screen. He could feel the plastic casing separate into several pieces, then he heard the tinkling of the tiny pieces clattering to the metal floor. The corner of the console screen now had long cracks spreading across it, accentuated by a growing black splotch that spread like an ink stain, devouring pixels as it went.

One of the Chechen's men reached out and gingerly touched the shattered screen as if he was a faith healer about to cure this injury with a touch. A spiderweb of cracks spread the instant his finger met the screen. With a feeble blip, the console went black.

* * *

Officer Pitts backed off as the man's head, neck, and throat continued to seize in this strange way. He watched as the man's face grew even darker bluish purple. Clueless as to how to help him, Pitts reached for his radio. As he did, a strange fluid began to run from the man's nose and the corners of his mouth. The fluid was clear and frothy.

Is he foaming at the mouth? Pitts thought. He had no idea what could be happening. More concerned now than he was a few minutes ago, Pitts called it in.

"Dispatch, this is 53902. I have 10-52 at my location. Subject is having trouble breathing, may lose consciousness."

The dispatch agent responded right away by first, confirming the location of his beacon then, advising Officer Pitts to clear the airway and begin chest compressions. Ambulance drones were en route.

"10-4," Pitts replied. "You hear that, buddy. They're coming. Don't sweat it, alright. You'll be fine." He patted the man's chest and grasped him under the arm pits and began lowering him down to the sidewalk. Passersby began clearing a hole around the scene. Laying the man on his back, Pitts attempted to clear the airway, but there was a major problem from what he could see.

"What the fuck?" Pitts said. The man's mouth was sealed

shut. It hadn't occurred to him before now because it was such an odd thing to see, but they were. Sealed. This man's lips were glued shut with some kind of adhesive.

Pitts had no idea what could have happened to this man or however he ended up like this, but if he didn't do something soon this man would die right here. Pitts knew with some degree of certainty that he had to open the man's mouth. The choking and the glued lips had to be connected. At that moment, the man's eyes rolled into the back of his head and his body went limp.

"Come on, pal," Pitts shouted.

Forgetting about the man's distended cheeks, he slapped the man's face to revive him. A hot squirt of fluid flew from the corner of the man's mouth onto Pitts's open palm. Jamming his finger into the small opening, Pitts worked the hole larger and larger with one, then two fingers until it was large enough to begin physically and grotesquely peeling the man's lips apart. Peel them apart he did. With both hands he forced his fingers between the man's crusted, dry lips and pulled. More hot liquid poured from the man's mouth as Jim separated bottom lip from top. Blood mixed with the clear liquid as the thin lip membrane tore and separated—what was once part of the bottom lip now adhered to the top.

Halfway around the mouth, Pitts stopped and turned the man's head, allowing the fluid to drain onto the ground. In one large splash, it landed and soaked into the knee of Pitts's dark blue pants. Inspired by little more than instinct, Pitts reached back one more time and let loose a slap hard enough to wake the dead. On impact, the man's eyes shot open and issued forth a raspy, deep inhalation arching his back high off the ground as if taking the first breath of life. He coughed and sputtered. He blinked several times and with fluid running from his mouth and nose, he began breathing normally again.

"Hey, you're alright now, pal. Breathe easy, but in a minute, I want to ask you a few questions. Hey, settle down..." The man tried to get up. He tried to move, making for the same direction as before. Pitts was having none of it, pinning the man to the ground.

With two hands flat on the man's chest, Pitts discovered what this must be, what it all meant. The blank look. The relentless movement. The glued lips. The strange shapes that he could now feel hidden under the man's shirt.

In a catastrophic impact, Pitts's above average intellect collided with his below average motivation. He knew there would be no skating out of this one.

With his hands on the man's chest, through the pressed shirt, Pitts could feel long rectangular shapes. He could feel wires. He had no idea how any of this had happened. He had no idea where this guy had come from. He had no idea what a poor, unlucky bastard this man must have been to wind up in this situation, but he knew what it all meant. Panic rising, he looked around at the crowd of onlookers that had gathered. He looked beyond them at the traffic. He craned his neck to look up at the building, imagining how many people were up there in those offices. Still somehow managing to hold the struggling man in place, he grabbed his radio and called dispatch.

"Dispatch, this is 53902 again, same location. Subject is one of the... one of the bombers. I say again, subject is one of the bombers. I have him restrained. Clear all wheeled traffic in this vicinity and..." Pitts looked around at the faces of the unlucky people who happened to be walking by this morning.

"I'll need assistance clearing foot traffic. And send the bomb unit. Quickly."

People around him screamed. Most of them began to run; those who didn't stood with stunned looks on their faces. "Bomb?" they murmured to themselves then to each other, searching for validation. "Did he say bomber? Oh my god."

A herd mentality took over as people began to trample one another to get away. Utter chaos broke out as they ran into the street flowing with speeding vehicles. People pushed and pulled to get away as fast as they could. Those not close enough to hear the officer's call took the hint from those fleeing and followed suit.

* * *

From the van, the Chechen and his men scrambled to get another monitor up and running while also fumbling with the shattered transmitter. The Chechen held a series of wires and pieces of circuitry between his meaty fingers while one of his men desperately tried to connect more pieces salvaged from the floor. They were nearing the edge of the city as things grew frantic.

"Got it," said a man from the back of the van. The Chechen turned to see the small handheld screen the man was holding. He watched as the tiny figure of the police officer pawed at the chest of the volunteer who was still squirming to break free.

"Fuck," the Chechen screamed, flinging the remains of the transmitter to the floor. "The switch, goddamn it. Where is it?" He couldn't take his eyes from the screen. Seconds later a small box was thrust into his hand. It was smaller than his palm and had four raised buttons running in one row across its middle.

Still watching the small screen—watching the crowd run, watching the panicked men and women get upended by speeding cars in the street, watching hair torn out, clothes ripped, innocents trampled by neighbors in pursuit of self-preservation—the Chechen entered a combination of buttons he knew by heart: 2, 4, 3, 3, 1.

The screen went white, and half a second later everyone in the van heard a low rumble from some distance behind them.

13

No More Volunteers

The footage was shaky but clear on the large monitor. The officers and detectives in the command center crowded around watching the footage having just acquired it from the cloud database. From his body cam, the late Officer James Pitts captured crucial evidence in his interaction with the most recent bomber. The footage was automatically streamed and saved to the cloud as it occurred. Pitts was the first and only person able to obtain up close footage of one of the bombers since Ralph Jacobsen, the first suicide bomber.

The recording was confusing to Aubrey at first. From the angle of the officer's chest, all he could see initially was a blur of gray and black as people rushed by on their way to work. Then, a sharp jostling of the camera and a turn to see an apparently drunk man in a sharp suit trying to make his way past the officer. The view was too close to get a good look at the drunk, then a quick ninety degree turn and the man was against a wall. From this angle, they all had a good look at the soon-to-be bomber.

"Facial recognition. Now, please," Chief Inspector Long

said over the silent watchers. "I want to know who he is."

"On it," came a voice from the fringes of the crowd. Then, a shuffling as someone made their way to a computer somewhere across the room.

On the screen, there appeared to be a short struggle. Then, the bomber's head shot back and he began convulsing.

"What's up with him?" asked someone in front of Aubrey.

"Looks like our boy got too rough with him," came another voice.

"Nah, I don't think so," replied another.

The man was on the ground, now. It appeared the officer was calling in the incident. After taking him to the ground for apparent medical assistance, the officer was now poking and prodding the man's face which was oddly distended. The officer attempted to insert a finger past the man's lips but struggled as they were clamped tight shut.

"What is going on? Is he drunk?" asked Lewis in an aside to Aubrey.

"Who gets a bomber drunk before they go boom?"

"Liquid courage?"

As the officer peeled the bomber's lips apart, a cloudy liquid poured from the man's mouth.

"See that?" Aubrey said. "They were stuck together. Actually, it looks like they were glued together. What do you make of that?"

"What the hell is that fluid? Vomit? Bile?"

"Saliva, I think." Aubrey leaned closer to the screen. He grabbed Lewis's arm and pointed at the screen. "I bet they glued his mouth shut to keep him from drooling. They didn't want him drawing attention—a clean cut guy in a nice suit drooling like a mental patient would definitely get noticed."

"Yeah, but why is he drooling?" asked Lewis.

"Drugs?" Aubrey and Lewis were now having their own conversation while the others stared at the action unfolding on screen.

"Maybe drugs. But again, why get your bomber drugged up before sending him out to go boom? What if he makes a mistake, goes to the wrong building or never detonates?" Lewis rubbed his temples.

"Right. You don't want his judgment impaired. So, why the drugs? And look at the way he's fighting. It's almost robotic. Why would you want your bomber acting like that?"

Lewis continued rubbing his temples. "Who knows? I'd rather have a robot wife sometimes. At least robots can't argue with you."

"HA." Aubrey slapped the desk in front of him. "They want them to be robots so they can't change their minds. So they can't resist. There's your volunteerism. It's drug induced. They're pumping them full of something that turns them into robots. Tell them where to go and they just do it. That's why he looks drunk. Drooling must be a side-effect, so they glued his face shut. Downright wicked, but clever. Pretty goddamn clever."

Aubrey stared at the screen as the man on the ground continued to struggle. "Pretty damn clever. The whole thing is pretty goddamn clever."

Almost every eye in the room had turned to Aubrey. No one spoke.

On screen, the officer was patting the man's chest. After a moment, the crowds in the video footage began running away, panicked. They were scattering as the news of a bomb spread. Seconds later, the screen went white.

* * *

"Facial recognition came back with a one hundred percent match for our bomber. His name is Blaine Winston. We're getting background info on him now and a team has begun questioning OFP detainees about him." Detective Lewis pointed to a large screen which displayed the photo ID of Blaine Winston. "Street surveillance footage just came in from the cloud showing Winston leaving a black van moments before the blast."

One hour after the entire task force viewed the body cam footage, team leaders gathered in a large conference room for the first of several hourly briefings to be held that day. The briefing leader role would rotate each hour.

On screen, Lewis showed video footage collected from one of the street's surveillance cameras. First, they watched the entire event in reverse. They saw the white nothingness recorded in the camera's last seconds materialize into a confusion of debris and plumes, then the reversal of the shrapnel as it went home to its place in the structure of the building. The street scene was now full of people and cars and buildings still intact.

Lewis zoomed in tight on the bomber, flat on his back with Officer Pitts attempting to restrain him. The drugged volunteer moved in reverse; his back against the wall. Now, they watched him shift to the officer's side. Finally, he was walking backwards on a direct path to a black van. Lewis stopped the footage once he reached the van and played it back in slow motion.

"Here," he pointed to the screen, "you can see a small drone leaving the van just after our guy starts walking. Based on the size of the van and the window it came from, we estimate there were at least three other people inside."

"Speaking of the van..." Chief Inspector Long started.

"The van leaves seconds later and drives west. They used some kind of film on the windows that interferes with our cameras and sensors. The footage we have does not give us a clear shot of the inside. After the blast, the van enters an eight-story parking garage several miles away. Here." Lewis pointed to a small square on a map, which he opened in a lower corner of the screen. "No surveillance inside. Several adjacent buildings use the garage, so lots of people coming and going at all hours. Uniforms are searching the van right now. So far, it's clean of prints and DNA."

"Was the van under Metro Traffic control?" the Chief Inspector asked.

"Yes," Lewis said.

"Then why didn't MTS stop the van? And can we get any data on the van from MTS?"

Lewis scratched his head. "MTS only interferes when something illegal is happening. At the time, the van was just parking on the side of the road, then moved to a parking garage. Nothing illegal there."

"And the data?" The Chief Inspector spoke with tightened lips and narrowed eyes.

"There was nothing, Chief Inspector." Lee stood in the back of the room. "Wherever the van came from, it was wiped clean prior to today. It's like it didn't exist."

"Any other ideas, people?" The Chief Inspector's voice was on the edge of shouting.

"Lee, can you run a search to see if anyone leaving the garage in the hours after the blast wound up going to the same place?"

said a female detective to Aubrey's right.

"Yes, but like I told you after the last four bombings," Technical Specialist Lee replied, "facial recognition only works if we can see most of the face. Very few of our street cameras are at eye level and on top of that, few people actually look ahead when they're walking." Lee stood and approached the screen. "And even if we get good angles, we're talking about looking for facial recognition matches for the few thousand people entering and exiting the garage against the millions of people captured in thousands of cameras in the city..."

"Well, this is the..." began the Chief Inspector.

"...that's if we even have good facial shots. These guys are pros, so they'll know facial recognition is what we'll try first. And we'd have to talk parameters. I mean how many people meeting together is significant. But if we had other criteria to cross-reference," Lee continued unimpeded, staring at the images on screen now, talking more to herself than anyone else. "Like age, gender, background, or..."

"Thanks, Morgan," Lewis said with the apparent intent of breaking her train of thought. "We get it. Maybe you and I could talk about it after this. Essentially what you're saying is, it can be done, it just might be slow. And we'll have to get pretty lucky to get a good face."

"No. I'm not saying that it can be done. Not definitively, anyway." Lee shook her head. "We'll have to be *really* damn lucky. I mean, we have the bomber's face, so we can track him, but we'll have to be pretty damn lucky to get the others."

Aubrey agreed that facial recognition tracking was great on paper, but in real life it was rarely foolproof. He had the feeling that everyone in the room except Lee was leaning on it because they hoped it would be the magic bullet to their case. Lee was right, however; these guys were pros and the likelihood was almost nil that they'd reveal their faces even partially. Then, Aubrey was struck with an idea and couldn't believe it took him this long to think of it.

"What if we don't need faces?" Aubrey stood. Everyone in the room turned in his direction. "My company has an experimental program, cutting edge tech. It can recognize patterns in nonverbal behavior—gestures, walking gait and pace, physical mannerisms—coupled with body size and shape to help identify individuals. It gives probability matches, I've never seen it hit a hundred percent, but it's been pretty useful in the past. This may be a perfect application for it."

Everyone turned from Aubrey to Lee who shrugged. "Worth a shot. Will your company let us use it?"

"It's a proprietary program, but I'll ask."

"Good. Let's make that happen," said the Chief Inspector.

The briefing ended a moment later and as the room emptied, Aubrey stayed behind to discuss the details of the body language recognition software with Lee. He was detailing the nuts and bolts of the program when the Chief Inspector approached.

"Aubrey," she said, "only a few hours in and you're already contributing. That's good, very good. Makes me feel like we're getting our money's worth."

She stood two inches taller than Aubrey's six feet and looked as though she was put together from head to toe with precision; every square inch of clothing had a purpose only she knew.

"Sure thing, ma'am. Happy to do it," Aubrey replied. He had difficulty telling if the Chief Inspector was joking with her comment about them getting their money's worth. It occurred to him that she must be unaware of his unpaid volunteer status. He couldn't imagine her telling a joke or anything close to it.

She stared off at the wall of windows as she spoke. "I brought you on to help with the syndrome. Let's keep your focus there. We've got plenty of people working the bombings." She looked back down at him and squinted. "Stick to BSS. Understand?"

"Yes, ma'am. Of course."

Without another word, the Chief Inspector turned and walked away toward her office.

14

Deep Dive

"So, there was maybe a couple of details I failed to mention."

Lewis and Aubrey were standing in front of an automated hot dog cart outside Police Headquarters. Lewis was making his selection from a narrow touchscreen on the side of the squat cart. Aubrey had no interest in hot dogs from a robot cart, but Lewis insisted this particular cart was the best in the city.

"Details such as..." Before leaving the station for lunch, Aubrey had shared with Lewis the odd encounter he had with Chief Inspector Long.

"She wasn't thrilled with the idea of bringing you on. She showed Ralph's footage to the task force so many times because she was trying to prove that her people, us, could have figured it out."

Lewis extracted a fresh, steaming hot dog from a small compartment in the side of the cart. Aubrey admitted to himself that it did smell pretty good before ultimately deciding to partake in a hot dog as well.

"Prove it to whom?" Aubrey began scrolling through the

hot dog types and their various toppings.

"Major Corser. Remember how he came up to us right after we figured out Ralph's surprise and all that. He was a big Marty Aubrey fan back in the day. Still is, apparently." Lewis started in on his hot dog, moaning with pleasure as he did.

"So, what? He's a fan, so what?" said Aubrey.

"He's the one who told Chief Inspector she should bring you on as a consultant. She was resistant and insisted that her people could have made the same discovery you did. When they didn't, she had to concede. Voila, you're here." Lewis devoured the rest of his hot dog with an expression of bliss.

"I see."

"No, you don't." Lewis shook his head and discarded his hot dog wrapper. "The real story, the one she would never tell anyone, is that she wants a cop to be the one to stop the bombing. The only way she gets real credit for it is if it's one of her people, one of us. If it's some outsider, then they'll say she couldn't get it done. Also, the rumor is the Chief of Police is about to retire. When he does, she should be next in line, but not if she can't stop all this craziness."

"I see."

"Now, you do." Lewis eyed Aubrey's uneaten hot dog. "You going to eat that or..."

***

Back inside the station, Aubrey tried to concentrate on Boarding School Syndrome, but Officer Pitts's body camera footage had left him unexpectedly shaken. The implications arising from the new theory—that the suicide bombers were in fact not volunteers and therefore not suicides, that they were being drugged with some unknown concoction and now controllable—were unnerving.

The ability to induce anyone into becoming a bomber against their free will changed the way he viewed One Front for the People. As criminals, they were brought to a new level of loathsome; they were also far more dangerous. He now felt that the bombings and Boarding School Syndrome were not the lowest forms of terror of which they were capable.

Later that day, he decided to make a call he had hitherto been reluctant to make. He called his boss at OWG Insurance and informed him of his new role as contract investigator for the Metropolitan Police Department working on the Boarding School Syndrome case. He also informed his boss that he would not be able to continue his assigned investigation for OWG. Aubrey told him all this knowing that he would also have to ask for access to the proprietary body language tracking software for use in his work with the police.

Aubrey let the bad news sink in first before getting to his favor. As expected, his boss did not take the news well. After all, his boss had a boss and responsibilities and deadlines. The calm demeanor his boss normally displayed was broken in a cacophony of curse words and angry questions that all started with "What the fuck…", "Who the fuck…", or "How the fuck…"

Aubrey endured the angry backlash for several minutes before he interrupted and asked for access to the proprietary software owned by OWG. To his surprise, his boss took the request with calm consideration.

"They need our help, huh?" his boss had said after a long pause. "I mean, the police need our help to find and catch the deadliest terrorists in a generation. This could be… an interesting opportunity. To help, I mean. To help. To lend a hand. I mean, we're at war here, right? We're just chipping in."

Catching on to the unspoken actual opportunity, Aubrey said, "I'm sure the Chief of Police and the Mayor would be very grateful. Grateful enough to publicly thank the company and... you specifically."

"Oh, well that... that would be appreciated, surely. But you know just the fact that we could... that the company could assist in apprehending these monsters, well that's... Martin, let me run this up the flagpole and get back to you."

It had only taken an hour for the top of the OWG food chain to get wind of the Metropolitan Police Department's request to use the company's software. Their answer was an enthusiastic yes. And when it became known that an OWG investigator was now playing a crucial role on the task force responsible for ending the terrible violence, Aubrey was given an open-ended and fully paid sabbatical to continue his work with the police.

Furthermore, his boss's attitude regarding the incomplete fraud investigation changed rapidly in the hours between their first phone call and the recent email with OWG's emphatic support of the investigation. He was given permission for full access to their proprietary body language recognition and tracking software. Access would be granted immediately using the cloud-based OWG system.

Later that evening, after working with Technical Specialist Lee to get the OWG software up and running on her computer, Aubrey sat down at the BSS desk. He, Reynolds, and Grant were combing through data on the sleeping victims. Reynolds and Grant were busy with their heads down, scanning hundreds of documents, discussing possible leads as they came up. Behind them, a brainstorming board held dozens of sticky notes, grouped by color, each color matching a potential theory or lead. On the board now were three main groups labeled water/food borne, gas, and reverse cerebral scan. The last, reverse CS, was the newest group.

Aubrey turned in his creaky chair and looked at the board for the hundredth time today. In its many-colored sticky notes, all he could see was desperation. They were reaching for straws with these ideas and he felt that Reynolds and Grant must know it even though they would never admit it to themselves for fear of the worst feeling an investigator can have—going nowhere fast.

At the far end of the command center, Aubrey could see the lead board for the bombing side of the investigation. He squinted as he stared at the web of items spreading across the wall. Although they had advanced tools at their fingertips, cops would always use cork boards and paper. There was something about it that helped cops solve crimes—the tangible objects laid out before you to form the skeleton of a story not yet told. What he thought about now was the story of this string of crimes, the author of which seemed to be many chapters ahead at all times.

He turned back to his own notes on BSS. He was making his way through a series of folders containing everything Reynolds and Grant had collected on BSS, so far. Coming in with fresh eyes, he began as if BSS were one of his cases. He began by looking into the victims themselves, their families, and any and all ties to Ventana and the Z pill—the alleged impetus behind the poisoning. He admired the work done by Reynolds and Grant thus far. They had laid out a thorough and complex web of ties between the victims, but the only one he could find was the one that OFP made public: the victims were children of prominent people who had ties to Ventana.

The victims' ties to Ventana, however, varied in depth of involvement and length of time affiliated with the company. One victim's father was retired, but had served in Ventana's C-suite, eventually going on to serve as a board member. One child's mother was presently serving as a board member becoming involved with Ventana as an early investor in Zentransa. The latest victim's father was an executive at Ventana who many believed served as James Sarazin's right hand.

The common thread throughout it all was the fact that the parents of the victims had a significant stake in Ventana, Inc. With Zentransa serving as its most important product, an investment in Ventana was essentially an investment in the Z pill. OFP knew this and was targeting them for it.

Based on some quick math by Aubrey, all three of the victims' parents had doubled their money several times over. The motivation was clear: One Front for the People felt ire, disdain, and animosity toward anyone who had profited so much from the Z pill—the one thing they saw as having caused significant social strife and upheaval.

As Aubrey flipped through pages of documents and briefs prepared by Reynolds and Grant, there was one obvious pattern that stood out to him. Maybe the fact that it was so obvious made it easy to look past. He was staring out the window when Reynolds interrupted his stream of thought.

"You look like you've got something."

"Oh, yeah maybe," Aubrey said, startled out of his reverie. "When we look at BSS, who is OFP attacking?"

"Kids. Kids of people with ties to Ventana, specifically the Z pill."

"Right. Kids. Only kids."

"So far." Grant set down his tablet.

"Only kids," Aubrey continued. "So, only people who have kids are being targeted. There are some key people who were involved in Ventana when the Z pill was developed and brought to market and they haven't been targeted."

"Yet. They haven't been targeted yet," Grant said.

"Maybe. Though you could argue that the people they've targeted so far weren't even that instrumental in Z pill's development. One was an investor, but the others just worked at Ventana. The only reason they had a stake in the company was because it was given to them as part of their compensation package. They didn't fund the project."

"They're terrorists. And at the moment, they're blowing up random people all over the city. I don't think being discerning about who they terrorize is a priority for them," Reynolds rebutted.

"BSS is different. The motive, the means, the timing, the scope, the scale. Everything about it is different. We can't look at it from the same lens." Aubrey stood. He walked over to the large board with theories and leads posted on it.

"The strangest part," he said, "is not what they are doing. It's what they aren't doing. I mean look at these people." He pointed to pictures of James Sarazin and two other men: Stanley Campbell and Lawrence Moore. "The top dog himself and his top lieutenants. You've got the CEO, the Chief Marketing Officer, arguably the guy responsible for making Z pill what it is today in terms of sales, and the President of Ventana, Inc, whose job, as I understand it, was to build the business around the Z pill. Not one of them has been directly targeted yet."

"Do they even have kids?" Reynolds asked. "Grant, check that out." Grant tapped away on his computer for a few seconds.

"Nope. None of those guys have kids," Grant said.

"There you go. They don't have kids, so no one to infect."

"If that's true, we're working under a pretty huge assumption. That they only want to infect children. Why not infect adults?"

"Hurting kids is scarier," Reynolds said. Leaning back in her chair, she stared at Aubrey. He turned to meet her gaze and could see from her expression that she was not being combative. She was playing devil's advocate, debating, doing her job as a detective to cover all the bases in an argument designed to elicit the most fruitful conclusion.

"So why not just kill them?" Grant asked. He was looking back and forth between the two of them, as if he were unsure of whose side to take.

Reynolds looked at Grant. "Because the state they're in now is more frightening. Their fate is unknown. Just like the bombings, we fear the unknown. The kids could live or die. People walking to work every day could live or die. Their building might be next. It's all about fear. That's their point. Directly attacking the people responsible for the Z pill, the great evil in society according to OFP, isn't scary and doesn't send the message they want to send. Sarazin and his cronies have to watch these people suffer. They have to watch it and think about it. That's worse than being blown to bits or being put in some sleepy-coma."

"I see your point," Aubrey said. He turned back to the

board. "It makes sense, but something seems off about this." A thought occurred to him. "Does Sarazin have any young relatives? Nieces, nephews, anything like that?"

Grant tapped a few keys on his computer and dragged an image to a large monitor on the wall. It was a family tree with a thumbnail image of Sarazin at its apex.

"One brother and two sisters," Grant said as he highlighted the respective branches of Sarazin's family tree. "On his brother's side, he has two nieces ages eighteen and twenty. His sisters each have one child, a boy and a girl. Ages are three and thirteen."

"And they're all fine, at the moment?" Aubrey asked.

"At the moment, yes."

"They're not the age range of the other BSS victims," Reynolds said. "They don't fit their target demo."

"That's a flimsy assumption. Why should age matter?" After a long pause Aubrey said, "We're missing something. Something important."

"Of course, we are. If we knew everything, we'd... know everything. That's why we're here—to figure this shit out." Reynolds took a deep breath and sighed. "Look, why don't you do what you said earlier and get to know BSS as a disease like a scientist. And we'll continue to track down threads and commonalities between the victims."

Aubrey nodded. He stared at Sarazin's family tree. He felt sure there was something he wasn't seeing.

* * *

Nori Tashima knew she was lucky. No one anywhere close to her age was in this room. She looked around, taking it all in—the boardroom, the table, the power of the men and women seated around it.

Along the walls on either side of the long ebony wood table sat others like her—assistants, one for each seat at the table of power. Alike to her in role and duty but she was younger than the rest by at least twenty years.

She inhaled deeply, arching her back and lifting her chin. Her small hands clutched the tablet in her lap, ready to access anything her boss might need during the meeting. So far, Mr. Hanson had only turned around to ask her for a tissue. They were just getting to know each other, but soon the old man would trust her. He'd known her since she was a child but had only recently begun to take her seriously as a professional.

She was lucky. Her father and Mr. Hanson were old friends, but as her father would say, "Luck will only take you as far as your own intellect and skills will let it."

Lucky or not, no one her age was attending a Ventana board meeting.

"Despite the violence, shares are steady and we still forecast a 7% gain on EBITDA this month over last year," said an ancient black man. He sat at the far end next to Mr. Sarazin at the head of the table facing the wall of windows. Mr. Sarazin wore a blank expression. The man delivering the financial report had a scratchy voice and every syllable sounded like it took a great deal of effort.

"Thank you," Mr. Hanson said, startling Nori. He hadn't spoken since the meeting started. "What of this fund, James? For the bomb victims. Where is that money coming from?"

All eyes fell on Mr. Sarazin. He adjusted his black necktie and cleared his throat. His gaze remained fixed on the windows. "Me. You. Us. What does it matter?"

The forty-odd people around the table exchanged glances. Board members, officers, and senior leaders were all in attendance for the quarterly meeting, making for a packed room.

Mr. Hanson coughed quietly then continued, "Everyone clear out except the board members."

Once again, everyone looked to Mr. Sarazin who waved a hand in affirmation. With angry looks toward Mr. Hanson and mumbled complaints, the room cleared leaving only Sarazin, his eight board members, and their accompanying assistants.

No one moved. The board members remained seated.

"James, you promised an unlimited fund for the victims." Mr. Hanson had turned his high-backed chair to face Sarazin.

Mr. Sarazin nodded, still facing the windows.

"If these attacks continue, there could be thousands of victims," said a woman on the other side of the table. Nori had yet to learn the names of all the board members. The woman's hair was short and white with age. "This could become very costly."

"I don't care about the money," said a small man at the opposite end of the table from Mr. Sarazin. "We have the money. What concerns me is the threat."

This caught Mr. Sarazin's attention. He turned his chair to face his board of directors.

"What threat?"

"The threat against this company and…"

"There is no threat against this company. The company is doing fine. You heard the numbers. People don't want us to cave in to those terrorists and their insane demands."

"I'm not talking about P and L here, James," said the small

man. He leaned in against the edge of the table and slapped its black surface. "And you know that. I'm talking about the fact that they're targeting the children of key people from this company and its history. You may not have children, but we do."

"You think I don't care about your children." Mr. Sarazin leapt from his seat and pressed his fists into the table. "You have no idea what I'd do to protect them if I could." He turned and skulked toward the windows.

Outside, the simulated daylight gave an otherworldly silver glow seventy-five stories up.

"What can we do?" said the small man. He pulled at his tie. Moisture blossomed on his prominent forehead. "Should we leave? Should we take our families and go abroad somewhere? We shouldn't even be in this building, it's not safe." He looked around for agreement, his eyes searching the faces of the others.

"This building is safe. That I can assure you."

"How? How do you know, Sarazin?"

Mr. Sarazin turned back toward the room and spread his arms in exasperation. "I'm the richest man in the country in charge of the most successful company in the country. You don't think I have measures in place to protect us? There are things going on around you, Uri, that you have no idea about. No idea." He smiled, but Nori could see it pained him. His eyes did not reflect what his mouth attempted to portray. "You're safe, Uri. You're all safe."

Mr. Sarazin looked into the faces of each board member, who nodded in turn. He leaned on the table, looking calmer now.

"Run if you want to, Uri, but I'm not sure how much good

it will do. Me? I'm staying right here. If those motherfuckers want me, they can come and get me."

15

Clues

April 26, 2043

Aubrey felt three quick taps on his wrist. Pulling his jacket sleeve back, he looked down. His watch displayed a reminder of his appointment in five minutes—*11:00 a.m., Dr. Corey, Dr. Uday @ St. Mary's.*

He looked up at the edifice of St. Mary MacKillop Children's Hospital. Like almost everything else in New Aberdeen, it reflected the ultra-modern style of a mid-21st century building—surfaces covered in glass and stainless steel. It shined in the morning sun, forcing Aubrey to squint.

Detective Grant cleared his throat and pointed his chin over Aubrey's shoulder. "Here comes Reynolds."

The two men stood at the base of the stairs leading up to the hospital's main entrance. Aubrey looked over his shoulder to see Deputy Inspector Reynolds walking toward them. She looked fresher and more alert than the last time he'd seen her. They'd all agreed to go home, shower, and eat a decent meal before today's meeting. In the past forty-eight hours, the three of them had barely come up for air while working on the Boarding School Syndrome case. The meeting they were about to walk into was meant to give them a better idea of the science behind sleep, Zentransa, and, most importantly, a possible cause for BSS.

After muttered greetings, the three of them climbed the steps to the hospital's main entrance. Above the wide double doors in tall gold script read a Latin phrase: *Bona Diagnosis, Bona Curatio.*

Moments later, on the thirtieth floor, they exited the elevator. This floor, much like the main lobby and various corridors they passed through on their way to the elevator, felt warm and welcoming with pastel colors on the walls formed into a mix of shapes, angles, and curves. Friendly looking cartoonish animals appeared here and there with giant, toothy smiles.

They stopped just outside the elevator at a touchscreen that doubled as a directory and a bulletin board. Reynolds scrolled through the names until she reached the U's. Aubrey read a few postings on the other half of the board. One read: *Movie Nights: Friday 7:30 Social Room 3.* The notice was superimposed on a picture of a film reel. Next to it was an animated stage with its curtains drawn. After a second, the curtains opened to reveal the words: *Talent Show Saturday May 4th—Kids, Doctors, Nurses, Parents—bring your "A" GAME.*

"Uday. Here we go," Reynolds said. "This way."

Reynolds led the way to Dr. Hassan Uday's office. Along the way, they passed a library, and one room filled with kids of various ages. They wore patient gowns and, it appeared, they were in various stages of their respective ailments. They all sat in mauve cushy chairs centered around a pair of kids clutching game controllers. All eyes were glued to an enormous monitor. The spectators cajoled and egged on the players. IV bags gyrated on their hooks as several of the kids pumped their fists. Aubrey didn't get a good glimpse at the screen as they passed, but it sounded like the two gamers were in the midst of decimating a civilization whilst trying to assassinate one another.

They arrived at a closed door bearing a plaque that read *Dr. H. Uday, Pediatrics*. Reynolds knocked. No answer. She checked her watch, as did Aubrey. 11:01 a.m.

They waited for several more minutes. Aubrey was going to knock himself when a voice called out.

"Detective Reynolds?"

Aubrey, Grant, and Reynolds turned to see a doctor in a white lab coat waving at them from a doorway twenty feet further down the corridor.

"Let's talk in the breakroom. I have no furniture in there." The doctor waved them over. "Come. I have tea. Robert is here too."

In the tiny breakroom, the three investigators sat across from Dr. Hassan Uday, a pediatrician, and Dr. Robert Corey, a sleep scientist brought in to help the hospital with BSS.

Under his lab coat, Dr. Uday wore a navy-blue t-shirt emblazoned with the Superman symbol. Dr. Corey wore a pale green Oxford shirt tucked into dark khaki pants. Dr. Corey's red hair was balding down the center of his scalp while Dr. Uday's thick black hair reflected the white lights above them with the health of a middle-aged man who took care of himself. The two men seemed to get along just fine and probably made an effective team.

Five paper cups sat on the table. Wisps of steam rose from hot water steeping with tea.

"So, any progress?" Reynolds asked, starting the interview.

Uday looked at his partner before replying. "Well, we haven't cured the kids yet if that's what you're asking."

"But," Corey interjected, holding up a finger, "we do know a lot more now than we did the last time we spoke with you."

Before setting out that morning, Reynolds told Aubrey that she and Grant had interviewed Uday and Corey as soon as One Front for the People claimed responsibility for BSS.

"You know more about Boarding School Syndrome or how it's deployed or both?" Aubrey asked.

Corey's forehead wrinkled and he shot Aubrey a look that bordered on disconcerted.

"Well," Corey cleared his throat, "first, it would be BSD or Boarding School Disorder if that were the name you chose to use. It's not a syndrome, it's a disorder or a disruption in bodily functions, versus a syndrome, which implies a series of signs and symptoms associated with some larger cause. We've come to calling it acute hyper-somnolence or AHS."

Aubrey nodded. Corey went on. "As far as how it's being deployed, as you say, or how the children come to be infected, that is still a mystery. We can say, however, that there is no *clear* indication that these children were poisoned or infected by anything or anyone."

"Other than OFP saying so," Uday said.

Corey closed his eyes and nodded in apparent exasperation. "Yes. The fact that OFP has claimed responsibility and the fact that this disorder has popped up suddenly with no other explanation means that we can't rule out nefarious infection."

Aubrey glanced at Reynolds briefly and when she didn't continue the line of questioning, he spoke up.

"Can we talk about sleep for a minute?"

Both doctors gave Aubrey surprised expressions, then Corey said, "Sure. What do you want to know?"

"How does it work? What actually happens when we sleep?" Aubrey pulled a small writing pad and a pen from an inside coat-pocket.

"As a certified expert on the topic, I can tell you sleep is as enigmatic today as it has been for a century." Corey leaned back in his chair. He looked comfortable. Aubrey could tell the words came easily to him.

"The basics of sleep science are easy enough to understand: molecules in the brain—adenosine and adenosine triphosphate, or ATP—work together on either end of a chemical seesaw." Corey held his hands up, mimicking the balancing action of the playground toy. "When the seesaw tips one way or the other, it triggers when someone should sleep or wakeup. Adenosine builds up in the brain over the course of a day while ATP degrades, tipping you toward sleep. While you sleep the reverse occurs—ATP builds back up and adenosine degrades. When ATP reaches a certain level, the seesaw tips and you wake up."

Grant leaned in toward the table and grabbed his paper cup of rapidly cooling tea. He said, "So, where's the mystery? Sounds like you have it figured out."

"We know what happens to make you sleepy," Corey said, "and we know that sleep restores your body physically and mentally. Without it, or without a pill that replaces it, your health declines rapidly—your organs will begin to fail, you'll hallucinate, eventually you'll die.

"The mystery is why we need sleep. Why can't the body restore itself while you lie still in a quiet room with your eyes closed. What is it about sleep itself that's so special? We think the brain may require that state of sleep in order to perform its own maintenance. Like self-repair."

Aubrey scribbled his notes inside the notebook, rapidly filling the pages. Looking up, he said, "What does Zentransa do? How does it replace what we get while we sleep?"

"Zentransa works in two ways." Corey grew animated. This was his field of study and it clearly excited him to talk about it. "There is an immediate effect and a delayed, time released effect. After you take Zentransa, it very rapidly tips the ATP, adenosine seesaw in your brain. It drops adenosine and raises ATP to normal waking hours levels. The sensation you feel…"

"Zoning," Reynolds interrupted, referring to the ten to twenty seconds of euphoria produced once the Z pill hits the brain.

"Right. Zoning," Corey said. "Zoning is the brain resetting itself. Zentransa tricks the brain into thinking it just slept eight hours and so it begins performing all the restorative functions it would normally do while you slept, except that you're awake."

Grant, having finished his tea, crumpled the paper cup in his hands and tossed it in a garbage bin behind him. He said, "What's the second way it works?"

"Oh, right." Corey adjusted himself in his chair. "Zentransa also slows the rise of adenosine throughout the day while keeping the degradation of ATP in check. That's why you need several days off Zentransa to get back into a normal sleep cycle. It stays in your system. And the longer you take it without an occasional night's sleep, the longer the weaning period."

"What about the nightmares?" Reynolds said tentatively.

Corey shrugged. "Another mystery. We're not sure why

it happens but during the first real sleep, after coming off Zentransa, you will experience vivid, often frightening dreams." He shrugged again and half frowned. "Some in the field of sleep science believe the brain *requires* dreaming, to some extent, to perform that self-repair that I mentioned. They believe staying on Zentransa creates a dream backlog of some kind. So, when you do sleep, they come rushing at you like a torrent."

"And what..." Aubrey never finished his question. Outside the breakroom, from somewhere down the corridor, came shouting—a man's voice.

The group in the breakroom exchanged looks.

Dr. Uday held up a finger and pointed in the direction of the commotion. "I'd better go see what's going on." He walked out of the breakroom and Aubrey, unable to help himself, followed the doctor.

Stepping into the corridor, the shouting grew clearer. Two voices could be heard—the very loud man and another, much softer, man's voice.

"Well, where the fuck is he? My son hasn't changed one iota and this doctor is hiding out somewhere."

"Sir, I'll go find him right now. If he knew you were looking for him..."

"He should be glued to my son's bedside, goddamnit. Go get him, for fuck's sake."

Aubrey walked ten feet behind Dr. Uday, who'd quickened his pace. They reached the end of the corridor where it intersected with another and Uday turned right. Aubrey soon followed him around the corner.

Aubrey stopped behind Uday, who spoke with a nurse in hushed voices. "He's very upset you weren't here. He wants to speak with you."

Over the nurse's shoulder, twenty feet away, a well-dressed man stood by the open door of a patient's room. His suit was impeccable—dark blue, well-tailored. Even as a former cop and someone who would never consider himself fashionable, Aubrey could tell this man's attire was expensive. Maybe more than Aubrey earned in a month.

The man's silver hair and smooth face with well-defined cheekbones also gave the impression of stature. He held a trench coat draped over one arm and a soft, tan leather briefcase dangled from the other.

The man visibly seethed. His eyebrows stitched into a deep crease down the middle of his forehead. His lips were drawn so tight they all but disappeared.

Uday approached the man. "Mr. Lattimore, what can I do for you?"

Aubrey knew the name. Lattimore was the last name of one of the children infected with BSS.

"You can help by planting yourself next to my son's bed and never leaving until he's awake and back to normal." Mr. Lattimore pointed with his briefcase hand into the open door. "I came up here to check on Charlie and no one has been in his room for over an hour. What the fuck am I paying for?"

Uday raised his hands in supplication. "Mr. Lattimore, I assure you we're doing everything we can for Charlie. This disorder is not completely understood…"

"What are you people doing with all the money I've donated to this place? I practically paid for this wing and I can't even get a doctor to stop by to see my son?" Mr. Lattimore spoke more to the walls than to Dr. Uday. His eyes were wide and his head shook repeatedly from side to side. The man looked hysterical.

A woman appeared in the doorway of what Aubrey guessed was Charlie's room. She wore a loose cardigan and jeans. Her once blonde hair was pulled into a loose bun on top of her head. Her eyes sat in deep sockets.

She uncrossed her arms and touched Mr. Lattimore's elbow, which nearly startled him.

"Honey," she said. "Let the doctors do their work and stop raising a ruckus." She turned to Uday and said, "My apologies, Dr. Uday. My husband is under a lot of stress."

Her touch seemed to calm Mr. Lattimore, who closed his eyes and let his chin fall to his chest.

"I'm sorry, honey." With his eyes still closed, Mr. Lattimore shook his still-bent head. He took a deep breath, straightened and looked at his wife. "I have to go."

"I know," she said.

After a quick peck from his wife, Mr. Lattimore walked past the nurse, Dr. Uday, and Aubrey, not making eye contact with any of them.

Once Mr. Lattimore had made the turn down the next corridor, Uday said, "Mrs. Lattimore, what can I do?"

She waved a hand through the air. "Nothing. Why don't you just come say hi to Charlie?"

Uday smiled. "I'd love to. I was about to make my rounds after I finished talking with the police." He gestured toward Aubrey.

Mrs. Lattimore turned to Aubrey with a half-smile. "You're more than welcome too. It'll be a party."

The central feature of the room was the bed on which Charlie Lattimore lay. It was a standard hospital bed—white rails, adjustable to various states of comfort and height, white sheets pulled to Charlie's chin, white pillows cradling his tow haired head. Charlie's face appeared completely serene. His chest rose and fell slowly in perfect rhythm. He really did look like he was just asleep and could wake up any minute.

At the head of Charlie's bed stood racks of instruments in the form of gray and beige boxes of various sizes with readouts and touchscreens on their faces. Tubes and wires ran from the machines, disappearing under Charlie's sheets.

Dr. Uday began his examination of Charlie. He passed over the medical devices around the bed, pulled up the sheet and inspected connections between wires and cuffs on the boy's limbs. He then began touching Charlie in different places on his abdomen and moved his limbs in various motions.

In the midst of all this, Aubrey felt like an intruder. This moment seemed unusually intimate and he was a complete stranger. He retreated to a far corner of the room.

It was then he noticed the wall of flowers. They covered the full length and half the height of the wall nearest the foot of Charlie's bed. From one side of the room to the other bouquets of lilies, tulips, sunflowers, and other flowers had been lain and stacked in half-orderly fashion. The newest flowers had been added on the right and the display gave an eerie real-time representation of decay. On the far left, pedals had dried and crumpled to the floor. Stems wilted, twisted, and bent as if the slightest touch would send them to their dusty end.

Moving along the wall, the flora gradually came back to life. Browns turned to dull yellows, reds, and whites. Dry turned to moist. Wilted turned to supple and firm. It was life in reverse.

Mixed in with the decaying plants were stuffed animals—bears, dogs, tigers, other creatures Aubrey couldn't name. Some were tiny while others sat waist high.

"So thoughtful, aren't they?" Mrs. Lattimore caught Aubrey by surprise. She'd sidled up next to him.

"Yes, very," Aubrey said. "Friends of his?"

"Oh, yes. Friends of his. Friends of ours. My husband's business associates." She placed a hand on Aubrey's shoulder. "You'll really have to forgive him for the outburst. He blames himself for this. Those monsters targeted our poor Charlie because of his dad's work with Ventana." Her hand clutched the fabric of Aubrey's coat. "Are you any closer to finding them? To stopping this?"

"Every day that we learn something new, we get closer." Aubrey didn't know what else to say. What do you say to a mother watching her child sleep for the rest of his life, not knowing when or if he'd ever wake up?

Mrs. Lattimore removed her hand from Aubrey's arm. She twisted her fists against her chest, pulling her cardigan closed.

"Ma'am, I'm very..."

"Detective?" She looked up at Aubrey. "I haven't eaten in I don't know how long. Would you mind if I stepped out for a moment to run to the snack machine?"

Aubrey nodded. "Absolutely. I'll keep an eye on your boy, Mrs. Lattimore."

She moved to the bed and patted Charlie's hand.

"I'll be right back, Char."

Dr. Uday continued his examination after Charlie's mother left the room. Aubrey felt more comfortable now and walked to the bedside opposite the doctor.

Uday was working a soft black cuff that covered the boy's forearm. Similar cuffs wrapped around the biceps while strips of the same material stretched across his chest and abdomen. Circular sensor pads dotted the boy's exposed skin on his chest, neck, and temple. Aubrey imagined there must be more cuffs, strips, and sensors on Charlie's legs and pelvis.

Uday tore at a Velcro strip on a forearm cuff, opening it to reveal the white skin beneath.

"I can do that, doctor." The nurse startled Aubrey who hadn't noticed him enter the room.

"No worries, Tommy," Uday said with a smile. "Us doctors need to do these things every now and again."

The exhausted looking nurse wore light blue scrubs with pockets across the front. Several small, unrecognizable instruments poked out of the top of the pockets. Near his collar, he wore a brightly colored flower pin with a button in its center. Aubrey imagined the flower would spin or light up if the button were pushed. Just a way to entertain a kid about to get poked with a needle.

"Will he survive, Dr. Uday?" Aubrey asked, careful to keep his voice low. "Will any of the kids survive this?"

Uday didn't look up. He examined the inside of the forearm cuff. Tiny silver disks reflected in the dim light. He rubbed the skin on Charlie's arm then held a finger to one of the silver discs as if waiting for something. After a few seconds, his raised his eyebrows and reclosed the cuff.

"See these?" the doctor asked. "Deep tissue stimulators." He waved a hand over the boy's body, pointing out the other cuffs and strips full of the stimulators. "We can simulate light activity in the muscles with these. We can't make him a body builder, but we can mimic some low stress movement. It keeps the muscles from atrophying to a great degree. And this," from the bedside he lifted a clear tube flowing with yellow liquid, "we can give him all the nutrition he needs—calories, vitamins, minerals. And this," he tapped the inch-wide disc on Charlie's temple, "allows us to stimulate his brain in ways we could never before. And these lights," he pointed up to an array of long rectangular tubes on the ceiling, "can provide UV radiation. I can give him a day at the beach, simulated, but very near what he'd get if he were actually there."

Uday pulled the covers back over Charlie and gently tucked them under the boy's arms and shoulders.

"In short, Detective Aubrey, we can create much of what the boy would experience if he were awake. He is perfectly healthy, at the moment, and will remain so. One could argue that he is healthier now than a typical child his age since he doesn't eat all the junk food and soda so common with kids this age."

Heat bloomed under Aubrey's collar. "Perfectly healthy except that he won't wake up. Can't move. Can't talk. I'm sure the Lattimores would trade all the junk food in the world to watch their son kick a soccer ball one more time." A pause. "And I'm not a detective. Just a private citizen."

Uday raised his head, looking sheepish. Aubrey could feel Tommy, the nurse, eyeing him from the side.

"Of course, Mr. Aubrey. I didn't mean to imply his current state is preferable. I just meant that when he wakes up, he won't be in any worse shape than when he fell asleep. And to answer your question, no, I don't think this disorder in itself is deadly. He is physiologically just… asleep. We have to find out why and, most importantly, how to wake him up."

Aubrey heard footsteps behind him. Expecting to see Mrs. Lattimore, he turned to find Reynolds, Grant, and Dr. Corey in the doorway of Charlie's room.

"Everything OK in here?" Reynolds asked. Her face fell as she took in the room. Her eyes lingered on Charlie before she said, "We need to go, Martin."

* * *

Aubrey, Grant, and Reynolds walked the fourteen blocks back to police headquarters.

The day was bright. The sun gleamed off the buildings around them and Aubrey felt the heat begin to seep into his bones.

The sidewalk traffic was lighter than usual for the lunch rush, but it had become commonplace since the bombings started. People felt, understandably, safer indoors.

"Get anything useful from Corey?" Aubrey asked. A red light flashed on a pole thirty feet in front of them. It stood twelve feet high and, along with the flashing, it emitted a low undulating tone. An identical light pole ten feet further along the sidewalk flashed and blared as well. Two red and white striped barriers lowered themselves from the building and stretched across the sidewalk.

The three investigators stopped walking. They were in the medical district, Aubrey remembered. Ten seconds later, an orange and gray ambulance sped past them in a blur. It made an impossibly fast ninety degree turn across the ramped sidewalk ahead of them, drove between the barriers, and disappeared into a newly opened entryway in the side of the building.

Once the ambulance had disappeared into the bowels of the hospital, the barriers lifted, the lights stopped, and the entryway closed. All this happened without a fuss, aside from the light poles and sirens. Ambulances in New Aberdeen had no sirens or lights. The Metro Traffic System cleared the roads ahead of emergency vehicles and coordinated with the hospitals' operating systems.

Aubrey looked up at the clear sky. A medical-drone buzzed from a hatch high up the side of a hospital. In the span of a few seconds, two more drones entered other hatches, delivering patients, he guessed.

"Aubrey," Grant said.

He lowered his head. His partners were waiting for him.

"Sorry. Let's go," Aubrey said. After a few minutes, he reiterated his earlier question. "So, anything from Corey?"

"Only more on the mysteries of that cosmically enigmatic thing we call sleep." Grant shook his head as he spoke. "Isn't it ironic that he takes Z so he can study sleep?"

Aubrey nodded his appreciation of Grant's observation.

"We also talked about possible deployment measures," Reynolds said. She rubbed her eyes with her long, slender fingers. "He was not very cooperative, at first. I think he believes that BSS…"

"BSD," Grant interrupted and shrugged as Reynolds cut him a look of impatience. "Sorry, but we know it's a disorder now. Or, as the doctors call it, acute hyper-somnolence."

"I'm not introducing another acronym to our Lexicon," Reynolds said. "Let's just stick with BSS. Anyway," she glanced at Aubrey before continuing, "I think Dr. Corey believes BSS is not weaponized or part of some attack. He thinks it's all biological, part of some new plague or something."

"We can't rule out the possibility, but we need proof first. Until then," Aubrey removed his blazer and continued, "we go with the most convenient explanation—OFP is making it and deploying it."

Reynolds nodded. "Sure. Eventually, he humored us and made a few suggestions we should look into."

They stopped as a line of a dozen children in blue and gray school uniforms passed. A teacher at the head of the line and one at the end each held flags with the school's logo emblazoned on it—an orange fox on a blue background. The children, around eight years old, bounced along in something resembling good order.

The investigators continued walking after the children passed. Reynolds went on to explain that Corey suggested reverse cerebral signature as a possible way of rewiring the brain to such a degree as to cause BSS.

"But that would require a huge device and you'd need to already have the kid's CS mapped in order to alter it," Grant interjected. "And mapping the CS of a child is illegal. How would they get the CS in the first place?"

Mapping cerebral signatures was a massive undertaking requiring time and vast resources. Huge machines were needed in addition to the complete cooperation of the subject being mapped. The three of them agreed it didn't seem plausible.

Other possibilities Corey suggested for BSS weaponization were ones Aubrey and his partners had already thought of—aerosol deployment, water, pills, gels, and direct injection. Most of the possibilities were all but impossible to infect one intended target without infecting others. So far, no BSS victims had prior contact or proximity to other victims.

"What about radiation?" Aubrey asked. "Have we thought about that? That can be directional. They used to use radiation machines for cancer treatment targeting very small areas."

The other two nodded at his suggestion.

They were leaving the medical district and entering the commercial area where police headquarters was located.

They made small talk for several minutes. Aubrey listened to Reynolds and Grant talk about a recent retirement party for a captain where more than one officer got overserved and made fools of themselves. As they went on about the debauchery, Aubrey's mind wandered to the school children they passed earlier. He had no idea if they came from wealthy families and if those families had ties to Ventana and Sarazin. What if one of them was next? What would he do right now if he were a parent with a child that age? He couldn't imagine the terror of going to wake up your child for school every day not knowing if they'd open their eyes. Not knowing if you'd already said your last words to them. Not knowing if you'd feel their embrace again, send them off on their first date, help them move into a college dorm.

Aubrey shook the thoughts from his mind. He needed a clear head if he was to be of any use to the BSS investigative team. Stuck inside his ruminations, he'd been walking with his head down for some time. Looking up, he noticed the massive beaux-arts style police headquarters building coming into view on the opposite side of the street, a quarter mile ahead. With brown, rusticated first-floor masonry, arched windows, and pedimented main entrance, the long rectangular block of a building stood in stark contrast to the rest of the modernist city.

The building only looked old. It was completely contemporary in materials, infrastructure, and technology. It was designed to be a connection between the futuristic city and the old world. Law and order, Aubrey thought, wasn't the world's oldest profession, but it was its noblest.

Something on the sidewalk near the opposite corner of the building caught Aubrey's eye. A pedestrian's sudden movement, an annoyed shout, people turning to stare. A break in car traffic gave him a split-second view of the area near the commotion.

His heart sank to his shoes. His mouth dropped and his heart jackhammered in his chest.

He watched a woman with filthy, matted blonde hair walk slack-faced toward the main entrance of police headquarters. She wore a bulky red raincoat and walked with apparent purpose, bumping into other people with no regard for them. She didn't change direction. She didn't slow down.

Without thinking Aubrey dashed into the street. Tires screeched; alarms blared from somewhere. He ran without regard for his own safety, vaguely aware, somewhere in his brain, that the MTS had safety measures built in to stop traffic if someone stepped onto the street.

In five seconds, he was across the street onto the sidewalk in front of headquarters. He threw himself into the middle of a small crowd, threw aside a man in blue overalls, and wedged through two women in track suits. He had a clearer path now and ran harder. He heard his name shouted over his shoulder. More feet pounded behind him—Reynolds and Grant were following him.

He caught sight of the back of three dark blue uniforms walking together twenty feet ahead.

"Officers," he shouted. The officers kept walking, not hearing him over their own conversation. Aubrey shouted again, "Officers!"

One of the cops, a baby-faced young man, turned and locked eyes on Aubrey. "10-89!" Aubrey screamed the numeric code for bomb threat and pointed toward the other end of the sidewalk.

"10-89?" Recognition crossed the young officer's face. "Shit. 10-89? Where?"

Aubrey ran past the trio, not waiting. "Red raincoat," Aubrey yelled over his shoulder. "Woman, blond hair."

"Clear the sidewalk." Reynolds's voice behind him barked orders. "Get these people out of here."

The bystanders in front of Aubrey began to clear a path, apparently sensing something was wrong after they saw cops running and shouting.

Dead ahead, he saw her—the woman in the red raincoat. Fifty feet away from him, thirty feet away from the main entrance to police headquarters, she trudged along relentlessly. Her dead eyes stared ahead with robotic determination. All he could think about was the same look in the last bomber's eyes, the one who nearly drowned in his own drool.

Twenty feet away and he moved his legs at full speed, determined not to let her reach the main entrance.

Ten feet away and their eyes met. Her face remained slack, expressionless. Aubrey lowered his shoulder and slammed full-tilt into her solar plexus.

The two of them flew five feet, locked together for a brief moment before impacting the sidewalk in a collision of flesh and concrete. The woman let out a tremendous gasp and wailed like a creature possessed.

Aubrey pushed himself up and snatched both her arms in a vice-like grip, pinning them below his knees.

He reached down, grabbed both lapels of the raincoat and

tore it open.

A dingey yellow t-shirt stared up at him. Through the stains, he could make out a word in faded blue block letters: *Michigan.* Below it a large blue letter *M*.

He patted the shirt, then lifted it up to reveal pale skin pulled taut against her ribs. Nothing. No bomb.

"Shit." Grant fell to his knees next to Aubrey. Together, they searched the woman. She didn't resist and they found nothing but an empty pill bottle.

Grant read the label. "Zentransa." He bent close to her face and lifted her eyelids one at a time, shining a penlight into each one. "Over-zoned. She's a zombie."

"Shit," Aubrey said, falling back onto his haunches. "I thought..." He couldn't catch his breath. It felt like it had been a lifetime since he'd run so far, so fast.

"I thought she was too, man." Grant stood and waved the uniformed officers over. "As soon as I saw what you were running toward and heard 10-89. I thought she was one of them too."

Aubrey watched the woman lying on the sidewalk. Her blank eyes stared upward at nothing. Her body moved like a newborn's, gently flailing with no purpose other than some deep, instinctual need to do so. She'd overdosed on Zentransa and was now stuck in a netherworld between asleep and awake.

* * *

Anatoli Rubinski always had a knack for being in the right place at the right time. As the Chechen sat at the bistro table baking in the midday sun, he watched the chaos unravel across the street and it occurred to him that, once again, fortune smiled on him for some ungodly reason.

He and Lev, one of his better men, had been sipping their drinks for nearly an hour at *Jespresso Caffè*. They sat outside on small metal chairs at a table that tried desperately to look Florentine but came nowhere near. The seating did, however, give them the best view of the sprawling police headquarters just across the four-laned street.

For an hour they watched cops, in and out of uniform, come and go. Police cars lined the curb. Civilians filed in and out. It was heavily populated and busy with foot traffic, but no real exterior security was present that he could see. There was no standoff force that would prevent his next attack from unfolding.

Just as the Chechen was about to stand up and announce they were leaving, something happened. A man on the sidewalk, not twenty feet from the Chechen, ran out into the street, right into lunch hour traffic. The man's two companions quickly followed. Cars squealed to a stop as the three dodged near-certain death several times.

The Chechen got to his feet for a better look. Through the heads of rubbernecking passersby, he saw the man and his two followers reach the other side of the road safely. The three of them were running directly toward police headquarters.

Was this an attack by some other group? No, he thought. These people were in a hurry, but not attack hurry. They were in a defensive hurry. They were trying to stop something.

On the opposite sidewalk, the man in the lead pushed several people out of his way, yelled something to some uniformed cops, then ran, no, sprinted toward someone at the opposite end of the block.

The sidewalk near the Chechen became thick with people and the cars on the road resumed traveling. He stood on his chair, felt it creak and sway under his bulk. From his new vantage, it became clear who the man ran toward. About fifty feet from the man, a woman in a red raincoat ambled through the crowd, clearly drugged out of her mind, bumping into other pedestrians and giving no indications she was aware of their presence. She could have been one of the Chechen's volunteers, if he didn't know better.

Seconds later, the man speared the woman into the sidewalk. A crowd of cops quickly formed and the Chechen lost his view.

He sat back down and lifted the tiny white cup to his lips. Sipping the bitter liquid, he stared vacantly at the yellow and white, tiled table, lost in thought. The implications of what he just witnessed were obvious. The police now knew what to look for in potential suicide bombers. And, more importantly, after this incident, security at police headquarters would now stiffen dramatically.

Maybe he wasn't so lucky, he thought.

He looked at his man, Lev, sitting across from him. The square headed bruiser breathed so loudly through a crooked nose that the Chechen wondered how the man couldn't hear it inside his own head.

"Vot's up, boss?" the man asked.

"Police station eez now going to be more complicated." The Chechen downed the dregs of his cup. "Ve must adapt to this new development."

* * *

Late that evening, Aubrey sat at his desk compiling the notes from the day's interviews. He'd spent the bulk of the afternoon giving statements to the police regarding the incident with the woman in the raincoat. After clearing the scene and officially declaring the woman wasn't a threat, they called in an ambulance to take her to a detox center. Most of the cops Aubrey spoke to about the incident seemed to view him in a different light now.

"You know, if she'd actually had been a bomber," said the interviewing officer at the scene, "you'd have been blown to tiny little bits. There was probably nothing you could have done to stop it."

To this, Aubrey simply shrugged. "I would have kept her from getting inside."

The officer nodded with arched eyebrows. "Yeah, I guess you would have."

Reynolds sat next to him at the desk. "You eat yet?"

"I think I ate yesterday at some point," he said.

She gave a half-hearted chuckle, then slapped Aubrey's shoulder. "Hey, you made the higher ups rethink physical security around her. Chief was really pissed a potential threat got so close. They're creating a cordon around the building and posting officers at checkpoints."

Aubrey leaned back and stared blankly at the desk. "I guess there's that. The bright side of me making a fool of myself."

"Hey, Martin, look at me." She paused until he complied. "You risked getting turned into a cloud of pink mist to save hundreds of cops. That's not lost on anybody here. I promise you that."

"Thanks, Liz," he said.

"I'm going to grab a sandwich. You want anything?"

Reynolds stood up and rested her hands on her hips.

"Sure. One of whatever you're getting."

After she left, he sat motionless for a moment. His eyes settled on the wooden inlay around the edge of the metal desk. It was two-inches wide, gouged and scratched all to hell. Every inch of it was marred with cuts, dents, or missing chunks. This was not normal wear and tear. He wondered how it could have ended up in such bad shape. Perhaps the deep frustrations of a detective lost in his case taken out on the wood.

Aubrey looked at his watch. 11:30 p.m. He reached into his pocket and pulled out a thin silver box not unlike an antique cigarette case. Opening it, he looked down on four rows of oval-shaped, pink pills. He picked one from the top row and held it in front of his face between his thumb and forefinger. He rotated it, twisted it, and rolled it between his fingers, examining every microscopic detail he could see—the hairline ridge down its edge, the nearly imperceptible depressions in its face, the identifiers imprinted in its center—*ZEN* on one side, *966* on the other. He wondered how many Z pills the woman in the red raincoat had taken to reach the state she had been in.

He took his pill with a sip of water from a glass on his desk.

Several minutes passed while he polished his notes. Aubrey had always been particular about his notes and his briefings, ensuring they were in a format that was well-organized and easily understood. One of the reasons he had been successful in the private sector was his ability to convey his thoughts and conclusions in a clean, straightforward manner.

When the pill hit Aubrey, it took him by surprise, as usual. His breath caught in his chest. A euphoric rush filled his skull, blocking out all surrounding noise. He tilted his head back and his body forced a deep inhalation as if he had just emerged from a deep, cold dive into dark water. The sensation traveled from his head and down his body in a pulsating wave which alternated from warm to cold, cold to warm. As the wave moved on to new, unexplored territory it left goose pimples in its wake. It reached his toes and, seconds later, Aubrey opened his eyes.

Blinking the effects away, he rubbed the bumps on his arms and took another deep breath.

The zoning passed in fifteen seconds. The drug hit his bloodstream and his brain with full force; and as quick as it came it was gone again. Aubrey liked to think he had just received eight hours of sleep in fifteen seconds, but he knew that wasn't true. He knew the immediate effects were there, but the real magic of the pill played out over the course of many hours.

The sensation one felt while zoning was a result of the brain resetting itself as it bypassed its normal sleep cycle. This very brief, euphoric state was the brain's adenosine levels crashing and ATP spiking. Zoning was felt differently by everyone, but almost everyone felt some form of a brief high. Some, on the other hand, experienced nightmarish pain and discomfort. Many people, even those that could afford the pill regularly, chose not to take it for this reason, but they were in the minority.

There were some who enjoyed the brief high so much they took the pill multiple times a day. This was the dangerous habit of which the woman in the red raincoat had almost certainly been a victim. One pill too many in a short span resulted in an overdose, or in street terms, an overzone.

Everyone was familiar with so-called overzoners. Depending on the severity of the overdose, an overzoner or zombie might wander like the living dead for hours or days until the pill wore off and they came to.

Zombies were no real threat to anyone due to their mindless nature, but they were a nuisance. They wandered into busy intersections, onto railroad tracks, or found themselves in other dangerous places that required extraction. It was not uncommon for them to stumble off roof ledges, step in front of trains, or walk into open construction pits. Other than accidental death, overdosing on Zentransa did not directly threaten the life of the individual. The threat came from time. An overdose could be so deep and last so long that one simply died of thirst. The hope was that the zombie would snap out of their trance before dehydration took its toll.

The Z pill delivered a full night's sleep in a few seconds, thereby rejuvenating the body physically, but it could never slow down thoughts or quell frustration. Mental exhaustion and burn out loomed on the horizon for Aubrey.

Exhausted or not, Aubrey was satisfied on a level he hadn't experienced since before he'd handed over his badge. His life had taken a major turn in forty-eight hours. He still had a long way to go, but he felt certain that his life was course-correcting back toward the path he wanted to be on. To where he belonged. To where he was supposed to be.

Somehow, his helping on this case would get him his badge back. Perhaps helping the BSS kids or thwarting the bombers would provide enough redemption for the abysmal mistakes of the past, enough that he could carry the weight of the badge again. Of this, he was uncertain. A large part of him knew this was too much wishful thinking and he chastised himself for allowing his mind to drift to that fickle realm of hope.

In need of a stretch and a change of scenery, Aubrey stood and headed to the tall windows overlooking the street. The public clocks displayed the time—11:55 p.m. People—pill takers—were just beginning to leave work for home and their compulsory four-hour break before returning in a few hours.

He watched the sidewalks fill with pedestrians. The street, in its turn, filled with driverless cars searching for their owners. Regarding the people below with a marked difference from many weeks ago, he felt compelled to see their faces—choosing to follow an individual until they disappeared from view. He watched their expressions, their gestures, trying to guess what they must be thinking and feeling.

"Aubrey," said a voice from the far end of the command center. He turned and saw Officer Shyla Peters standing by the large lead board. "Going out for coffee. Want some?"

"Yeah, thanks," Aubrey replied. He watched Peters walk around the large room scratching orders on a handwritten list, making her way from one desk to another.

Two things occurred to Aubrey as he watched Peters. First, he felt honored to be considered for the coveted coffee list. It was his first time on the list that was usually reserved for full time officers. Second, he was again reminded of the old-school tendencies of cops. Peters was using paper and pen, as did most of the rest of the police force for mundane tasks like these. Even with access to all the technology in the world, cops still preferred paper and pen for most things. As his former team leader had told him, "Paper can't be hacked." This made sense to Aubrey, but he struggled to think of anyone desperate enough to hack a cop's coffee list.

Another reminder of the refusal to fully adopt modern technology was the lead board for the bombing investigation. More of a wall than a board, it was dominated by a massive touch-screen, which seemed modern enough until one took a closer look. Covering almost two-thirds of the monitor were pieces of paper, photographs, and bags holding 3D printed duplicates of evidence—the actual evidence stored safely away. Covering the touch-screen's fringes and the rest of the wall were cork-boards with their assortment of similar items tacked to them.

Remembering the Chief Inspector's words from two days ago, Aubrey looked around for any sign of her before walking to the leads board. Compared to the dinky leads and evidence board for Boarding School Syndrome, it was downright vast. He moved from one end to the other and back again, his eyes scanning the many photographs, timelines, written statements, and clear evidence baggies containing exact replicas of shards of metal, plastic, and clothing.

Aubrey stood back and took it all in. It told the same dichotomous story of so many other unsolved crimes: tons of evidence telling the story of exactly how it was all going down, yet no way of stopping it.

The police knew what the bombs were made of, they knew how the killers were getting the bombers to "volunteer," they knew the motive, and they even knew the group claiming responsibility—a round dozen were locked up in county jail. When considered as a whole story it all said one sad thing—they were so very close and there was still no end in sight.

The leads and evidence board Aubrey admired in that moment told the story of what had happened all the way up until that very second. But with serial crimes you had to know the next move before it happened, which they did not. The bombing investigation was further along than BSS, but both sides were equidistant from putting an end to either string of crimes.

Leaning against a heavy desk near the center of the leads board, Aubrey continued scanning. Times like these called for openness of mind. He felt that when you did not know what you were looking for, you often stumbled on an unexpected discovery.

After several minutes, his eyes settled on a section titled *Statements* on the large touch screen monitor. This section had been partitioned from the rest of the monitor and had its own touch-screen controls. Tabs at the top of it separated the database into *Witnesses, Victims, Experts, Suspects,* and a final one labeled *Persons of Interest*. It looked like nothing was being held tight to the chest around here. He figured that everyone was frustrated with their own lack of progress to the point that they displayed evidence like this in the hopes that someone might fall into a theory or connect the dots when no one else could.

He tapped *Witnesses* and a list of names appeared. Next to each name was a time a date marking when the statement was taken and next to it a shorthand code indicating to which bombing it referenced. They appeared to be ordered in descending order from the most recent blast. The entire first page of witness statements was marked with MID128-32 or midtown near the intersection of 128th street and 32nd avenue.

Aubrey scrolled through the long list of witness statements, eventually finding his own toward the bottom grouped with those from the first bombing. Choosing a few at random to read, he found they all told the same story—they saw a guy who looked suspicious, wore a nice suit, looked kind of like the guy they showed on the news.

He tapped the other tabs, finding nothing of real interest until he reached the *Suspects* tab. What struck him as interesting was the sheer volume of names on the list of suspects. He knew members of One Front for the People had been rounded up, their names were here, but he was staring at a list of around a hundred names.

He tapped a column titled Status to group the names by their status. The list now began with those whose status was marked *In Custody*. Scrolling down the list to find the last line on the *In Custody* names, he stopped at the row numbered 105. Close to ninety percent of the names on the *Suspects* list arrested or detained were not known to be members of One Front for the People. Hoping it wasn't true, it looked to Aubrey as if the Metropolitan Police Department's strategy was to detain every person who had both a criminal record and had ever uttered a word against the Z pill or Ventana Inc, hoping they could put enough pressure on the criminal underground to squeeze out answers.

Unable to resist, Aubrey dove head first into the sea of data in front of him. He lost track of time while he stood there poring over the interviews. At first, he selected them at random from the *In Custody* column, then he became more systematic. Each file contained an interview transcript, a list of diagnostic tools used during the interview, a short conclusion by the interviewing officer, and a section titled *Actionable Intelligence*. He scanned every interview transcript, read the detective's conclusions with great care, then jumped to the next interview. About halfway through the list of those in the *In Custody* column, clear patterns started to form.

Every detained OFP member had a lot to say. Each statement of theirs was pages and pages of text. Aubrey did the math and concluded that the team of investigators must have spent tens of hours with each OFP detainee they had in custody. In this case, as in so many others, it was clear that quantity was not quality.

Most of the statements rambled on about the cause of One Front for the People, touching rarely on the bombings themselves. The sentiment of the statements ranged from helping the poor and feeding the hungry to offering a brotherhood and sisterhood to those that society forgot. Without exception, the members of OFP were stalwart in support of their cause. Also without exception, all of them opposed the Z pill, Ventana Inc, and in some cases the CEO of Ventana himself—James Sarazin.

Strangely enough to Aubrey, every OFP detainee decried the bombings and Boarding School Syndrome as tragedies going against the virtues of their organization. When pressed hard with questions they were predictably evasive and unforthcoming while still condemning them. To a man, they would not supply information on either the bombings or BSS.

Aubrey stopped and re-read one interview. It seemed to drive home the loquaciousness of the detainees and their seeming opposition to the bombings.

Suspect:... *the pill is the fundamental cause of every problem we have in this society. It IS the reason people are poor and getting poorer. It IS the reason there is so much crime. It IS the reason people are starving. We have a cause to help those people while you simply defend the pill's right to exist. We give people who have been ostracized a home. We offer a place of understanding. We offer brotherhood. We teach people to question what society hands them.*

Officer: *And the bombings are supposed to solve all those problems you mentioned? You people think killing hundreds of innocent people is somehow going to get people to agree with you. Right now, the homicide rate is through the roof due, in no small part, to your little gang. Care to explain how making more crime is going to somehow solve the problem of crime?*

Suspect: *What they're doing is... well, people are listening aren't they. But, no... these attacks are tragic. They're brutal. And frankly, they go against the reason many of us sought refuge in One Front. I'm often very saddened by what they're doing. But... they can't be stopped. You can't stop them.*

Officer: *Why not? Why can't we stop them? Why can't you help us stop them?*

Suspect: *And the kids are... the sick children... I wish...*

Officer: *What? What do you wish?*

Suspect: *I wish you'd let me go home. I can't help you.* End of interview.

Aubrey skipped to the section titled *Conclusions.* The interviewing officer kept his brief.

Suspect denies any connection to bombings or Boarding School Syndrome. Refuses to speak about either beyond his belief that they are tragic. I, the interviewing officer, believe the suspect to be untruthful.

The officer's conclusion was pretty typical. All the cops he knew usually assumed a suspect was lying because they often were.

Aubrey was struck by the way the suspect used "we" and "they." He re-read the interview and, on a hunch, went back and re-read several more from OFP detainees to confirm his theory. The references to "we" and "they" came up over and over. One suspect after another used the same type of phrasing in their statements. We and they. They used "we" when referring to the general OFP causes and philosophy and "they" when referring to the bombers. This seemed like a flimsy theory at best and one he would not hang his hat on, but he logged the note in his memory as something he should come back to later.

The other ninety-three detainees revealed virtually nothing in their interrogations. No matter how hard the interviewing officers pressed, no matter what threats they issued, no information of any real substance could be gleaned.

The ninety-three non-OFP detainees proved Aubrey's previous theory that the Chief Inspector was at least as concerned with what the police appeared to be doing as much as she was with what they actually did. The OFP arrests, Aubrey felt, were justifiable. The others, the ninety-three poor souls caught up in the random sweeps, were for show.

Toward the end of his second pass through the interviews, he glanced at the diagnostic tools section for one detainee interview. It listed the various means by which the interviewing team measured cerebral activity and biological signs to detect levels of honesty. Biologics and cerebral scanners coupled with pupil dilation sensors made up the bulk of the diagnostic tools. The readouts were all there, displaying everything from body temperature and blood pressure to pupil size differentials and which areas of the brain were most active during the interview.

At the bottom of this section was a single line giving the aggregate result for all of the tools. This particular suspect was given the grade of *Moderately Truthful.* Aubrey broke down the diagnostic tools' readouts with a few taps until the screen showed him a line graph representation that spanned the entire time of the interview. He could see, based on the line's peaks and valleys, when the suspect was truthful or not. Based on what he was seeing, Aubrey concluded that the suspect had been so-called *Moderately Truthful* for the entire interview.

He checked every one of the dozen OFP interviews and found similar results. Every suspect was rated as *Moderately Truthful* overall and for most of their interviews. The interviewing officers' conclusions, on the other hand, consistently disagreed, stating that the suspect was being dishonest.

He tapped at the screen, backing out of the individual interviews to the main screen. He wanted to see the big picture. He needed a high-level understanding of what the investigative teams had gained from all of the interviews. What had they learned that had real value, Aubrey wondered.

With a few more taps on the screen, he managed to filter the interviews by the section *Actionable Intelligence.* On the screen appeared twenty-six rows. Twenty-six interviews with twenty-six suspects uncovered good intel. Considering only twelve of the detainees were known OFP members, this seemed like a pretty high number to Aubrey.

He tapped the first on the list and quickly scrolled to the section labeled Actionable Intelligence.

Suspect personally knew first bomber, Ralph Jacobsen. Gave address of Jacobsen's home before bombing.

Aubrey thought that this was a loose interpretation of Actionable Intelligence, but the search of Jacobsen's home could have turned up something. However, Jacobsen would have been easy to find—he had a job, paid rent, had food delivered to his home. Moving on, Aubrey selected the next interview and found *Actionable Intelligence.*

Suspect was associated with second suicide bomber, Royce Bayez. Suspect gave name and address of Bayez's life partner.

This last one came from a non-OFP detainee. Despite what Aubrey thought about the non-OFP arrests, there were fourteen interviews with non-OFP detainees that found actionable intelligence, all of which dealt with bombers two through five. All intelligence from OFP detainees dealt with Ralph Jacobsen.

Aubrey went through the rest of the list. After reading through interview number twenty-six, he decided the investigative team had two types of what they considered *Actionable Intelligence*: intel on Ralph Jacobsen and intel on the last four suicide bombers. All the *Actionable Intelligence* entries fell into one of these two categories. This fact worried Aubrey—what the investigative team considered "actionable" was suspect at best and this was the best they could get out of one hundred and five detained suspects. Either the investigators were profoundly ineffective, which Aubrey did not believe, or there was no intelligence to be gained from these particular individuals.

As Aubrey pondered over all of this, Detective Lewis joined him at the monitor.

"Any big 'AH HA' moments yet?" asked Lewis.

"Not really. Though I did have a couple of thoughts. Have you considered the popularity of our bombers inside OFP?"

"Popularity? Why? Are they running for prom king posthumously?" Lewis loosened his tie and settled heavily next to Aubrey onto the edge of the desk.

Aubrey laughed and continued, "No. What I mean is, other than our first bomber, Jacobsen, not one of the OFP detainees knew the other ones. They were pretty open about knowing Ralph, but not the others."

"No?" Lewis approached the screen and began to tap at the many tabs displayed. He scanned and scrolled like a practiced hand. It was clear to Aubrey that Lewis had spent quite a lot of time at this monitor. "Looks like a couple of people knew them. Look at these." Lewis pointed to the suspects' interviews that mentioned the bombers by name.

"Yes, but those are non-OFP detainees. They knew the bombers, sure, but they weren't affiliated with OFP."

"That's what they tell *us.*" Lewis cocked his head at Aubrey. "Besides, if you take them at their word, we only have twelve OFP members. They're supposed to be a couple hundred strong. Those bombers could have been fringe members or something."

"Ralph wasn't a fringe member. Everyone knew him. And we know at least one of the bombers after him was drugged. And we know Ralph didn't want to blow himself up or he was at least surprised it was going to happen."

"OK. So, they use Ralph as an unwitting source of inspiration for the others, then they run short on volunteers, so they use the drugs. We already know they're assholes, now they're just bigger assholes. So, what?"

"So," Aubrey tapped the screen and selected an interview transcript at random. He read the words on the screen, "'*We provide people a home. We give people who have been cast aside a place of refuge. We welcome all and the only thing we ask is they never take the pill.*' All this talk of refuge and home. They're selling themselves as this welcoming group, so why would they have members that no one knows? These bombers are giving their lives for the cause yet no one in the organization actually knows who they are?"

"Are you circumnavigating the globe to reach your point?"

"I do have a point. Look, we know they drugged the last bomber, right? *At least* the last one, but maybe more. Probably more. Well, I think they're grabbing these people off the street." Aubrey paused to take a breath. "I think they're having a hard time finding willing suicide bombers so they're just grabbing people, people nobody will miss. And they don't have to convince them to join the cause at all, they just drug them."

"Drugging them certainly makes things easier, doesn't it? And you could argue that other than Ralph," Lewis said, folding his arms and squinting as if looking for something, "the other bombers had very few connections with the outside world. Let's check something." Lewis walked to another section of the wall-sized touchscreen and began tapping and scrolling. He waved Aubrey to come closer. "Let's see." He was pointing at a screen split into a mosaic of six windows. Each window had a profile of one of the six bombers. He tapped on one window to expand it, scrolled to a section toward the bottom. "This is Ralph. Says he was a member of OFP for six to twelve months."

"We knew that. Every OFP detainee you have fessed up to knowing him."

"Right." Lewis closed that window and tapped on the one below it. "Here's Bayez—second bomber. Looks like he was in OFP approximately six to ten months... we think." He closed the window and moved on to the third bomber. "Jeffs was third. Says here, '*approximately three to four months with OFP*.'"

Lewis opened the fourth window. "Mills. Number four. Says '*less than six months*.' OK, let's look at Van Weisen, our last one... same thing '*less than six months*.' And our latest guy, the drooler, Mr. Winston... guess what?" Lewis looked at Aubrey.

"Less than six months," Aubrey answered.

"You got it."

"So, what's the deal? Why use the maddeningly vague '*less than six months*'?"

"Well, based on the notes here..." Lewis took a moment to read more notes from the last three windows. "They could not have been with them for *more* than six months. That determination is based on activities in their personal and professional lives and interviews with the current members we have detained."

"OK so, based on the data, they could have been with OFP for any amount of time up to six months." Aubrey crossed his arms and sighed. "Or... not at all."

"Look, I'll run this down with the team and put the new theory out there. See what we can dig up." Lewis put a hand on Aubrey's shoulder and his tone was non-committal. Aubrey felt patronized.

"OK. Just do me a favor and don't give me credit. I don't need the Chief Inspector..." Aubrey's watch chimed. He looked down to see a five minute reminder for an appointment to interview Dr. Amy Longfellow, a sleep scientist. "I need to go. I'll catch up with you after this call, but I think this points to something..." He was interrupted again when another detective, one Aubrey did not recognize, stepped up and grabbed Lewis's upper arm.

"Another raid," the detective said, his eyes wide and his

breathing hard. "Good intel on this one. Chief Inspector thinks we might get 'em this time."

16

The Raid

"SWAT is suiting up now," the detective continued. "Chief Inspector wants you and me to get two teams together and come in right behind SWAT to start sweeping the house."

"Got it. Where did the lead come from and where is the Chief Inspector?" Lewis asked.

"I don't know, but I think it just came in. She's briefing SWAT."

"Was it a CI or…"

"I don't know." The detective was turning to leave. "I have to go get ready. I'll meet you at the staging area." He was halfway across the Command Center when he turned back. "Bring the BSS team. She wants them there. She specifically mentioned them." He exited the large room through the door Aubrey first entered several days ago.

Staring at the empty BSS desk, Lewis then glanced sideways at Aubrey. "Where is your team?"

"They went to interview some chemical weapons expert out at the Navy port. Won't be able to get back for at least a couple of hours."

With a half-smile, Lewis said, "Well, as the ranking present member of the BSS investigative team, you're going to have to go for a ride."

"I guess so." Aubrey couldn't help the wide smile now plastered across his face. "Let's get going."

* * *

In the driver-less Metro PD van, Aubrey sat toward the front on a shallow bench along the bulkhead. In addition to Aubrey and Lewis, five other officers sat silent. The tension in the van was noticeable; everyone had been working on this case with more focus and intensity than any case before it. The possibility that they could be on their way to a turning point or, better yet, an end to the entire case, had piqued everyone's adrenaline.

Aubrey's mind was still working over the discoveries he made in the last hour—the use of "we" versus "them" in the detainee statements, that every bomber since Ralph Jacobsen might never have belonged to OFP and could have been snatched off the street and drugged. More so, he ruminated on the approach the Task Force had adopted in recent weeks. The sheer number of detainees and the inverse proportion of evidence and leads gained disturbed him.

Aubrey looked out of the front of the van. In the artificial light of early morning, the cars ahead of them magically parted. Each of them fitting neatly into gaps appearing out of nowhere in the lanes of traffic next to them. He knew that the Metropolitan Traffic System was working to clear the lane ahead of them by adjusting the placement and speed of every car on the road ahead and those nearby. A few inches forward or back for thousands of cars could free up a lot of room in short order.

"I don't think I'll ever get tired of watching that," Aubrey said, staring ahead. "I feel like Moses."

Lewis, who was not paying attention, said, "Moses?"

"The Red Sea."

"Oh, right. I get it." Lewis paused. He looked to be considering something unknown to Aubrey then asked, "Did you get any other ideas from looking at the big board? You were there for a while before I walked up."

"A few." Aubrey was unsure how to proceed, then decided it was best to dive right in. "Though, one thing I noticed is how many people you all have detained in connection with the attacks."

"We've been busy," Lewis said as the others seated in the back of the van shot glances toward them. "OFP has been tough to round up. They're in deep hiding right now, obviously. Rounding up the others has been a task too, but I think it's been worth it."

"How so?" Aubrey felt that he must be careful with how he continued his questioning. He knew Lewis was on edge, the staging area was only a few minutes away. While he didn't want to push Lewis too hard, he knew that people on edge tended to be more candid. More truthful. It was a calculated gamble.

"How so?" Lewis said with raised eyebrows. "Where do you think the intel for this raid came from? Probably one of our detainees."

"Not this one," a voice to Aubrey's left said. He looked over to see the young female officer he recognized from the first briefing. She gave Aubrey and Lewis a complacent look then continued staring out of the window across from her. "Chief Inspector said it was an anonymous tip. Came in on the hotline."

The two men glared at her for a moment. The vibrations of the electrically powered van buzzed under their feet.

"What are they charged with? All the non-OFP members you've detained," Aubrey asked. "How long can you hold them before their lawyers get antsy?"

"They're charged with affiliation," Lewis replied. He stared at Aubrey across the otherwise silent space. The other riders' sideways glances were now coming more frequently. "Look, the powers that be want to see results. They want to see progress. The arrests and... and these raids show the civilians that we're working on it. That we're hunting these fuckers down."

"So, they're guilty by association?"

At this, Lewis crossed his arms and stared out of the front window of the van. He shook his head for a moment before turning back to Aubrey. Lewis's face was stony, more determined than before. Lewis had drawn a line in the sand and he would now defend it.

"Yes. Fuck yes." Lewis jabbed the air with his finger. "Goddamn right, Marty. They're guilty of being associated with the most loathsome, the most violent criminal organization this city has ever seen. I don't really give a shit if they were directly involved with the bombings or BSS or not. They want to go around preaching OFP's bullshit or they want to be buddies with these bombers? Well, guess what—we're going to find you. And we're going to lock you up."

Lewis looked back at his fellow officers in the back of the van, as if searching for agreement. There was some; a few heads nodded. "Oh, and to answer your other question, I don't know how long we'll keep them. And once again, I really don't give a shit."

Aubrey bent forward and stared at the floor of the van. He had been afraid of this. He knew that when a situation went bad, when people were dying and you couldn't do anything to stop it, those in command got desperate.

He'd seen it serving in uniform overseas. He'd seen it as a cop. This was why villages got torched. This was why petty criminals got beaten to a pulp.

Soldiers get sick of seeing a lack of progress in war, they get sick of an enemy who has refused to show themselves and stand up for a square fight. They start to grab anyone that resembles the enemy and vent their frustrations. Some of the good cops of the Metropolitan Police Department had started resorting to the same tactics.

"Are you really just arresting everyone who is remotely connected to OFP or the bombers?" Aubrey knew he was pushing his friend, but he wanted to give Lewis an outsider's perspective. "What do you think is going to happen, the bombings will just stop? Have you considered that OFP are committed to this cause and if you do arrest the right guys, then new guys could just take on the mantel and carry on with the mass killing? This isn't a war of attrition. This is terrorism. You can't just kill or arrest more of them in the hopes they'll give up. They don't give up, that's what makes terrorists… terrorists. They just keep going."

Lewis looked away, staring out of the front of the van again.

Aubrey continued. "And we know they're drugging them now, so how do you…"

"We're still looking for the same people," Lewis said without looking at Aubrey. "The guys building the bombs are the same ones drugging those poor bastards. The same ones blowing people up."

"And what if I'm right about them grabbing people off the streets? Then, they aren't part of OFP at all and..."

"We're still looking for the same people."

Aubrey shook his head. "What I mean is, arresting people just for being associated with the bombers doesn't make sense anymore. They're victims just like the other people killed in the blast."

"What should we do then, Marty?" Lewis threw up his hands. "Our leads get us nowhere. Our witnesses are shit. Even our confidential informants can't give us anything worth a damn. Meanwhile, the city is being blown apart. So, what should we do?"

Aubrey knew that anything he said now would fall on deaf ears. He allowed his friend a moment to vent his frustrations.

Lewis continued. "The Mayor and the Chief of Police want to see progress. The *people* want to see progress. They want to see that we're getting close to the end of all this. So, this is search and destroy, not wait and see. We don't have the luxury to be patient. This investigation, this war, weighs on our shoulders—the cops. You must have forgotten what that feels like, Martin."

"Have you forgotten what happens to people in our justice system?" The heat under Aubrey's collar was rising. "Those people will be brought up on charges predicated on the evidence you've put up to arrest them. Most of them will be flushed through the system just to free up space in cells at county. A lot of them will end up in the Keep, you know, prison."

"I'm not sure why I should care about that," Lewis said, shrugging.

"Because once they get to the Keep, their fate is in the hands of those whack-job executioners." Aubrey half rose from his seat. "The ones who dole out the death penalty like it's a milkshake at a diner. Like they're just taking out the trash. You haven't forgotten about those maniacs running around the prison, have you?"

"Once again," Lewis said, "I'm left wondering why I should give a shit."

They stared across the van at one another. Each knew they were at an impasse. Something between them had shifted in the last few minutes. Their renewed friendship was on the precipice.

Aubrey wondered whether he would have seen things the same way had he been on the case as long as Lewis. The longer you're in the shit, the less you smell it, he thought. Coming in with fresh eyes gave him the luxury of a non-jaded perspective. Aubrey had the esteemed privilege of sitting atop his high horse in order to better survey the landscape.

He didn't blame Aaron Lewis one bit and was on the brink of telling him so when the van suddenly lurched to a stop.

"We're here," said the young female detective.

They all began to file out. Lewis went before Aubrey and turned when his feet hit the pavement before Aubrey was halfway out the rear doors. "We'll call you if we need you," he said.

Aubrey sank back onto the bench seat and watched Lewis move off into the growing crowd of police personnel. He knew he had pushed Lewis too hard. He had tested his old friend's faith in himself and now Aubrey turned that same test inward. Who was he to question their philosophies? He had committed a sin far more egregious and was in no position to cast judgment. How hard would it have been for him to keep his damn mouth shut?

Perched on the end of one bench, he kept the rear doors of the van open to better survey what was going on around him. He could see down a street crowded with police cars and vans. The bulky SWAT armored personnel carrier formed the centerpiece of the display, looming high over the marked and unmarked police cars. He could tell that they were among the last groups to arrive.

Small gatherings of officers and detectives huddled around various centerpieces of their own. Some had paper maps and photos on tablets to look over, others had cups of hot coffee and casual conversation. The SWAT team in their urban camouflage and assault gear crowded around a small monitor mounted to the inside of the rear door of the APC. Aubrey assumed the leader with shiny brass on his collar was leading them through the details of their assault plan.

Everywhere, everyone was waiting for the word "go" so they could get down to business—whether it was kicking down doors, searching for evidence, or observing. Everyone secretly happy to be there to earning the right to say they were there when it all went down. No matter what *it* turned out to be.

From snippets of conversation around him, Aubrey learned that the target for the assault was half of one floor of a thirty-story apartment building three blocks away. It was suspected that a dozen or so members of OFP would be there.

The purpose of the safe house was unknown. Scanners could not pick up any evidence of weapons or explosive materials, but all options were still on the table for the assault.

The plan was for drones to fire flash-bang and pulse grenades through windows while SWAT Team 1 burst through one of two entry points to the safe house. The second door would be guarded by SWAT Team 2 to pick up anyone trying to flee. A simple plan. All inside the home were to be considered armed. Resistance was to be met with force.

Lewis stood some distance away holding a large tablet and his team of investigators were gathered around. Aubrey could not see what they were looking at, but he imagined it was images of the safe house, blueprints, and pictures of the OFP members believed to be in the safe house. Aubrey wondered if this had started to become routine for them at this point. Lewis did not look his way.

Near the SWAT APC a small group gathered around Chief Inspector Long, who stood quite still with her hands clasped behind her back. Over her shoulders hung a traditional style leather holster.

As always, the Chief Inspector looked imposing and not as a result of her height alone. She stared into the distance even as the SWAT team wrapped up their briefing and began to mill about. Occasionally, she would whisper orders to a nearby officer. Suddenly, she turned and looked in Aubrey's direction—not at him, but at something near him. She stared for the briefest of moments then turned and gave orders to her nearby officers and the SWAT commander. As orders were being given and taken, Aubrey heard the quiet hum of another vehicle outside the one he sat in.

Aubrey stepped to the pavement to get a better look at the latest arrival. At first, he thought they must be a vital part of the assault team as the Chief Inspector was apparently waiting for them before giving the "go" order. The new van pulled abreast of his own and as it moved along, its sides came into view. Bands of blue, gray, and red stretched across it and emblazoned in the center of the side panel in large bold print read *Metro News Network* with the subscript *The City's Source of Truth.*

Aubrey couldn't believe what he was seeing. Lewis's words now rang louder than they had when he first heard them. "The Mayor and the Chief of Police want to see progress. The *people* want to see progress. They want to see that we're getting close to the end of all this."

They want to see. And now they will, no doubt about that, he thought. He had seen the footage of early raids and thought the news coverage was fortuitously timed, and thorough. He had chalked up the media's luck to an inside leak, as per usual. He was right, of course, but he never imagined the leak's source was the Chief Inspector herself.

Aubrey watched the SWAT Team divide into two lines and jog off between two tall buildings in the direction of the safe house. Other teams gathered, waited, then trotted off themselves.

Four police drones took flight from atop the APC. They buzzed and purred at different heights, their human pilots sitting comfortably back at the station. The drones took off toward the target just as a hatch in the top of the news van opened up to Aubrey's right. A dozen small round drones rose into the air from the hatch, tiny cameras attached to their bellies. They hung there for a few seconds, twenty feet above the MNN van, before flying off in the wake of the police drones. The news crew's drones would keep their distance, but only just. They would hover close enough to get a great shot, but not close enough to get caught obstructing.

The rear doors of the news van were open. Aubrey stepped closer and peered inside. Two men and a woman sat on stools bolted to the floor of the van. One of the men and the woman wore t-shirts and jeans while the other man wore a suit; he was the on-air talent, Aubrey guessed. The walls of the van's interior were covered in flat panel monitors. Shallow benches covered in various types of remote-control stations and computers sat below the monitors. The van's occupants watched three monitors on the left side of the van with rapt attention.

Aubrey moved closer to get a better look at what the crew was watching. The woman looked down as he approached. Her hair was shaved into a white mohawk and she had a long earring hanging from her right ear.

"Want to watch, sir?" the woman said. The others didn't seem to notice or care that Aubrey was there.

"Sure," Aubrey said. He assumed she thought he was a cop. He didn't feel like correcting her.

He hopped into the van and stood behind the three news people. The monitors displayed footage from the dozen news drones stationed in what looked like a semi-circle formation around the corner of the building where the raid was about to take place. Each screen showed four drone video feeds, each from a slightly different angle. Ahead, just outside the windows of the OFP safe house, the larger black police drones hovered.

"AI controlled?" Aubrey asked after he noticed the drones weren't being controlled.

"Yeah," the woman answered. "Observe and report mode. Give them a location and they wait there until something cool happens."

For a moment nothing happened. The police drones hovered in mid-air in the near distance.

Aubrey glanced outside toward the Chief Inspector. Next to her, a short, uniformed officer wearing black fatigues stood. The Chief Inspector stood stock still, then looked at the officer and gave the slightest of nods. The officer touched his ear piece and said something Aubrey couldn't hear.

Aubrey looked back at the monitors. White puffs burst from the bottoms of the police drones. In front of the drones, windows shattered as the flash-bang grenades flew into the apartment.

The news drones repositioned and zoomed in on the apartment windows. From several angles, Aubrey watched black shapes rush past the windows. Each had weapons drawn.

"Audio?" the man in the suit asked.

The other man pushed a button and the van filled with noise.

"...on your knees. Hands behind your head."

"Clear."

"Sierra-Lima, move into rear bedrooms."

"Roger."

A pause.

"Clear."

"Clear."

"Clear."

"Two blue coming out."

"One blue coming out."

"Roger."

"All clear."

"All clear. Roger. Romeo actual, we're all clear up here. Four suspects detained."

"Ordinance?" said a voice. Aubrey looked outside at the officer next to the Chief Inspector. He was speaking to the team inside.

"Negative. Nothing obvious anyway," came the reply from the SWAT team commander.

"Weapons?"

"Negative."

"Roger that. Uniforms and forensics are on their way up."

The radio chatter continued, but the action was over so the man in the t-shirt switched off the audio.

The raid itself had lasted only a few minutes. Before long, a line of detainees, flanked by uniformed officers, were led back to the staging area.

In single file they walked with zip-tied wrists. All four detainees were men—two white, one black, and one Asian. Their clothing looked as if they had just been roused from bed.

Half the news drones remained floating around the crime scene while the other half followed the line of detainees, buzzing in and around them like large insects. The officers in charge did nothing to prevent the cameras' intrusion, as if they were unaware of the cameras' presence.

The SWAT Team returned after the detainee train. They shook hands and slapped each other's backs for a job well done and the safe accomplishment of their mission.

Aubrey watched the investigative process unfold inside the apartment via the news drones, which had moved closer to the crime scene, mere feet from the apartment's three windows.

An officer entered the empty apartment and held out an

object the size of a baseball. It sprouted tiny rotors and floated above his hand. Once he left, the object moved around the apartment, scanning as it went. This would create a 3D representation of the safe house.

Once the scan finished, the DNA team entered in their white hazmat suits and masks. They methodically worked the apartment, preserving and collecting the delicate and vital invisible evidence. Next came the forensics team to pull fingerprints, collect and bag physical evidence, and photograph key areas of the safe house.

Two hours passed and the investigation was in full swing when a young uniformed officer approached the rear of the news van.

"Mr. Aubrey?" the officer said. Aubrey nodded and the officer continued, "They're ready for you up there."

The walk to the safe house went quicker than Aubrey had anticipated. The neighborhood was middle class residential and single-unit commercial. The apartments had no lobbies or doormen. Twenty-four-hour storefronts occupied the first floor of every building with apartments on the floors above. The target building was no different. A quick-serve restaurant offering everything from chicken wings to tofurkey sandwiches stood adjacent to the resident entrance.

The officer led him upstairs to the safe house and upon entering it was exactly as he had expected. Detectives combed every inch of the space for any sign of evidence that might help their case. In gloved hands they carried powerful flashlights, small mirrors, and clear baggies marked with large bold numbers. In the center of one room, stacks of clear containers held physical evidence already cataloged.

Black scorches marked several spots on the floor. Curtains

had been singed, windows shattered and furniture toppled, but otherwise the safe house appeared no worse for wear after the raid. SWAT had been swift and efficient; no blood had been spilled.

In the front room, the largest in the apartment, a couch sat under two windows with a recliner to either side and a TV in the opposite corner.

Aubrey did a walk-through of the safe house before beginning a detailed, painstaking search. Off the front room was an open-plan kitchen from which a hallway led to a single bathroom, and two bedrooms. During the walk-through, Aubrey spotted nothing remarkable, but several cabinets, drawers and a closet that he saw would need further inspection.

He didn't know exactly what he was looking for as it was obvious there was no chemical lab in the safe house capable of producing whatever caused BSS. He'd be limited to paraphernalia or supplies.

Doing his best not to get in the way of the other investigators, he gathered the necessary supplies—latex gloves, flashlight, clear baggies—and began his inspection.

17

Blood and Oil

"Nothing?" Deputy Inspector Reynolds asked.

"Nothing," Aubrey confirmed.

"Damn," Detective Grant said. "Another one comes up with nothing. How many of more of these raids do we need before we find something?"

"Well, the bomb guys found something useful. Right?" Reynolds looked at Aubrey with a hopeful look.

"I don't think so. I didn't see or hear anything to that effect. Then again, I can't know for sure." The three of them were sitting around the BSS team desk. Papers and tablets were scattered across the desktop. He glanced back toward the large monitor at the opposite end of the command center. Aubrey had spent the last half hour describing everything he saw and heard at the raid, but he left out the argument with Detective Lewis. "Honestly, the place was clean. If they took anything away, they removed it pretty quickly because I didn't see anything worth mentioning."

"You said they had some electronic equipment. Could some of that have been used for the explosive devices?" Reynolds said.

"Probably not. The tech guys are searching them now along with some laptops, tablets, and phones found at the scene, but it just looked like old computers. They were most likely trying to pawn the stuff." Aubrey thought about the way the entire apartment appeared to him as he had been walking around it, conducting his investigation. "No, it was clean. The whole place. You know, if I didn't know that place belonged to suspected terrorists, I would have thought it belonged to a bunch of college kids."

The three members of the Boarding School Syndrome investigative team sat in silence for a moment. The absence of anything remotely useful from the raid was a major disappointment. The investigation had been stagnant since the beginning, but they'd all hoped to come away from the raid with something to give them a boost. Every other lead had been a dead end or a nonstarter altogether.

Aubrey contemplated telling Reynolds and Grant about his argument with Lewis and his own thoughts on their approach to the bombing investigation on the whole. He decided against telling them in part because he now questioned his own theories, but more because he didn't feel like burning more bridges.

Lewis had given him the cold shoulder since they returned from the raid several hours ago. There had also been a memo sent around to the task force outlining who had access to which case files. Lewis had not made any attempt to have him fired or excluded in any way, but Aubrey had damaged his most important lifeline into the bombing investigation.

Aubrey stood up and left the other two, making the excuse that he was going to check in with Technical Specialist Lee on progress with the body language recognition program. More than anything he wanted to escape their looks of defeat. Both sides of the investigation had made little progress and gone on long enough to make anyone feel defeated.

The BSS team had been dealt a particular blow with Aubrey's failure to turn up anything at the raid. The bombing investigation had at least detained suspects. The BSS team, on the other hand, had zero to go on. The interviews could still turn up something, but they all knew it was unlikely. Aubrey had helped them realize the complexity of developing and delivering BSS. This had only made their task seem all the more impossible.

Speaking with Lee did not make him feel any better. The software itself, she had told him, was difficult enough to configure on the back end. Integrating it into the data stream of all the surveillance cameras deployed throughout the city was titanic in its complexity.

"We're making progress," she said, trying to reassure him. "But don't hold your breath. Chief Inspector isn't even really on board with me spending so much time on it, but I happen to believe in it. We ran several test-runs on a couple of cameras just outside the building. I went out and walked around, caught the footage on both cameras, then ran the program to see if it could find me in the second camera's footage only using body language caught in the first. It came back with ninety-two percent accuracy."

"Yeah, I told you it works. I've nailed a handful of investigations using it. Did you tell Chief Inspector about your test?"

"Yes. She didn't seem impressed. I have a hunch that even if we find someone using this tech, she won't throw much in the way of resources behind it until we have facial recognition or DNA to verify."

Lee's office was just off the main room that made up the task force's command center. Aubrey left her office feeling somehow worse than before he went in. From outside her door, Aubrey was close to the large evidence monitor board. He stared at it, trying to pick out anything new that might have been added since the last raid. He could see no major differences except for a small red circle on a map screen around the location of the last raid.

Aubrey thought about going home. He thought about taking a break for a few hours. He needed to clear his head and figure out what to do next. The idea of returning to his apartment for anything more than a quick shower and a meal made him nauseated. The feeling of defeat was creating a sizable pit in his guts, siphoning off important resources from the rest of his body. He knew he had to do something quick to curb the pit's appetite. He needed a quick win or a small sign of forward progress in his case, whether it be BSS or the bombings.

He was massaging his forehead when his pocket buzzed. Pulling out his phone he saw an email from Dr. Amy Longfellow replying to his email in which he apologized for having to miss their previously scheduled call.

Mr. Aubrey,

I will be out of town on international travel for the next ten days. I can talk today before I catch my plane. I'm afraid that is the best I can do before I return. Let me know. —Amy

* * *

From the corner of the room, the Chechen watched his men working. It was an assembly line designed to manufacture pain, fear, and death. The Chechen didn't like to romanticize his work, but he also didn't sugar coat it. His role was to terrorize. That's what he was paid for and that's what he'd do.

This would be the first time in quite a while that the Chechen had used this particular method of mayhem. He could teach his men the particulars, but he had to be doubly sure they followed his orders to the letter.

"Don't forget the rods, Vasiliy," he said.

"Yes, sir. Apologies, Anatoli." Vasiliy sat hunched over a square card table packing the fingers of a surgical glove with polysemtex-d and two-inch long black rods, each an eighth of an inch thick.

When all five fingers were packed, Vasiliy handed the glove to the man on his left, who inserted a tiny cylinder into the PSD, twisted each finger, and tied them off, then cut them free from the glove. A pyramid of several dozen finger-length eggs sat on the end of the table.

Against the wall, five new volunteers sat in a row of folding chairs. IV tubes ran from their arms to bags of *voodoo* hanging from hooks in the wall. Small blocks of wood held their mouths open. A strip of duct tape, stretched tight from the middle of their foreheads to the backs of their chairs, kept their dead eyes facing the ceiling.

The Chechen had figured out what went wrong with the last batch of *voodoo* and the troublesome drooling that caused him so much anxiety days ago. He vowed not to repeat the mistake. Having solved the imbalance in the delicate mixture, the Chechen fine-tuned his solution and even verified its effectiveness on one of his own men.

"Careful, Lev, you don't vant them to choke to death," the Chechen shouted. Lev was forcing strips of a cream-colored, cotton candy-like material down a volunteer's throat. The Chechen's man reached for another strip, dipped it in a bowl of clear liquid and began feeding the end to the open-mouthed volunteer.

"Wait, Lev." The Chechen walked over and picked up the bowl of clear liquid. "Is this mineral oil?"

"I believe so, sir," Lev said. The oily strip dangled over the volunteer's gaping mouth, dripping onto his face, down his nostrils, and into his unblinking, unflinching eyes. The volunteer continued staring at the ceiling; lines of drool and oil ran down his cheeks.

"Mineral oil vill make him shit himself," the Chechen said. "That will make the contents of his stomach move too soon."

"You said oil, Anatoli. I didn't..."

"I know vot I said." The Chechen waved a hand through the air, swatting the accusation away. "Git something else. Olive oil, motor oil, I don't give a fuck. Just something else."

Lev nodded and set down the dripping strip. "I'll check ze kitchen."

A moment later, he returned with a plastic bottle of amber liquid and showed it to the Chechen. The Chechen nodded. "Continue."

Lev went on feeding strips to the five men, who sat drugged and helpless.

"Svallow," Lev commanded every few seconds.

After each volunteer had been filled with enough strips of the insulating material to satisfy the Chechen, he said, "Enough. Move on to ze next step."

* * *

Aubrey dialed as fast as he could. Dr. Longfellow picked up on the first ring.

"Dr. Longfellow, thank you for agreeing to talk to me," Aubrey said.

"No problem, Detective. I'm actually in the car right now on my way to the airport, so I'll have to make it quick. You had some questions for me?"

"Yes, I do." He tapped an icon on his phone screen to activate the recorder function and informed her he was doing so. "Dr. Longfellow, can you start by telling me a little bit about what you do for a living and your expertise as it pertains to sleep and sleep disorders?"

"Certainly," said the woman's voice. She had a smooth but serious tone. "In short, I'm a somnologist, so I study sleep. But, I'm also a professor of sleep science at Hutton University and director of the Millstein Sleep Laboratory here in the city. My expertise primarily deals with sleep, sleep related disorders, and circadian rhythm disorders. I'm actually traveling today to visit several colleagues overseas and deliver several lectures on circadian rhythm disorders."

"I see. Doctor Longfellow, I'd like to talk about the so-called Boarding School Syndrome," said Aubrey as he scribbled notes on a nearby yellow legal pad. "Are you familiar with BSS beyond what you've heard on the news?"

"I am," she said. "I've been asked to consult with one of the doctors whose patient is currently affected by..." A pause. "...The unknown sleeping disorder."

"One of your contemporaries informed me of the misnomer being used in the media. I take it you don't care for the popularized name that's being used."

"I do not," she said. "First, it's not a syndrome... it's a disorder. Second, the part about boarding schools implies that only the wealthy should be concerned for their children's safety. Everyone should be worried about this."

"Can you tell me what the doctor called you in to do?" Aubrey asked.

"I can tell you some of it," she replied. "But I can only go so far without violating confidentiality." A pause, then she continued. "The doctor mostly wanted to know about sleep, how this disorder was similar to sleep, how it was different. Their chief concern, naturally, was whether I thought this disorder could possibly be fatal."

***

In the basement of police headquarters, Pamela Bauer sat at her work station behind a thick pane of ballistic glass. Fidgeting mindlessly with her hair while she read a romance novel on her phone, she twisted in her chair. Every few minutes, she'd grab another piece of chocolate from the bowl on her desk and add its wrapper to the growing pile next to her console's screen.

The console alarm snapped her back to her job. She tossed the phone to the side and leaned forward in her chair, scanning the screen. It displayed several video feeds. Most were from the holding cells down the corridor. One showed the area just on the other side of the glass—a twenty-by-twenty square of black tile flanked by five scanning booths on one side and two sets of doors, on the other side, that led out into the subterranean garage. A final feed showed her the exterior of those doors. On which, she watched two uniformed police officers escorting a man in cuffs. When they reached the door, she waited for their cerebral signatures to be confirmed on screen. A second passed and then green haloes flashed around their heads. Satisfied, she tapped a square on her console and the entry doors swung open.

"Afternoon, Bruce, Tom," she called through the speaker in the glass. "What do you got for me?" The officer's names had appeared on her screen as soon as their cerebral signatures had registered, but after fifteen years, Pam knew everyone anyway.

"Morning, Pammy," Officer Bruce Horn said. He foisted the suspect forward by the elbow, "Sam Bush here kicked my cruiser and busted out the headlight. Then, the car's scanner pinged him with an outstanding warrant. So, here we are."

The suspect wore a tan bomber jacket and jeans. His white face, covered in tattoos, gave no reaction to anything they said. To Pam, he looked out of his mind drunk or totally resigned to his fate. Maybe both.

"Another one?" she asked. "Already had a few dummies today do something purely stupid and get themselves popped for open warrants. Something must be going around. We had a guy spit on a cop, one slap a cop, and a couple more try to bang up a car like your guy. And they all had warrants. Idiots, I tell you." She shrugged. Criminals being stupid was nothing new and didn't faze her in the slightest. "Take our friend Mr. Bush to booth number three."

Officer Tom Vincent walked Sam Bush to the middle booth and placed him on the two yellow footprints inside. Automatically, a ring the width of the booth lowered splashing green light on Sam's body.

As the ring progressed slowly down, a picture emerged on one of Pam's console screens. It showed a 3D image of his body. Bright white areas showed where any solid objects appeared on or in Sam's body. White spots shined from his teeth and one from his thigh. His stomach, appearing light gray and larger than usual, looked full to bursting.

The ring returned to the ceiling of the booth.

"Anything?" Vincent asked.

"Just some dental work, maybe a bullet or an implant in his thigh, and a full belly. Must have helped himself to a last meal before deciding to come visit you boys."

"That true, Sam?" Horn said, leaning an elbow against the glass in front of Pam. "Didn't invite us to dinner?"

Sam Bush didn't say anything.

From inside the booth, a robotic arm extended two cotton swabs. It moved toward Sam's face as a computer voice said, "Please open your mouth and remain still."

Sam did as he was told. The arm rubbed each swab on the inside of his cheeks then disappeared.

A second later, a window appeared on Pam's console that read: *DNA CONFIRMED. SAMUEL JAMES BUSH.*

"Congrats, Sam. You're you," Pam said. The officers laughed. Sam remained stone faced and placid.

A small orb in the corner of the scanning booth blinked to life and, although nothing could be seen by the naked eye, Pam's console gave her another alert that read: *CEREBRAL SCAN CONFIRMED. SAMUEL JAMES BUSH.*

"Second confirmation complete. He's good to go. You guys take care of yourselves," Pam said. She waved at the officers as they walked through the scanning booth to the other side. Pam picked up her phone and resumed reading.

In five minutes, she had completely forgotten about Sam Bush and his full belly. The oddness that, in the last ninety minutes, four other suspects were brought in with overly full bellies, compliant dispositions, and similar arrest stories faded before she turned to the next steamy page of her novel.

* * *

"Can it?" Aubrey asked. "Can Boarding… can the sleeping disorder be fatal?"

"I don't know with any certainty," came her reply. "The disorder looks identical to sleep. Everything about it: brain activity, organ function, all the body's restorative cycles are there. We haven't had enough time to see any measurable degeneration of major systems, so as far as I can tell, the patients are in an un-waking state of sleep."

"So, is it fatal?" Aubrey repeated.

"I don't think so," she said. "I think… if they keep them well-nourished, they should be fine."

"One Front for the People claims responsibility for BSS," said Aubrey. "How could they have done this?"

"I'm just a doctor. I'm not a detective," Dr. Longfellow answered flatly. "Medically speaking, first blush is no, it should not be possible for them to have done this. But these days… who knows. So many impossible things have occurred in the last fifty years. The Z pill itself shouldn't be possible, but it is."

"Strange that two seemingly impossible things have occurred and that they are so closely connected."

"Not really."

"Not really?"

"No," the doctor continued, "One Front for the People, if they're actually doing it, are pretty clear why they're doing it. Philosophically, it's some sort of... balancing of societal scales for them. It's a reaction to the pill. One has caused the other. In a world where the Z pill is possible, however unbelievable it may seem, this disorder is also possible. It's not so strange that they've both occurred and it's not so strange that they're so closely tied to one another."

"I see," said Aubrey. "Could OFP have re-engineered the chemistry of the Z pill so that it had the reverse effect?"

"Possible in theory, but I think they'd have to administer it every day, just like Zentransa is taken normally. How do they do that while the children are under lock and key in the hospital? And how do they get it into the system of the target kid initially without infecting other people?"

"Maybe one huge dose for each kid?" asked Aubrey.

"No. I think that would kill them. Much like when someone overuses the Z pill—too much adenosine, ATP or some of the other sleep related hormones can be fatal."

As Aubrey heard this, his mind wandered to the open mouth of a hunched overzoner wandering aimless down an empty street.

She continued, "With a properly dosed Z pill, the brain is at least tricked into thinking it has already slept. In an overdose of any kind, the brain is trying to frantically fix a problem it doesn't know the cause for. So, you get chaos in the brain and in the body. In some cases, in an attempt to fix a problem, the brain inadvertently causes permanent, irreparable damage to itself and the body's systems."

* * *

Officer Tom Vincent slid the steel cell door closed by hand. He could have done it with the push of a button but he always preferred to feel metal slam home against the jamb. He nodded to a man in a booth behind him and the deadbolts shot into their housings, locking Sam Bush in the holding cell.

Nine suspects, all male, sat on benches around the twelve by twelve concrete room. A toilet in the corner was currently occupied by an enormous dark-skinned man who bared his teeth when Vincent made eye contact.

Sam Bush unnerved Vincent. He just stood there, six inches away from the cell door, staring ahead with disinterested eyes. A line of spittle began falling from the corner of his lips. He was on something, of that Vincent had no doubt. His bloodwork was clean of Z and the other common substances, so they'd have to send the blood sample to a specialist.

"Sit down," Vincent said through the steel bars.

Sam Bush fell to the floor. His legs stretched out in front of him, his back slouched forward. And those eyes continued staring.

"No, I meant..." Vincent shook his head. "Whatever."

Tom Vincent turned and left for the exit. Along the way, he passed the remaining nine holding cells, having put Sam Bush in the last cell. They rarely needed all ten cells on even the worst days.

The occupants of the other nine cells were a mixed bag much like Sam Bush's new roommates. Most sat or slept on the benches. A few sat in the middle of the floor, just as dazed and confused as Sam Bush.

Vincent exited the holding area and entered a long room with workstations lining the walls. He logged into an unoccupied station and proceeded to complete the processing for Sam J. Bush.

The room was mostly full. Three dozen cops sat at computers doing the part of the job everyone hated—paperwork.

Twenty feet away, five suspects with unusually large bellies sat quietly in their holding cells.

* * *

"Dr. Longfellow, I've spoken with quite a few people regarded as experts in the last week. There are a lot of theories out there about BSS. What do you think? How are they doing it?"

There was a long pause in which Dr. Longfellow could be heard breathing and letting out an audible sigh. "As I mentioned earlier, I am not a detective. I don't study the criminal mind. I don't study, nor do I have any interest in, terrorist motives or means. Even in the medical field, I have very little knowledge or experience with disease vectors or infectious diseases. Sleep and the study of its disorders simply doesn't regularly deal with those things."

"Doctor," he said, "could you just give me a..."

"I won't give you a guess," she said, finishing his thought. "No matter how uneducated it would be. I don't deal in guesses. I deal in science. And frankly, from a scientific perspective, I don't know how they're doing it. I really don't. And it scares the shit out of me."

"Well," he said after a pause, "I appreciate your help. Do you know of anyone else we should speak to?"

"The only person," she said, "the best person, in fact, is... well, you won't be able to reach him."

"No?" Aubrey said. "I have extensive resources at my

disposal. I'm sure I could figure something out if I knew their situation."

"Sorry, but I'm afraid he's in the one place you can't go."

Aubrey thought he knew what she meant. "Dead?"

"No, prison. Or what do they call it? The 'Keep?' Anyway, quite a shame. He knows more about sleep, sleep disorders, and most especially, Zentransa than anyone else alive. Really a shame what happened to him."

"Who is he? Did he have a team? Someone close to him that I could reach out to?"

"His name is Dr. Leo Alkorn. Formerly the head scientist at Ventana Inc. A real bastard if I ever met one—just a bitter, miserable old man—but he was a genius, just brilliant. And no, his team is gone too. Convicted along with him. Apparently, they were all caught up in some web of financial fraud."

"Ventana?" Aubrey asked. "As in…"

"Yes, the makers of Zentransa."

"What did he have to do with Zentransa?"

"He invented it, of course. James Sarazin gets all the credit for architecting the pill's rise, but Dr. Alkorn was its creator. He worked with Sarazin from the very beginning. He came on some hard times, apparently, and somehow coaxed his team into going along with this plan to rob the company. Brought them down with him. Anyway, they caught him and…"

Aubrey stopped listening. He stopped breathing. His heart pounded on his ribs so hard he could see his shirt pulsing to the beat. He stared at his yellow legal pad, scribbled with notes. The words on the pages blurred as his thoughts swam.

Here it was. Motive. Rock solid motive. The pieces of the puzzle started coming together for him. This was the break they needed; he knew it; he felt it. Yes, the scientists were locked away, but someone motivated enough and duplicitous enough could find a way to operate from within a prison. All they would need was a means of communication with willing actors on the outside.

"...Sorry, Detective, but I will have to go. My flight is..."

"Sure. N-No problem." He ended the call with his brain in knots. He'd just uncovered an enormous puzzle piece.

His first thought was that he had to talk to Dr. Alkorn and the other scientists. His second thought was: how in the hell would he be able to do that?

* * *

The Chechen sat outside Jespresso Caffè sipping from a tiny white ceramic cup. In spite of the police standoff zone, his new favorite coffee shop was just as accessible as it always had been. The biggest difference was the presence of uniformed cops patrolling the area—five on this block alone—and the total absence of cars on the roads around police headquarters. Even though cars were nearly silent these days, the street felt eerily quiet in their absence.

The benefit, however, was an unobstructed view of the building across the street. Ironic, he knew, because the part of the building with which he was concerned was underground. Nonetheless, he wanted to be present for the excitement that was about to rattle the boys in blue.

He checked his watch—3:35 p.m. If his estimated timing for everything was near correct, the party would begin in roughly seven minutes.

* * *

As a cop, Aubrey had arrested many people who ended up at the Keep, a monolithic behemoth of a prison. He knew the justice system in and out, so he knew the difficulties and near impossibility of acquiring permission to see a prisoner. When a criminal was sent to the Keep, they usually stayed there. They might become one of the lucky few to be released, but most inmates died there. A few died of old age; most of them were executed.

If you found yourself guilty of a major crime, the system was straightforward. The court's job was to decide guilt. The prison's job was to house you while your sentence was decided. The executioners, who lived and worked in the Keep, decided the sentence. They could set you free, they could let you die behind bars, or as was believed to be their preference, they could execute you.

The mysterious league of executioners, officially referred to as the Order of the Coppice, were highly revered and feared both in and out of the prison complex. It was known that Members of the Order skulked around the Keep, in near silence, judging and assessing who would be next to die by their hand. Their judgments on the inmates were unannounced, unexplained, and unquestioned. Prisoners referred to them as Tappers due to the rumor that they killed with the touch of their finger.

Aubrey knew that the duties of the administrators of the prison and those of the Tappers were kept separate for the most part, but he also knew that the Order held a great deal of sway over the day to day running of the Keep. The decision to visit an inmate was left to them and they rarely allowed it. Their reasons were unclear, but most outsiders felt that it was to keep their practices from becoming widely known.

The Tappers' power went unchecked due, he guessed, to the services they provided society at large. They kept the inmate population down to a controllable, sustainable level while keeping the dirty work of culling the prison herd out of the hands of lawmakers and politicians.

Aubrey found their mystique unrealistic and their power unsavory. He recalled encountering Tappers on two separate occasions. The first time was on the subway as a child. His father pointed to a short, thin man standing in a tight black cassock near one of the train doors. The Tapper stood still and silent in his cloak with shiny black buttons running from neck to waist.

Aubrey remembered, even as a child, the strange juxtaposition posed by the scene of the stoic Tapper surrounded by men in expensive suits speaking in business-like tones, waving their arms about in what looked like a heated discussion. Even today he had no idea what business they could be involved in together.

Aubrey's father would later tell him what the man was and what he did. Young Martin Aubrey was, at the same time, horrified and fascinated.

The second time Aubrey saw a Tapper was more recent and more personal. It happened several years ago during the trial of Victor Hamburg, who was accused of a gruesome triple murder. Victor, in an apparent jealous rage, smashed in his wife's head with a claw-hammer, then sought out her lover.

Victor found his wife's lover, who happened to be in the middle of an amorous exchange with a second woman. Victor dispatched both of them in the same manner as his wife. It was apparent, however, that Victor took his time with his wife's lover, concentrating his blows to the head and genitals.

Aubrey was the lead detective on the rather open and shut case of Victor Hamburg and appeared before the court to give his testimony. The trial was swift, as most were. When the guilty verdict was delivered, Victor was promptly sent to the Keep where his true sentencing would take place. As Victor was escorted out of the courtroom, Aubrey, from his seat behind the prosecutor, saw a man in black watching from the rear of the room.

As the crowded courtroom began to empty, people avoided this man like the plague, giving him a wide berth around his seat near the center aisle. Aubrey and the man stared at one another for a moment. He had black hair just starting to gray at the temples and he looked at Aubrey and no one else. His expression was that of understanding; it was a look of professional appreciation. Without warning, the man stood, and Aubrey realized why so many people went through great pains to avoid him. His tight black cassock was unmistakable. Here stood death.

Why had he come? The Tapper could have waited until Victor arrived at the Keep to judge him. Did he plan to Tap Victor here and end his life inside that courtroom?

Aubrey never got an answer. The man in black left without speaking to anyone and, as far as Aubrey knew, not another Tapper was seen in a courtroom ever since.

His mind lingered on the memory of that Tapper. For several minutes, he thought of little else. Suddenly, a vibration in the floor broke him from his thoughts. A sustained rumble in his feet, then the entire building seemed to jolt in place.

A man walking past lost his footing and fell. Tablets slid from desks. Light fixtures swung in circles on their tethers.

Someone nearby yelled, "Earthquake."

"Take cover," screamed another.

Aubrey was moving to crouch under his desk when it stopped as abruptly as it had begun. The building was still again. The rumbling tremor had lasted maybe a few seconds.

A moment passed in which no one spoke. Then, the screaming started. It came from below him, up through the floor.

* * *

The Chechen sipped his coffee until the tiny dregs touched his tongue. He spit the sour shards back into the cup. Setting it down, he checked his watch—3:42 p.m.

A few seconds passed. Everything about police headquarters across the street seemed normal. He wasn't sure how much he'd hear or feel when it happened, but he was confident he'd notice something to indicate the bombs had detonated as planned.

Another minute passed. Then another. Had he miscalculated the timing? Had he misjudged the amount of PSD he needed to use? Another moment and no signs from across the street that five bombs had gone off inside the building.

A twist in his guts. The *voodoo* drugs would wear off soon. If the police found the devices inside the volunteers...

An almost imperceptible tremor coursed through the ground under his feet. It only lasted a second, but it was enough to satisfy Anatoli Rubinski. He sighed with relief and let himself relax a little. His shoulders loosened

After another moment, smoke rose from somewhere on the backside of the building—a dense black plume flowing upward over the building.

* * *

Officer Tom Vincent clicked *Submit* at the bottom of the final form. Sam J. Bush had been booked and processed and he was now someone else's problem.

Vincent stood. The sound of quiet chatter and the clicking of keyboards filled the room. The smell of coffee drifted into his nostrils. He wanted some, but the thought of drinking the police station swill made him shudder. Just across the street, the good Italian coffee place would have just what he needed.

Vincent bent to gather his things when the wall crashed into him. A wave of drywall, metal, plastic and wood drove him back across the room. He flew through the tables and computers and other officers.

He landed with a crunch.

His eyes opened but he saw nothing. In the blackness, random patterns of light flashed across his retinas.

He was buried. His arms pinned. His chest constricted. Something pressed down on him. Some enormously heavy and immovable thing trapped him. Each exhalation of air allowed the weight to sink into him a little deeper.

His eyes began to clear. His vision was restored. Faint light came from somewhere. He could make out what was on top of him.

Bars.

Intact bars of a holding cell lay on top of him. In spite of being immobile, he could still feel the pain. He could feel it in his legs as it pulsated and throbbed. He could feel it in his chest as breaths became harder and harder to suck in. His head pounded. Something flowed into his eyes and mouth. Blood. He could taste it.

He tried to call out but he could barely muster a whisper under the weight of the bars.

Then, he smelled it. The smoke. A second later, he saw it. Black clouds collected above him. What little breath he could draw burned in his chest.

The smoke grew. Darkness gained on him.

* * *

Aubrey walked the scene with Detective Julian Winger. The basement of police headquarters was comprised of ten holding cells, several offices, and a few control booths. The entire floor had become a crime scene.

"Video footage is pretty clear," Winger said. "The explosion originated from five suspects in holding cells ten through seven. Which," he waved his hand over a scorched section of concrete wall, "would have been over here."

Glass crunched under Aubrey's heel. He kicked at what was once a light bulb and cleared a spot with his foot to stand amongst the rubble. Lanes like animal trails had been cleared for people to walk through the debris. Teams carried it away in wheelbarrows to be sorted and sifted for residual evidence.

Forensics specialists sifted through the wreckage wrought by the explosions. A dozen of them in white clean-suits combed the area. The bars on the last three cells had been blown clean off their mounts. The walls separating cells ten through four had been blown out. All inmates therein were dead. The back wall that lined every cell also served as the main footing for the entire building above them, which meant it was several feet of reinforced concrete. The footing wall acted as a funnel for the blast, like a giant shape charge focusing its force out and up from the cells.

Thin layers of gray fire-suppressant powder coated everything. Black scorch marks covered the walls and ceilings surrounding the last four cells. All the rooms and offices adjacent to the holding cells had been demolished. This included a workroom, two control booths, several offices, and a breakroom—their occupants killed or wounded.

Fortunately, this area of the station was built for security and strength. Every door was made of heavy steel and most of the walls were concrete or cinder block. The original architects had never planned for an explosion of this magnitude but, for the most part, the building had held together.

"How did they get the explosives in?" Aubrey asked. "How did security scans not pick them up?"

"Audio and video recordings and the scanner files show the suspects each had some sort of bulge or mass in their abdomens. We think they swallowed the explosive materials. Like drug mules except they were bomb mules."

"Jesus," Aubrey said. The scene had been cleared of all casualties, the dead and wounded, for hours. Ambulances and fire trucks had appeared within minutes, emergency services pulling together to help the cops in need. Medical-drones did most of the heavy lifting, but every able body in the building had contributed to clearing debris and pulling out the bodies of the dead and wounded. "This is our guy." Aubrey cleared his throat. The air was still thick with dust. "Has to be."

Winger nodded grimly. "Chemical analysis will tell us if it was PSD and where it came from. But yeah, I think you're right."

Aubrey looked up. The blast had stripped the ceiling of

everything except a few dangling wires and exposed pipes. The concrete girders and floor above looked to be relatively unharmed minus some cosmetic scarring.

Aubrey said, "Do the engineers think that'll hold after..."

Shouting cut him off. "We got another one."

Aubrey and Winger hurried over to a far corner. At first glance, it looked to be nothing more than a mound of brick and dust.

A crowd of people had already gathered and as he got closer, Aubrey noticed a black boot protruding from the rubble. Everyone leapt into action. A chain gang was created, the mound cleared piece by piece until a section of bars was revealed. Under them, the ashen face of a man in a dark blue police uniform.

"Let's get these bars off," said a woman in white coveralls. Aubrey ran forward, stumbling through the mess. He and eight others strained to raise the twelve-foot wall of cell bars. After a final heave, they dropped the bars onto the floor where it fell, raising a cloud of white dust.

A stretcher was brought over and the officer loaded onto it. His arms dangled over the edge of the plastic board. Two officers carried his limp form away and as they passed, Aubrey saw an eyelid flutter open.

18

The Father of Z

"Chief Inspector Long?" Aubrey sat across the oversized wooden desk from the Chief Inspector. She leaned back in her chair, resting a cheek on her fist. She'd been staring absent-mindedly at the wall ever since he made his request.

"What?" she said, not looking in his direction.

"I was asking if you could help us get out to the Keep so we can question Dr. Alkorn and the other scientists from Ventana."

She sat up straight and looked at Aubrey as if just realizing he was in the room with her. "You know how the system works, Aubrey. You know how those... *Tappers* run that prison. Families barely have access to inmates."

"I know. But if the Chief of Police or the Mayor were to..."

"First of all," she interrupted, "I've got every cop available to me kicking over every rock in this damn city hunting for OFP. I can't spare the bodies to go on some wild goose chase. Second, there's no guarantee the Chief or Mayor would make a difference even if they did make such a special request. Lastly, why should the Mayor or the Chief make such a request? OFP just blew up half of police headquarters, right under our nose! Do you think BSS is top of mind right now?" Her fist pounded the top of the desk. "And your theory is that these disgraced scientists are somehow operating a major terrorist operation from inside a prison. And not just any prison, from inside the Keep, which is *exceptionally* secure."

"Ma'am, it's the best lead we have on Boarding School Syndrome. And I think it's a good one—there's definitely motive. I just have to find the means and opportunity. And if we can tie them to BSS, I think we can make a logical leap to tie them to the bombings."

She waved her hand, batting his ideas away like so many flies. She sank back in her chair once more. Her face looked worn and stretched. "I'm not going to bother the mayor with this. Or the Chief. I'll make the request to the prison administrator myself. But don't bank on anything."

"Thank you, that's… it'll have to do for now. I do have another idea to run down the lead."

She sighed and crossed her arms. "Oh yeah, what's that?"

"Sarazin. I need to talk to him too. He knew these people well—they worked for him for a long time. He and Dr. Alkorn were probably pretty close, so he might know something that could help us."

She gave a slight chuckle and turned to look out of her office window considering something, weighing her options before replying. "You know that request doesn't actually sound so crazy compared to your prison field trip." She waved a hand without looking at Aubrey. "Fine. But use the proper channels and take an *actual* cop with you as lead on this."

Her emphasis on the word "actual" stung Aubrey, but he left with renewed hope. For once, they had a solid lead to track down.

The Command Center was nearly empty. Almost every able-bodied officer and detective was out in the city chasing down every possible lead to find OFP members. The attack on police headquarters had created a feeling of total war against the terror group. All resources would now be deployed to capture the killers.

He found Reynolds and Grant at the BSS desk. They were having a quiet conversation when he started toward them. Like everyone else in the building, they'd been shaken up by the attack. They both had known several of the casualties and had wanted to join the citywide manhunt with the rest of the force, but Aubrey had convinced them to stay back. He didn't say it out loud, but he knew a show of force when he saw one. The BSS investigation needed to stay focused.

He briefed them on his earlier conversation with Dr. Longfellow and his request of Chief Inspector Long to question the Ventana scientists being held at the Keep.

"I mean, it makes a lot of sense," Grant said. "Alkorn was pissed about getting caught in his little financial scheme and blamed Sarazin and the other officers at Ventana. Plus, he'd have intimate knowledge of the people working closely on Zentransa's initial release to the public, therefore, knowing who to target. Makes sense."

"Let's find out exactly what he was convicted of first. And to your point, that only answers *why* he'd do it," Reynolds said. "It tells us nothing about how he actually infected the children and, most importantly, how he did it from prison."

"Alkorn would know all about Zentransa and would probably know how to manipulate its properties to create BSS. We just have to figure out how he got it into the kids," Grant offered. "And don't forget that some prisoners are allowed to communicate with the outside."

"Communications are traced and recorded. We could find out easy enough," Reynolds said. "But the bigger question is how does a scientist, angry at his old boss, convince a terrorist organization to start poisoning kids and bombing buildings? Because we have to assume that he is behind both. Don't we? It can't be a simple coincidence that OFP decided to start doing BSS with the mad doctor and randomly bombing innocent people at the same time."

At this, Grant and Aubrey had no response. For a moment, the two looked at one another, apparently hoping the other had a suitable answer.

Finally, Aubrey said, "I don't know, but that doesn't matter right now. We finally have a place to start and the rest of the answers will come. I know they will. We just have to run this down and the rest will come."

"I agree. Either way, we need to talk to Alkorn and his team," Reynolds said. "And we need to talk to Sarazin." Aubrey and Grant both nodded. "Alright. We're waiting on the Chief Inspector to go visit our pals in the Keep. Grant, see if you can set up a meeting with Sarazin."

"Yes, ma'am."

* * *

Several hours were spent digging into the cases of Dr. Alkorn and his associates while Grant worked on setting up the meeting with James Sarazin. The cases were pretty straightforward based on everything Aubrey read. Alkorn and his team were found to have mountains of evidence on their personal and work computers implicating them in the fraud scheme. Their bank accounts showed them to be the beneficiaries of a sudden influx of income plus correspondence between them that painted the whole picture.

The crime itself involved the use of a sophisticated computer worm installed on the Ventana servers; Aubrey didn't quite understand how it worked, but somehow it took fractions of pennies from financial transactions, pooled them together, and deposited them into an offshore account that eventually fed Alkorn's and his team's personal bank accounts.

The case against Alkorn also laid out his financial troubles stemming from an addiction to gambling compounded by alimony owed to three ex-wives. Getting his team involved, it appeared, amounted to simple intimidation on Alkorn's part and greed on theirs. Alkorn and his team, however, remained defiant, maintaining their innocence throughout the entire trial.

Aubrey was reviewing the character profile on one of Alkorn's team members, Natalie Shoeman, when Reynolds pulled her chair next to him.

"Grant got word from some other cops of a good lead on an OFP safe house," she said. "People are pretty dispersed right now so he and I are going to join a few others to raid the place."

Aubrey stood. "Alright, I'll be ready in two minutes. Let me just..."

"No," she shook her head. "Sorry, Marty. Just me and Grant. They said something about it being a liability to have civilian personnel at the scene."

Aubrey shrugged and tried to sound as casual as possible. "Sure. Yeah, that's fine. I'll catch up with you afterwards." He sat back down. Reynolds and Grant stood and nodded their goodbyes.

"Hey, where did the lead come from?" he asked Reynolds. "Tip line?"

"Yeah. Anonymous call on the tip line. How'd you know?"

"Lucky guess," he shrugged.

She squinted at him. "What is it? What are you getting at?"

"I don't know. Probably nothing." Aubrey turned in his chair to face the windows of the large room. Light spilled in painting the floor in harsh white rectangles. "Keep your heads down. I'm going to work for a while longer and then take off for a bit. I'll meet you back here later."

* * *

Martin Aubrey left the empty command center for home, deciding he'd clear his head with a quick workout and a hot shower. He hoped his partners uncovered something worth mentioning, but he had a profound feeling that they would come up empty… again. He sympathized with them. They wanted to work out their anger and frustration by kicking in some doors. He would too, if he was them.

Looking up through the artificial lights, the sky was dark, appearing as a strange veil hanging over the city. Blackness waiting to smother out the light of the wayward populous of New Aberdeen.

People never looked up anymore. Why would they, he thought, when the sun was down on the street now. It was put back into the sky when the city was through with it. The world of the Z pill told the sun where to be. Money, power, authority, shot-callers, and world builders—they were the ones who determined the time of day. Those without the luxury of the pill lived in a world perpetually saturated with sunlight—real or fake—whether they liked it or not.

Aubrey made his way home on foot, deciding the walk and the burnt calories would be good for him. His mind clung to the prospect of visiting the Keep and the imminent—he hoped—meeting with Sarazin. He made a mental list of questions to ask Sarazin, which seemed far simpler and more straightforward than the imaginary conversation he kept having with Dr. Leo Alkorn.

What to ask the prime suspect in a string of child poisonings, he thought. Should they go in guns blazin' or play it slow? This was all assuming they would get access to the man and his team. The Chief Inspector was taking on the request personally, which made him feel better. He did not appreciate her motives at times, but he felt sure she was a solid professional looking to stop this violence and save their city.

Home was a comfort. A quick intense workout followed by a long, hot shower did wonders for relaxing his mind and body. He threw back a Z pill and lay like a statue on his bed while he waited for the zoning to commence. It passed over him like a warm breeze. The hairs on his skin like so many leaves on the ground rustled by the wind. With great care and mindfulness, acutely aware of all of his nerve endings, he sat up.

With the euphoria still on him like a light blanket, his body felt good. His mind felt good—relaxed and nimble.

A glass of bourbon later and he felt focused and sharp.

The call from Detective Aaron Lewis could not have come at a more perfect time.

"Why aren't you at the station?" Lewis asked.

"Needed a recharge. Came home for a bit while you all were out rounding up bad guys." He thought his attempt to sound blasé came off as authentic.

"You need more Z? We can put you on the health plan if we need to, since you're technically a contractor. Also, since we're not paying you... it's the least we could do."

"No, I'm good, but thanks." Aubrey appreciated the olive branch, no matter how camouflaged it may have been. "Hey, why aren't you still sniffing out OFP in all their hiding places?"

A pause. "Marty, let's get a drink. Come back down here but don't go to the station. Meet me at Winky's bar. You remember where it is?"

"Of course, I remember," Aubrey said, recalling the tiny watering hole two blocks from police headquarters. "I'll see you there in thirty minutes."

* * *

Winky's was a spot only real veteran cops knew about. "A place for cops to drink with cops away from all the other cops," was how his first lieutenant had described it. "Rookies aren't allowed. Get some salt on your shoulder boards and we might let you in."

He saw Detective Lewis sitting in a dark corner of the bar. He was halfway through a tall mug of amber beer with an empty one beside it. Aubrey made his way across the almost deserted bar, long and narrow with scarred wooden floors and a beat up bar top. The place felt like it had been there a thousand years, with tables that looked to have been cleaned at least that long ago. He sat across from Lewis at a small high-top table. Lewis looked up in apparent surprise, having been lost in thought.

"How'd the raids go?" Aubrey asked almost as soon as he sat down. He was intensely curious as to the progress of the day's operation.

After a deep sigh, Lewis said, "Same as always. Nothing to write home about. Some known members of OFP got detained. But that's about it. They're all out there. Dispersed. Still hiding out. We'll never get them all." He took a long pull of his beer. "Look, I want to talk about the other day." Aubrey thought for a moment Lewis would bring up their argument in the back of the van. "The other day, just before that raid, you and I were talking about the last three bombers: Mills, Van Weisen, and Winston. We were looking at how long each of them was affiliated with OFP. Remember?"

"Yep, I remember." Aubrey waved to the bartender and signaled they'd need two more beers.

"Right. And you were saying how OFP was all about giving people a place where they felt like they belonged. But then these bombers are barely known inside OFP. Ringing a bell?"

"Yeah, it rings a bell." Aubrey remembered the conversation perfectly but wanted to give Lewis plenty of runway for where he was going. He kept the interruptions to a minimum.

"So, basically, we had little to no idea how long they were with OFP. Well, since you and I talked in the van," Lewis coughed and continued, "it's been nagging at me. So, I did some digging for answers to that question. I gathered everything I could find on these guys: internet metadata, activity logs from personal and residential security cameras, social media posts and records of personal interactions from as far back as six months before the bombings started—as much as I could get anyway." Lewis paused to down the rest of his beer. "I'm telling you, Marty. I looked at every damn thing. Then, I crammed all that data through our AI system, which is second only to the federal government's."

"And?"

Lewis just shook his head looking defeated. "I couldn't find anything. Nothing solid, anyway. The AI couldn't pull anything from all that data that showed how long they'd been members of OFP. Which says a lot. But what says even more is that the AI couldn't show they were actually *ever* in OFP. Not using the data I fed it, at least. Then, I realized I had to change the question. I wasn't asking the AI the right question."

Aubrey liked Lewis's change in tactic with the AI system. Artificial Intelligence was incredibly effective at using a compilation of data streams to answer questions, give probabilities, and make predictions, but you had to ask the right question in the right way. Garbage in; garbage out.

"I looked at the profiles we had on these people. Nothing in common. I mean nothing based on what I could see. I deepened their profiles using every aspect of their lives I could find: love interests, hobbies, education, work, eating habits, workout preferences, everything I could think of. I then ran those deeper profiles through our AI system and asked it to use all that data and tell me the *likelihood* that these people would have joined a domestic terror group like our good friends at One Front for the People."

"And?" said Aubrey

"Less than a ten percent probability for all of them. Highest probability was eight-point-five percent for one of them—Winston, I think." Lewis raised his hands in a gesture of deference. "Looks like you were dead on. Other than Ralph Jacobsen, and maybe Bayez too, I don't think any of them were ever actually in OFP." Lewis tipped back the fresh beer dropped off by the server. "And this last attack at the fucking station." Lewis looked away at this, forehead creasing. "No claims have been made yet and nothing has come back as definitive on whether it was the same bombers. And we don't know yet what possible ties those guys had to OFP, if any."

"Let's pretend I am right. Let's say that the bombers, including the ones at headquarters, aren't in OFP. What does that mean for us?"

"It's like you said before, it means that the terrorists are snatching people off the street." Lewis leaned across the table at this point, his tie soaking up the ring left by his last beer.

"Yes, but it's also like you said in the van. We're still looking for the same people. They just have a different weapon now. They're weaponizing people. Remotely guided human-borne improvised explosive devices." Aubrey snapped his fingers and pointed at Lewis. "Hey, I just invented a new acronym: RGHBIED. Look at that." Aubrey couldn't help the joke; he was in too good a mood now that he and his friend were talking again.

Lewis laughed into his beer. "That's pretty good. Bit of a mouthful but... look, my question is why? Why are insiders getting skittish? They don't want to give it all up for the cause or what?"

"Could be. Or..." Aubrey paused. A memory from the night he and Lewis were looking at the big board came back to him. "We and they."

"What? We and who? What are you talking about?"

"I'm talking about 'we' and 'they'. That day, before the raid, before you and I talked about the last three bombers, I was reading the interview transcripts for the OFP detainees."

"Yeah? Spit it out please." Lewis was growing impatient, and drunk.

"Well, in all that talk about providing a refuge and a home, et cetera, they used the pronoun 'we.'"

"So?" Lewis said, unimpressed.

"So, when the detainees mentioned the bombs or Boarding School Syndrome, they used the word 'they' exclusively. There's a separation there. 'We' for one thing, but 'they' for another. Seems odd, doesn't it?"

"Again, maybe those guys just don't believe in the cause. But someone does because they're still blowing this fuckin' city the hell up." Lewis was now working on his fourth beer.

"But not one of the OFP detainees would use 'we,'" Aubrey continued. "That seems off to me. You'd think they'd claim the credit, at least to spread their message."

Lewis burped and asked the bartender for pretzels. "Gotta slow down if I'm going back to the orifice. I mean, office. Keep going, I'm listening."

"What if they're some rogue group *within* One Front. Operating in the dark. You won't catch them with OFP, because they've separated themselves from OFP."

"Interesting theory." Lewis rested his head on his fist.

"I think they're still run of the mill terrorists with a political agenda and all that." Aubrey let his mind wander, allowing the theories to come as they were. Lewis was a good sounding board in any state, but especially with several beers in him. "But they must have either been members and splintered away from the mainstream OFP... after becoming too radical, or they joined as radicals adopting the OFP doctrine or..."

Aubrey paused and pointed at Lewis. "Or they just hijacked the OFP name altogether."

"What? What hijack? Why do that?"

"OFP had some street cred. People knew who they were. The name is recognizable. Why not steal their brand and run with it?"

"Buddy," Lewis croaked, "Terrorism 101 teaches us that taking credit is their whole thing. Why blow people up just to give some shitty old hacks credit?" Lewis swayed in his chair, shoveling handfuls of pretzels in his mouth. "Dovvent may senf." After a long swig of beer, he continued. "They must have been a part of OFP, then," he made a gesture with his hand, "splintered off. That just makes good sense to me, man."

"Credit. Why give them credit?" Aubrey stared at the tattered dart board behind Lewis. It had been hit with thousands of darts over its lifetime. The metal rings separating the scoring brackets hanging on for dear life. The black, green, and red circles blurred as his eyes unfocused and he let that question bounce from one side of his brain to the other. Why would they let OFP take credit? It made him think of something his dad used to say—"If you're in a position to take credit, you're also in a position to take blame. Best you be man enough for both, son."

"Blame." Aubrey shot up out of his seat, sending it toppling over and drawing attention from the bartender. "They want OFP to take the credit because it also means they take the blame. They don't want credit. They don't want anyone to know they're doing it at all. Giving credit to OFP is deflecting blame from them. Why would the cops go after one suspect when another one has already confessed?"

"Again, Terrorism 101, buddy." Lewis's head swayed from

side to side. "Taking credit is their thing. It's part of their whole... deal." He threw a wild hand up for emphasis. "Why preach a... a message for someone else? Why risk getting caught the whole time? What's the point of being terrorists if you don't have a message?"

Aubrey had no answer. He knew he was close to something, but he didn't know what that something was. He had the overwhelming feeling that the answer was very near, but he had no good ideas on what he was even looking for. He was in the dark groping and searching, but everything he touched felt like the thing before it.

Lewis let out a long, loud breath. "OK, let's recap. There's a group of psycho killers with a penchant for destruction and poisoning kids, but they don't want credit for any of it. And they don't really have a message, which means they're not really terrorists at all. They just hijacked the pre-existing cachet of a bunch of whiny hippies to make it look like *they* did it. Which again just makes them psycho killers. Frankly... that scares the piss out of me. Killing for no reason at all is just..." Lewis cut himself off and reached into his jacket pocket. Reading something on his phone, he said, "Shit. Speak of the devil. Guess who just claimed credit for the bombing at police HQ?" He raised his eyebrows. "I have to get back. C'mon let's go. Oh, by the way, genocidal maniacs who operate on this scale generally have a message and are happy to take credit for it. Most of them enjoy the spotlight."

At that moment, Aubrey's pocket vibrated, shocking him out of his thoughts. He pulled it out to see a message from Ryan Grant. Their meeting with James Sarazin would start in two hours.

***

To all media outlets,

The police of this city have obviously chosen sides. They choose to support the evils that plague the people, the corporation that poisons society, the pill that destroys the fabric of all that we once held dear. One Front for the People will continue to target all who participate in the perpetuation of the existence and spread of the drug Zentransa.

Death will spread like a cloud over this city until you come to heed our words.

***

April 28, 2043

The large reception area outside James Sarazin's office was designed to impress. The space was an enormous circle with impossibly high ceilings. Aubrey estimated that the entire command center at police headquarters could fit with room to spare. Most of the floor space was empty except for the two small rectangular couches, on which the trio were now sitting, in the room's center. Massive contemporary art pieces hung on all but the exterior walls, which were all glass. Everything but the vibrantly colored art was starkly minimalist, bright white, and high gloss. Aubrey felt as if he were in the middle of a modern art museum that doubled as an office. The receptionist's cylindrical desk even looked like it could be the podium of an attentive docent, patiently waiting to explain that the piece you were admiring is a "comment on American consumerism."

As Aubrey looked around, he noticed the absence of anything related to Ventana Inc, which contrasted with the rest of the building where visitors and employees were bombarded with branded imagery every few feet. He was considering the myriad of visitors, suitors, peddlers, and ass-kissers who sat on these couches on a daily basis, when the dark mahogany, oversized doors to Sarazin's office flew open.

James Sarazin stepped through them with a cheerful expression and strode over to meet his guests. The father of Zentransa was shorter than Martin Aubrey had expected. He approached with effortless, airy confidence. Every move said this was a man in a hurry, yet in the moment, ready to capitalize on every efficiency in movement and conversation. In a black suit and black tie, Sarazin extended a hand to each of the three guests, giving what Aubrey considered an overtly firm shake. Aubrey was under the impression that despite his small stature, this man could shrink people at will. His power and influence were worn like a scent. Besides, Aubrey thought, Sarazin would see his shortness as a strength, something that was a contributing factor to his success; he would tell you that if he were tall, he would never have tried so hard to become who he was.

"Thank you so much for coming down," said Sarazin. "Can I get you a cup of coffee or anything?"

Without waiting for an answer, Sarazin turned back toward his office. The three investigators followed the founder of Ventana Inc inside. The office looked like a smaller version of the room they just left. Only here, framed by massive windows and spotlighted by the artificial sunlight's beaming bright rays, stood the man's colossal glass and metal desk.

Looking around, Aubrey saw none of the normal accoutrement of an executive's office. There were no sculpted awards of excellence from the local business bureau, no framed gifts of congratulations from his employees, no pictures of Sarazin glad-handing with politicians and power brokers, or any pictures at all. Expensive looking art covered most of the walls, except for one which held four large television monitors tuned to four different financial business news channels from around the world. This office, much like the waiting area outside, was all about one thing—the man himself.

"I'm so glad you're here," said Sarazin, sitting behind his massive desk across from the three of them. He leaned back in his sleek black chair. "I've been telling the Mayor and the Chief that I want to help. We have some pretty impressive technology here plus some really smart people. Whatever you guys need I'd love to contribute. I mean, this violence is... well, it's just evil. Pure, downright evil. And I can't tell you how sorry I am about what happened at the police station. Simply tragic. I told the Chief my offer of financial assistance to the victims' families extends to the police as well. Especially them."

Reynolds nodded slowly as if taking the man in. "Thank you, sir. All we're really here for is some information. We have a few questions for you and then we'll be out of your hair. That's it."

"That's it?" Sarazin asked with a look of surprise. "I thought you might want to borrow some of our artificial intelligence systems to run some modeling or something."

"Just questions, sir." Reynolds placed her phone on Sarazin's desk. "I'm going to record our conversation. If that's OK?"

"Absolutely."

"Mr. Sarazin, what can you tell us about Dr. Leo Alkorn?"

she said.

Sarazin's face made no reaction to the mention of the man's name. His lack of reaction was so complete that it puzzled Aubrey.

"Dr. Alkorn?" Sarazin smoothed his black hair back and shrugged. "What can I say? He was a brilliant scientist who was an integral part of this company's success for a long time..."

Grant interrupted. "He was recently arrested and convicted of a number of financial crimes. All of them against this company."

"I'm *very* aware of that, of course. You didn't let me finish," Sarazin said with a look of eternal patience. "He was an integral part of this company's success until he came on hard times and made some unfortunate choices."

"You don't appear to harbor any bad feelings toward the doctor," Aubrey said, speaking for the first time.

At this, Sarazin's expression took on a noticeable change. "Bad feelings?" he asked. He paused and turned in his chair and face the sun, now blasting the desk and its four occupants. "I'm filled with regret about Dr. Alkorn. And his team. He and I had a... special relationship. He didn't get along with most people, but I felt like we understood each other. That made working together very... productive."

"Why are you filled with regret?" Aubrey asked.

Sarazin stared off into space for a moment longer, then turned back to them. "Because I feel like I could have helped him before his situation got out of control. I tried. I tried to help him, but by then it was too late. He'd gone too far. Something had to be done."

"Why did he steal from you?" Aubrey asked.

"They said it was a gambling problem spun out of control. He hatched this crazy scheme of his and bullied his team into going along with it." Sarazin steepled his hands on the desk. "Listen, I really do want to help, but what's this all about? I'd rather not relive this part of my life. There is nothing I know that isn't already on file with the police."

"Sir." Reynolds leaned forward in her chair and pushed her tablet across the desk toward Sarazin. "Take a look at this. This shows all the victims of the so-called Boarding School Syndrome." Aubrey knew the image she was sharing with James Sarazin. Resembling a family tree, the web of connections between the victims was illustrated with linkages between them. Several were connected with one or two links between them, some had many more. One common link ran through all three of them, however. "Can you tell me what you see here?"

Sarazin stared at the screen with a blank expression, which Aubrey assumed had been practiced and perfected through years of experience negotiating multi-billion-dollar deals.

"They all have one thing in common." Sarazin let out a deep breath he'd been holding. "Me."

"That's right," Aubrey said. "Every victim has a connection back to you in one way or another. Most of them pretty direct."

"What are you getting at?"

"Would you say that Dr. Alkorn knows more about sleep, sleep science, and the development of sleep related drugs than anyone else alive? Many of his colleagues believe so."

"Of course. He may have been an unruly asshole, but he was certainly a genius. He was brilliant in many fields, but especially in his chosen specialty. I say again, what are you getting at?"

"Mr. Sarazin." Aubrey paused. "You had the man arrested. Had him sent to the Keep. Have you ever felt that he may blame you for all that? That while he's rotting away in a prison, which he's never likely to leave alive, he may have some ill will?"

"It's occurred to me, sure."

"So, you have this guy—this brilliant scientist—who knows all about sleep and drugs and chemistry. Then, you catch him stealing and he gets sent to the Keep." Aubrey paused to let Sarazin catch up, but he had a feeling Sarazin needed no catching up. "Then, you start to have people around you, people connected to you in one way or another, become targets of some strange poisoning. Are you smelling what I'm stepping in here, sir?"

"Obviously." Sarazin adjusted himself in his chair. "And how is he supposed to be carrying out these acts of terror, because I assume you're blaming him for the bombings too."

"That's crossed our minds, yes," Grant said. "He was, or is, a chemist. Bombs are just chemicals and wires. But we're more interested in BSS. If he did one, then he probably did the other, but our focus is the poisoning happening to these kids."

"How am I supposed to help?"

"Did he ever threaten you?" Aubrey asked. "Did he ever say he'd get back at you? Anything like that?"

"No, not really," Sarazin said, gazing at the far wall. His face had lost all emotion. "He just stared. He wouldn't take his eyes off me. I was there when they arrested him. I… I wanted to make sure they weren't rough with him, you know. Then, in the courtroom, again he just stared. He wouldn't stop staring."

"And his team?" Reynolds asked. "How did they treat you? What did they say to you?"

"They were… less stoic. Livid. Infuriated. They denied everything of course and blamed Alkorn for getting them mixed up in all of it." Sarazin coughed and straightened himself in his chair again. "No, they weren't as quiet."

"Sounds like they had a motive," Aubrey said. "Sounds like they could probably put their heads together and figure out how to poison those kids."

"Detective, trust me…"

"I'm actually not a detective," Aubrey corrected. "I'm a private citizen."

"Oh, I thought… what are you, some kind of consultant or something?"

"Something like that," Reynolds replied, cutting off Aubrey. "Back to what you were saying, Mr. Sarazin."

"Oh, right. I was saying you should trust me. There is no way these people, these scientists are blowing people up or poisoning anyone. You're barking up the wrong tree on this one."

"Do you still have any computers or hardware that belonged to them?" Grant asked. "Any papers, notebooks, or ledgers? Journals even?"

"No. All of it was seized by the police." Sarazin spread his hands, palms up toward the officers. "You guys have it all."

"Have you received any correspondence from Alkorn or the others at all?" Reynolds asked.

"No. I've not communicated with them in any way whatsoever," Sarazin said.

"Have you…"

Sarazin held up a hand. "Detectives and private citizen, I really have to get going. But I'd be happy to answer all of your questions. Maybe you can send my receptionist an email with your questions. I promise I'll answer every last one of them to the best of my ability."

"One last thing, Mr. Sarazin," Aubrey said as he and his partners were shown the door. "We'd like to go speak to them. To Alkorn and his team. Do you think you could help us arrange that?"

Sarazin stopped short of the tall mahogany doors and turned back toward the three of them. "Arrange… I mean, how could I possibly help you do that?" Sarazin emitted a slight laugh. "I don't know… I mean, I have absolutely no connections with the prison system. I don't know how I'd be of any help."

"You're very friendly with the Mayor, aren't you?" Grant said. "You could talk to him. We think that if the request came directly from him, in this trying time, we may have a shot."

Sarazin's face relaxed. "Sure… sure, yeah I can do that. No guarantees though." Sarazin turned back to the door and upon opening it appeared lighter and much more charming than he had only a moment before. "Detectives, I hope you have a wonderful rest of your day and good luck on the case."

19

The Keep

The command center had come to life with a new vigor since the previous day's raids across the city. Whether it was rage, frustration, or dogged determination, the energy in the room made the air hum.

While the BSS team was interviewing James Sarazin, the rest of the officers and detectives on the task force had been busy wrapping up interviews with the detained members of One Front for the People.

In small groups, the detectives and inspectors pored over every syllable of interviews in the hopes of finding some nugget that would help them. The pressure to find a resolution to the death and destruction had come to a near breaking point.

"They won't find anything useful," Aubrey said as he and Reynolds watched the other detectives in the command center. He spoke only loud enough so Reynolds could hear him.

"Why do you say that?" Reynolds asked.

"Just a feeling," Aubrey told her.

His feeling was that he and Lewis had stumbled onto some version of the truth at Winky's, though he wasn't ready to share their theories just yet. He needed a little more time to process it all.

He mentally ran through it to make sure he had their ideas straight. OFP had been hijacked by someone looking to either use OFP's established street cred, or to saddle blame on the ignorant members of One Front for the People.

Why did this other terror group want to push blame onto OFP? What was their ultimate end game for the bombings and BSS? These questions were beyond Aubrey's reckoning at the moment. Then, there was the question of Dr. Alkorn's involvement. Aubrey had thought Sarazin would yield more helpful information during their interview, that he'd want to make Alkorn pay for what he did and therefore be more forthcoming. More than anything, the CEO seemed to want to protect Alkorn, the same person who tried to rob Ventana for tens of millions of dollars.

Aubrey could understand Sarazin's affection for the scientist. After all, Alkorn had been the science behind Sarazin's bold ambitions; their relationship was symbiotic in many ways. The CEO and the mad doctor had a powerful connection which, Aubrey assumed, made the shock of discovering Alkorn's betrayal difficult for Sarazin.

Aubrey looked at a conference table across the crowded command center. There sat Aaron Lewis, leaning far back in his chair with arms crossed while five detectives around him argued over some piece of evidence, probably some snippet of an interview. Lewis did not take part in the argument but stared out of the nearby window until something made him turn his head toward Aubrey. They exchanged a knowing nod.

Earlier, Lewis told Aubrey that he shared their theory

with Chief Inspector Long and her lieutenants—how they believed a rogue group within OFP or outside it carried out the bombings and were spreading BSS, and pushed blame on OFP in order to remain hidden. He told the Chief Inspector how they should pursue another strategy, one that looked at possible impostors and other sleeper cells operating within the city.

She did not receive the information well. As Lewis explained it to Aubrey, "She basically told me never to question her strategy again. That without anything more concrete than the use of pronouns, she didn't have the time or the money to start over. The public wanted to see people being arrested and that we are bound to catch them in one of the round ups. Oh, and if I liked being a cop, I'd better forget all of 'my bullshit theories.'"

Now, Aubrey sat and thought about Reynold's rather simple question. How did he know they wouldn't find anything useful from the raids? Should he divulge to her any part of his and Lewis's latest theory? After some consideration, he decided against telling her.

Lewis had not told the Chief Inspector that Aubrey had played a key role in developing the new theory. That little omission, Aubrey believed, was the only reason he was still employed with the police. He thought it best not to get another of his allies in hot water by selling them on one of his harebrained ideas.

He stood behind a chair at the desk where Reynolds and Grant sat. He leaned with both hands on the back of the chair, bending at the waist to face the floor. Without looking up, he said, "Let's go over the Alkorn case one more time. Tell me what we have so far."

"OK," Grant said. He leaned in to read from the tablet in front of him. "Dr. Leo Alkorn… arrested January 24, 2043; convicted on March 1 of multiple counts of embezzlement and an attempt to defraud Ventana Inc… blah, blah, blah… conspiring to defraud shareholders… blah, blah, blah… along with three members of his team: Rajesh Imanpor, Natalie Shoeman, and Stanley Winthorpe." Grant paused then looked up. "Talk about quick processing, right at one month from arrest to trial. Quick trial too—only two days." Grant looked back down and pointed at the screen. "Looks like he was immediately sent to The Keep on March 1. That gives them a month before the bombings and BSS started."

"More than a month," Reynolds said. "They would have spent all of February in county lockup awaiting trial. And at some point, Alkorn enlists OFP to carry out these attacks." Reynolds sounded unconvinced. "Again, the question is how does he convince these once glorified hippies to become killers?"

If it was OFP at all, Aubrey thought.

"OFP already had an anti-rich people thing," Grant answered. "And they were well-known Z haters, blamed it then, and blame it now for all the world's problems. They were kind of a perfect fit."

"Alkorn wasn't a Z hater. He was a Sarazin hater, we think," Reynolds corrected. "How does he communicate with OFP? Then and now," Reynolds asked.

"I told you," Grant said, "some prisoners are allowed to communicate with the outside world."

"And I told you," Reynolds retorted, "all comms in and out of the Keep are traced and recorded. So, what? He sends coded messages?"

"Maybe," Aubrey said. He'd been quiet, attempting to fit the puzzle pieces together in his mind.

"He could also have help smuggling his messages out," Grant said.

"That's true. And it doesn't mean that he's been running the show," Aubrey speculated. "It could be that he just got them started, showed them how to infect kids with BSS, maybe build the bombs, then let them run with it."

Reynolds leaned heavily in her chair with crossed arms and exhaled a long sigh. "None of this matters unless…"

"Reynolds, Grant," came a shout from behind Aubrey. He turned to see the tall, thin form of Chief Inspector Long standing in her office's threshold. She waved the two detectives over.

Aubrey watched their conversation. Long stood stiff with her hands on her hips, not emoting one iota of her thoughts through facial expressions. Grant and Reynolds, on the other hand, exchanged looks of tense excitement—their faces stiff but purposefully so, as if attempting to contain something.

After the brief exchange, Aubrey's partners returned, Grant ahead of Reynolds. When he was five feet from Aubrey, Grant's face turned into what Aubrey could only call a shit-eating grin. "Well, Marty, let's go to prison."

* * *

They made it onto one of the first trains out early that morning. The sun had just crept over the northern fingers of the Chesapeake Bay when their train began a rapid acceleration to reach its top speed of nearly five-hundred miles per hour. It would make the one-hundred-mile journey in a little over twenty minutes.

Several minutes into the ride and the g-forces finally relaxed enough to allow Aubrey to pry his head from the compressed foam of his headrest.

Whatever strings the Chief Inspector called in and whatever leverage she applied to grant them permission to visit the Keep must have been significant. Aubrey knew it was no easy feat to make the trip happen and he was grateful. He also knew the Chief Inspector didn't make it happen out of the kindness of her heart or through some sense of professional courtesy. But he didn't care. They were on their way to the Keep to chase down the only promising lead in the BSS case and that's all he cared about.

"What else do we have on Alkorn and his gang?" he asked.

"Gang?" Reynolds scoffed. "They didn't rob a train, Marty."

The three of them had a row to themselves near the rear of the first car. Aubrey took the window, Reynolds on the aisle, and Grant sat in between them. The rows were six across with a wide aisle down the middle. Aubrey estimated twenty-five to thirty rows in total. With the exception of a handful of empty seats, the rest of the car was filled with various types of prison workers on their way to start a shift—maintenance workers in coveralls, administrative clerks in civilian clothes, guards in light blue uniforms. Train attendants standing at the front and rear of the car wore crimson coats over black vests and slacks.

Passengers rode in the first car of the ten-car maglev monorail prison transport. The last nine cars were dedicated to the prison's number one import—inmates. Aubrey could only assume what was inside the windowless cars behind them. Steel benches, shackles for wrists and ankles, armed guards pacing, soon-to-be prisoners in the standard gray uniform on their way to a new world they'd likely never leave.

"Anything you want, I got it." Grant said, gesturing to the tablet on his lap. "The only thing is, these folks were clean. Squeaky clean." He tapped the screen a few times with his finger. "Alkorn was the worst of them and even he wasn't that bad. Twice divorced. No kids. And we have his performance reviews from Ventana, done by Sarazin himself."

Out the window, Aubrey watched the scenery below them change from suburban sprawl to forests of tall pine trees. Watching the green treetops whip past below the monorail, he suddenly became disoriented. The ride in the maglev train was virtually silent and incredibly smooth, giving almost no sensation of movement… until one glanced out the window.

Aubrey leaned closer to Grant's tablet for a better look and to turn away from the view out the window. Alkorn's performance reviews went back for years, but they were all the same. Most of the review would regale Alkorn's accomplishments for that year then the review would end with the same line: *Dr. Alkorn is seen as abrasive and hard driving by his team members. He is encouraged to attend sensitivity and emotional intelligence training.*

"Try explaining that to the Board," Grant said. "'Our major pharmaceutical initiatives are on hold this year because Dr. Alkorn is attending sensitivity training.'"

Aubrey leaned back. The faux leather creaked under his back. "What about his team? What do you mean by squeaky clean?"

"I mean squeaky clean," Grant said. "They all have multiple PhDs and according to testimony taken during the case, they were the most sought-after scientists in their field. Any guesses on the one reason they all gave for wanting to work at Ventana?" Grant waited, looking back and forth between Reynolds and Aubrey. When no one answered, he said, "Dr. Leo Alkorn. They may have been among the best in their field, but Alkorn was actually *the best.*"

"Makes our case even better," Reynolds said. "They look up to him, idolize his intellect, tolerate his known abrasiveness just for the chance to work with him. Tyrants have a knack for easing people into a sense of normalcy around their sociopathic, destructive behavior. I bet this is a similar situation. After a while, they have something like Stockholm Syndrome. Then, when he needs their help in this plan to steal from Ventana, they just go along with it."

Grant nodded, looking convinced. "So, why wouldn't any of them turn on him after they were arrested? Why not turn state's evidence? They were all as quiet as little mice at the trial."

"Shame can be a powerful motivator," Aubrey said. "Their careers were basically over whether they snitched on Alkorn or not. Or maybe, perhaps likely, Alkorn had something on them."

"Maybe he isn't even the ringleader," posited Grant. "Maybe it's one of the other three. We don't know for sure he crafted this thing by himself or that he originated the idea."

Minutes passed and none of them spoke. Some of the other passengers talked in quiet tones amongst themselves. A group of maintenance workers two rows in front of Aubrey whispered to one another, laughing at an unheard joke. The back of a bald man's head bounced with mirth. The guards appeared to keep to themselves for the most part, but a few chatted loudly toward the head of the train, just behind the engineer's booth. Most of the passengers sat quietly, probably contemplating the day ahead and anticipating the ride home ten or twelve hours from then.

At the front of the car, a young man with a pale face stood in a red train attendant's coat gazing with wide-eyed wonder out the windows. The other train attendant at the rear, a grizzled looking man in his sixties whose faded uniform broadcast his years on the job, chatted up the passengers like they were old friends—cracking jokes, shaking hands, slapping shoulders.

Somewhere near the halfway point of the ride between the city and the prison a hundred miles away, Aubrey saw something strange. His eyes and brain had adjusted to the rapid, silent pace of the train and in a pause of conversation he watched the trees outside zip past below them. The tall conifers stood in soldier like rows, neatly spaced, uniformed. A moment passed as he watched the endless forest wash under them like a green, bristly ocean. Something caught his eye. Ahead, many hundreds of feet in front of the train, a brown metal platform appeared from the forest. Maybe twenty feet square, it stood level with the monorail track with a set of stairs along its backside. There was nothing else around it other than trees. No buildings. No civilized structures of any kind.

"Who on earth would board the train out here?" he wondered out loud.

"What?" Grant looked up as the platform zipped by in a blur of brown and black.

"Nothing." Aubrey shook off the strangeness of the sight and said, "We only have a few minutes left. What's our plan? How're we going into this?"

Reynolds looked up from her notes. They spent the next

ten minutes discussing their plan of approach. They agreed on the planned sequence of questions and pressure points.

Aubrey opened his mouth, about to speak, but stopped short and forgot all about what he was going to say.

The train began a gentle curve to the left. The track ahead began to come into view for miles. In the near distance, a dark monolith towered above the forest and rail line. Their speed made it grow before his eyes as if he were watching a giant sequoia go from a sapling to an ancient and massive sentry of the forest.

The Regional Corrections Center grew to life in front of him. The Keep, as it was known to most everyone, was a giant, featureless cylinder forty-eight stories tall with an ash-gray exterior. Not totally featureless, Aubrey noticed, as the miles ticked away. Around the top rim, small square windows reflected the early morning sun, glinting yellow light like the diseased teeth in a hyper-extended jaw of some terrible beast ready to devour the sky.

"No wonder they call it the Keep," Grant said, stretching his neck to see over Aubrey's shoulder.

Grant was right. It looked like a medieval keep. A castle's last line of defense. Where you fended off your enemy or perished trying.

"It looks," Reynolds paused, "ominous. That's the only word I have."

"You guys are two for two," Aubrey said. Ominous was a perfect description for the monstrous building. It didn't appear inherently dangerous, but you didn't feel safe near it either. He wondered what it would feel like when they were inside it.

One more feature broke the skin of the Keep—a two-story

opening near the ground where the monorail line pierced it.

Aubrey watched the Keep quickly grow in size as the train headed toward the entrance. Soon, it loomed, casting a dark shadow over them and the train.

He barely felt the train slow as it began entering the interior depot platform. He squinted at the sudden change from the dark shadow to the bright white lights of the interior of the Keep's train platform. He registered passing a massive open room to their left, a wall, then a smaller one where they appeared to be stopping.

This fifty-foot long platform was occupied by the same types of people that rode the train with them to the Keep. Guards in uniform, maintenance workers, and people in civilian clothes milled about waiting to board. Some wore their shirts untucked, others slumped against a wall or column, or shouldered bags across slouching backs. Most of them yawned with exhaustion.

The train gave its final gentle bump and stopped completely. The doors on the left side of the car hissed open and the attendants stepped off to stand outside each set of entry doors.

Aubrey, Grant, and Reynolds were among the last passengers off the train. The crowd on the platform thinned as folks boarded to go home or left on their way to start a shift. Standing in the middle of the almost empty, square platform, Aubrey looked around wondering what to do next.

The platform was a giant box with three exits along the wall opposite the track. There were no signs or markers for where to go. Another moment passed then the three of them were alone.

"I didn't expect a welcome party," Grant said, spinning slowly in a circle with his arms spread wide, "but they really pulled out all the stops for us, didn't they?"

As if on cue, a nondescript gray door gave a thunderous *clunk* that echoed in the emptiness. They all turned toward it and watched as the thick metal door swung open. Its hinges creaked like a banshee in the still air and its bottom corner scraped with a sound that reminded Aubrey of nails on a chalkboard.

From behind the door stepped a small man in a tight gray suit that wasn't far off from a perfect match with the gray walls, gray doors, and gray floor. The man stopped halfway out from behind the door and scanned the empty platform before laying eyes on Aubrey, Grant, and Reynolds—as if it were possible to somehow miss the three lone humans who stood in its center.

The small man waved them over. They walked toward him and Aubrey could soon see the man's pinched face and tiny, pointed nose. He wore his black hair slicked back and plastered to his scalp with product. Not helping his small stature was his waif like physique.

"Detectives," the man said as they reached him. His voice sounded more like a kazoo than a natural human sound. "I am Seymour Chalmers, a senior administrator here at the RCC. I'll be escorting you to the... um... interrogation room." He smiled and raised both eyebrows. "This way please."

They followed him down a corridor, passing many hallways that branched off from the main. After several minutes, they reached an elevator flanked by two guards in pale blue uniforms.

Chalmers stopped short of the elevator and turned to face the three investigators with his hands perched in front of him. "These gentlemen will escort you up to meet with the inmates.

You have one hour. I will meet you down here when you've finished."

All three protested in unison, but Aubrey spoke the loudest. "What do you mean 'one hour?' You can't put a time limit on these things. We need as much time as we need, end of story."

"Sir, I've worked here for seventeen years." Chalmers pushed his spear-like chin up at Aubrey and spoke in his nasal, whistling voice. "And I have never seen police, or anyone else for that matter, be allowed to interrogate a prisoner. Much less interrogate four of them. Someone called in a serious favor to get you here today." He prodded the air in front of Aubrey with a ghoulish finger. "Don't look a gift-horse in the mouth."

"Why is that? Why don't you let people talk to these inmates?" Aubrey didn't know what else to say. The curiosity overwhelmed him. Why were no other cops or investigators allowed to come to the Keep? Chalmers cocked his head with a confused look.

"Do you know what we do here? If someone is suspected of a crime *after* they arrive here, having been convicted of another crime, what difference does it make? They will be selected or they won't. The Order decides that, no one else."

"Selected?" Reynolds asked.

"He means executed," Aubrey answered for Chalmers. "What if they have information about another crime? What if they can help bring another person to justice?"

"Do the work before they arrive here." Then, Chalmers shrugged. "And aren't we all brought to justice one way or another?" He shrugged again and gave Aubrey a smug grin. "Now, you better get going. They'll be waiting for you."

Chalmers spun on his heel and left back down the main

corridor.

Inside the elevator, Aubrey watched one of the guards, a young black man with a tight crew cut, push the button for level twenty-six. He turned to Aubrey and said, "Don't mind Chalmers. He doesn't get out much." The guard's name tag read Rogers.

Aubrey nodded. "Do we really only have an hour?"

"Afraid so. Strict orders to get you out of here in one hour." The guard turned to stare ahead.

A ding signaled their arrival to the twenty-sixth floor. The doors slid open and they were greeted with another gray walled corridor. The wall ahead of them had the number *26* stenciled on it in black paint.

"This way," Rogers said and led them down a wide, curving corridor that, Aubrey guessed, followed the contour of the exterior of the prison. Tube lighting hummed overhead and the air smelled like cleaning chemicals mixed with sweat.

They followed Rogers further into the corridor. When they came abreast of a perpendicular hallway, the three detectives stopped cold. At the end of the hallway, natural light poured in from some unseen source. The sunlight spilled through the lattice work of a cage at the end of the hallway.

"What's down there?" Reynolds asked.

"Great Atrium," the guard bringing up the rear said. He was a squat, swollen man with no hair. "Runs the whole prison, top to bottom. Helps with sanitation."

"It's open to the elements?" Aubrey asked.

"No," the guard replied. "Big glass skylight up top. Come on, let's go before the natives get wind of you."

The guards led them further down the corridor and stopped at a door on the right. Rogers opened the door and stepped inside. Aubrey, Reynolds, and Grant followed him. The room was about twenty feet long, ten feet wide, and slightly curved like the corridor. It was filled with small tables, chairs, book shelves, a television behind thick glass, and a rectangular plastic card table where sat four inmates in white prison uniforms. Even with their shaved heads, Aubrey recognized them all as the four Ventana scientists. Down the middle of each of their heads ran a tattoo of a black barcode.

Alkorn sat on the far left of the table, hands crossed in front of him. His chubby red face stared at Aubrey behind thick glasses. Next to Alkorn sat Natalie Shoeman, the only woman. She was pale with almond shaped eyes and thin lips. Then sat Rajesh Imanpor whose brown cheeks bore the sheen of sweaty work. On the far right end of the table sat Stanley Winthorpe, tall and thin as a rail with a pinched face contorted into what looked like a permanent scowl.

Aubrey turned to Rogers. "We need to speak to them one at a time."

"Not possible. It's like this or not at all. Those are my orders." Rogers didn't flinch.

Aubrey was on the verge of appealing to the guard lawman to lawman, when the door to the rec room opened.

Aubrey's jaw dropped.

An older man entered the room. Approaching seventy years of age, with a head of disheveled white hair and a two-day beard on his face, he wore a black cassock with shiny black buttons down its front.

The Tapper took no notice of anyone in the room. He didn't make eye contact with Aubrey or anyone else. He quietly skulked to the darkest corner of the room, sat on a plastic chair, and crossed his legs.

Aubrey turned back to Rogers. "Can we speak outside?" He gestured to Grant and Reynolds to join them.

Outside the rec room, Aubrey pointed to the closed door. "What the fuck is he doing here?"

Rogers's forehead wrinkled in apparent confusion, then he said, "Oh. Him. The Member." He threw his hands up. "They go wherever they want. Everybody knows that. Best not to pay any attention to him. I don't even notice them anymore." He rubbed his chin. "They do have an observation room he could watch from, but… who knows why they do what they do. Again, just try not to pay attention to him and you'll forget he's there."

Aubrey closed his eyes and dropped his head. He took several deep breaths.

"We have to rethink our approach," Reynolds said.

"To say the least," Grant added. "We're not going to get anything out of them now that they're together, especially with an executioner sitting in the goddamn corner."

"We have to talk to them. We can't just go home." Reynolds looked at her watch. "And we're preciously low on time."

Aubrey knew she was right. They had to try. "OK, so what's the plan?" he asked.

"Let's just start asking them questions," Reynolds said. "See who we get a reaction out of and then peck away at them until we draw blood."

When they re-entered the rec room, Aubrey tried to take Rogers's advice and ignore the Tapper sitting in the corner of the room. He found it impossible. The man was an aberration of the law. He sat there in his black outfit, black gloves, judging everything these inmates said. He delivered his version of justice when he felt like it, to whom he felt like.

His very presence made Aubrey nauseated.

Aubrey tore his eyes away from the Tapper, who didn't seem to notice or care about anyone glowering at him. Aubrey and the detectives pulled up chairs and sat opposite the table from the four scientists turned inmates.

For a moment, no one spoke. The Ventana four displayed mixed emotions. Alkorn looked bored. Imanpor and Winthorpe both appeared incensed. Shoeman was visibly upset and anxious—constantly rubbing her neck and the side of her bald head.

Reynolds leaned forward slightly and turned toward Aubrey with an expectant look. He took that as his cue to start.

Aubrey crossed his legs and tried his best to steady his breathing, pushing out all the frustrations from the last several hours, the last several days. He needed his mind sharp.

He began. "We don't have a lot of time, unfortunately. So, we'll skip the preliminaries and jump right to it. That OK with you all?"

The four prisoners sat stock still. No one spoke. A couple of them sighed.

"Tell me what you think about James Sarazin."

No words. No movement from the scientists.

"Tell me what you think about Ventana."

Nothing.

"Tell me what you think about Zentransa."

Nothing.

"Tell me what you think about the Ventana Board of Directors."

Nothing.

With the same rapid-fire cadence, Aubrey continued.

"Tell me what you think about One Front for the People."

Eyes moved at this question. All four sets now locked on Aubrey's. Imanpor twitched in his chair.

Aubrey had hit on something.

"Do you believe in their cause?"

Imanpor's eyes left Aubrey's and shot toward Alkorn.

Aubrey waited. When no one spoke, he continued. "Do you believe in what they're doing out there?"

A shadow of confusion seemed to pass over the Ventana four. More eyes ventured toward Alkorn, who continued to lock eyes with Aubrey. His face held the same complacent expression.

"I'll pretend you don't know what OFP is up to since you aren't *supposed* to get news or communications here at the Keep." Aubrey nodded to Grant, who held a tablet. Grant tapped the screen then slid it onto the table in front of the inmates. It showed a carousel of news articles about the bombings, BSS, and OFP.

Alkorn was the only one who didn't glance at the tablet. The others bent forward to watch the articles slide past in succession. Winthorpe's hands shot out for the tablet and he pulled it toward himself. He tapped the screen to stop the carousel. After a moment, he passed it to Shoeman whose face fell. She passed it to Imanpor who gave no reaction, but the twitching seemed to intensify. When the tablet reached Alkorn, he didn't reach for it or look down. He continued to glare at Aubrey with those bored eyes, like he'd rather be getting a root canal.

"Did you communicate with anyone from One Front for the People before being sent to prison?" Reynolds chimed in.

Subtle expressions that bordered on perplexity passed between the Ventana four. More eyes slid in their sockets toward Alkorn. It was as if he were a magnet and the eyes of the other three scientists were filled with iron filings.

No one responded verbally, but Aubrey noticed Alkorn's face had grown a shade darker. His eyes squinted.

Grant's turn. "Have you been communicating with OFP since your incarceration?"

"Jesus." Shoeman broke the unspoken vow of silence among the Ventana four. She stared at the table with wide eyes, then buried her face in her hands. "Jesus," she whispered.

"Dr. Shoeman, have you communicated with OFP since you were sent here?" Grant pressed her.

"Jesus." Face still in her hands, she shook it back and forth against her palms and fingers. "Jesus."

"Dr. Shoeman, is there anything you want to tell us?" Renolds asked.

Shoeman continued shaking her head behind her hands, but said nothing other than, "Jesus."

The rest of the hour passed in a similar fashion.

Aubrey, Grant, and Reynolds continued to pepper them with questions, but not one of the Ventana four responded. Winthorpe and Imanpor sat defiant and angry. Shoeman remained distraught and exasperated, hiding her face and whispering, "Jesus," every few seconds.

Alkorn just glared. For the interview's entirety, his eyes bored into Aubrey's with that same look of profound boredom and complacency.

When their hour was up, the shorter guard ordered the inmates to their feet and began escorting them out. The four scientists were halfway to the door when Aubrey's desperation reached a breaking point.

He snatched the tablet from the table and searched until

he found the picture he needed. He zoomed in tight on the face of a young girl stricken with BSS. He jumped from his seat and strode toward Alkorn, who turned toward him in surprise.

Aubrey threw an elbow into Alkorn's chest and pinned him against the rec room wall. A bookshelf between Alkorn and the wall spilled its contents, causing him to slip and almost lose his balance. The sudden violence caught Alkorn off guard and for once in that interminable hour, his face broke from the bored, blank stare and scrunched up in alarm and fear.

"Is this you?" Aubrey shouted at him, holding the photo in front of his face. He felt arms pulling at his elbows and heard voices pleading with him to stop. Aubrey ignored it all and pressed the tablet closer to Alkorn's face. The screen showed the little girl in a hospital bed—tubes and wires connected to every part of her. "Did you do this, Alkorn? Are you poisoning these kids?"

Alkorn stared at the screen. At the little girl.

Something crossed the man's face. Some emotion Aubrey couldn't pinpoint. At least, in the context of the moment it made no sense. Alkorn's face went slack. His entire body seemed to relax. He sighed heavily. His eyes fell, then he closed them for a moment. When he opened them again, the bored look had returned. His body became rigid against Aubrey's arm.

Aubrey relented and allowed himself to be pulled back. Alkorn turned to the door once more and followed the guard out.

"Dumb move, sir." Rogers stood in front of Aubrey. "Dumb move. I have to report this to your Chief Inspector. You know that, right?"

Aubrey let out a breath he didn't realize he was holding. "I guess it's a good thing I'm not actually a cop."

He glanced back into the rec room as they were leaving. He eyed the corner where the Tapper sat with his legs still crossed, bouncing his foot in the air.

The nonchalant nature with which the Tapper sat there, silently judging the world on his own terms made the already substantial knot in Aubrey's gut turn over on itself.

Aubrey opened his mouth, not sure what he was going to say but feeling like he had to say something. His blood hot in his veins. His heart thumping.

The Tapper's head turned. His eyes met Aubrey's. A cold fist gripped Aubrey's lower spine. The Tapper's eyes were not menacing, not malicious, or malevolent. They were empty. A doll's eyes. Lifeless. Was this the price you paid for ridding the world of so many souls? Your own soul escaped you whilst your physical self lived on?

"You have a question for me, detective?" The Tapper's words were soft. He could have been an old man speaking to his grandchildren. In spite of terrible eyes, the rest of him portrayed a rather gentle disposition.

All intention of speaking drained from Aubrey's mind. Yes, he had so many questions. So many.

But not today.

Aubrey turned and left the room with the others.

* * *

On the ride back to the city, the three detectives sat in silence. Aubrey was deflated. By the looks of it, so were his partners. He stared out the window at the passing forest below. His eyes lost focus; the trees became a green blur. The near imperceptible vibrations of the train hummed through his feet into his legs.

On the way out of the Keep, Corrections Officer Rogers did the three detectives a favor by not informing Chalmers about Aubrey's aggression toward Alkorn. Rogers might report it to Chalmers later or he might not report it at all. Aubrey naturally preferred the latter. When the Chief Inspector learned that the meeting was a failure, she'd be pissed. If she learned Aubrey got physical with one of the inmates, she'd go ballistic and probably fire him.

The day had been a near total loss. They gained no new information and were no closer to any real answers. Before they left the prison, they inquired with Seymour Chalmers about the scientists' communications with the outside world.

"None," Chalmers replied after searching a database via his tablet.

"What about contraband communication devices?" Aubrey had asked him.

"They certainly exist," Chalmers declared. "There's no denying that. But I cannot account for them. I can only tell you that, through official channels, the four inmates in question have not spoken to a soul outside this prison."

There were, however, glimmers of signs of clues. Only glimmers, but they were unmistakable—the looks shot toward Alkorn during the questions, Shoeman's obvious distress when BSS and OFP came up, and finally Alkorn's reaction when Aubrey confronted him with the photo of the little girl.

What was that look in Alkorn's eyes? Regret tempered by resolve? Firmness of purpose? Stubborn persistence laced with sadness? Whatever it was, it threw Aubrey. If he'd only had a few minutes alone with Alkorn, he thought, he could have gotten somewhere.

Aubrey's pocket vibrated. Startled from his reverie, he pulled it out to see a call from Technical Specialist Lee incoming.

He answered.

Breathless, she said, "Where have you been? I've been trying to get a hold of you."

"In prison," he said.

"What? Did you get arrested? What do you mean in prison? Where are you now?"

"Long story." It wasn't a long story, but Aubrey didn't feel like going into it. "I'm on a train. What's up?"

"I need you to get back here as quick as you can," she said. "I have something to show you."

"What is it?"

"I think I found something. We got a ping on the body language recognition software. A few pings actually. Just get here soon."

* * *

"OK, let's recap." Lee sat in front of three massive computer monitors atop an ancient wooden desk inside of her closet sized office. "I took all the video footage from outside the parking garage where our bombers parked after the last attack. I then created a program that took that footage and told your body language recognition software to search the entire metropolitan surveillance system for matches."

The office was dark and cramped but he managed to find the corner of a metal cabinet on which to perch himself.

Random technical equipment littered every shelf and flat surface—memory sticks, tablets, cables, plastic boxes, and objects whose purpose he could only guess at.

"And?" Aubrey asked.

"And I found a lot of matches, which we expected."

Aubrey nodded then spun his finger in the air as a sign for her to speed up, but Lee carried on, apparently insisting he understood the entire process.

"So, I told the program to find groups of people who left the garage separately and then were found to be entering and or congregating in or around the same location somewhere else." Lee's face brightened as she spoke.

"And?" Aubrey asked again.

"And it took a while. It took almost every terabyte of processing power I have, but we found a match. A group of three people, three men, who left the garage at separate times on the day of the last bombing and are now all seen entering the same building here." Lee pointed to one screen. It was a bird's-eye view of a building from a slightly forward angle. It looked to be in rough shape with many windows boarded up and graffiti covering most of its brick exterior. "Program says the matches range from sixty-five to eighty percent probability."

"Where is that building?"

Lee zoomed out and Aubrey saw that the building was located in the heart of one of the poorest neighborhoods in the city. This was significant because the parking garage the bombers used was in the heart of the financial and commercial district, which meant it charged daily rates that were likely outside the range of someone living in the neighborhood Aubrey was now looking at.

"Oh, and one more thing." Lee turned in her chair to face Aubrey. "I've been looking at footage of these guys coming in and out of this building. They never look up. Everyone else does, but not these three. They've been trained not to look up. They're dodging our facial recognition capabilities."

"How many more people from that building don't look up?"

"I'm glad you asked, because I checked." Lee tapped at her computer's keyboard and pulled up a mosaic of eight photos. All of the photos were of men hunched over with hats or hoods pulled up to block any cameras. "Eight people total. And these eight are repeat offenders for not looking up. Could be there are more in their group and they're just lazier."

"Eight people." Aubrey had a hard time believing that eight people could cause the mass carnage taking place in their city. "I need to get Aaron Lewis."

* * *

"Holy shit." Aaron Lewis stared at the large monitors. Lee had taken him through the same rundown she had given Aubrey with only slightly more embellishment. Aubrey chimed in from time to time to explain how the body recognition software worked. "So, three to eight people we think are in there. And by the looks of the building, they may be the only ones living there."

"No." Lee was scrubbing through video footage to show them that more people lived in the building. "They may be squatters but there are others in there." She pointed out several men and women entering and exiting the building's front doors.

"Do you have anything on the inside of the building? Any

scans?" Lewis leaned in close to the monitor that showed the bird's-eye view of the building.

"No. This is just standard satellite stuff," she said. "I can't dispatch a drone without the Chief Inspector's say-so. But once we tell her what we have, I'm sure she'll at least let us take a look."

"No," Lewis said. Aubrey and Lee shot each other a look. "We check this out on our own." He didn't look away from the monitor, leaning ever closer as if trying to fall into the screen and be transported to the site of that building. "I'll grab a couple of people." Lewis whipped around to Aubrey. "You grab your team. And Lee," Lewis said. Lee looked up in surprise. "Can you bring some of your toys? We need to get a look inside that building before we take it to the Chief Inspector."

"Me?" Lee pressed a hand to her chest. "I… uh… I'm not a field person. I'm just a tech. I don't go into the field. I took this job so I didn't have to go into the field. I…"

Lewis cut her off. "I need someone who can operate this equipment. That's you. No one is going inside the building. I just need a few people to judge what's going on in there and back me up when I call back and tell the Chief Inspector what's going on." Lewis looked at Aubrey. "She won't listen to just me or Aubrey. She likes you, Lee. She'll listen to you." Aubrey didn't know if this were true or not, but it had the intended effect on Technical Specialist Lee.

Lee swallowed hard. "OK. Let me get a few things together." She began rummaging around her office, pulling open drawers and placing objects in a duffel bag.

He turned to Aubrey. "Get your team and meet me outside in ten minutes." Lewis started walking away.

"Aaron," Aubrey said in a loud whisper. "Lewis," he said again, lunging out of Lee's door and grabbing Lewis's arm. "This is reckless, buddy. We can't just go down there by ourselves. We need to at least tell *her* first."

"No." Lewis shook his head; his eyes darting around the command center looking for someone. "She won't listen to us. She already told me what would happen if I went back to her with any more bullshit. We have to check this out ourselves first."

Lewis started to pull away and Aubrey tightened his grip. "If anything happens, you'll lose your badge. You know that, right?" Aubrey recalled how he felt the day he handed in his badge. Along with the immense shame and remorse, total despair had consumed every cell in his body. The feeling of complete uselessness and failure was something he did not wish on anyone he cared about.

"Nothing is going to happen," Lewis said. "We're not going inside. We're just going to take a look."

20

The Volunteer

Anatoli Rubinski's latest volunteer sat droopy eyed on the sofa. If he didn't know better, the Chechen would have assumed she was an overworked mid-level manager at some thankless job in the commercial district. He did know better though. He knew she was under the magical spell of his homemade *voodoo*.

The Chechen sat on a dusty recliner in a dusty living room staring with pride at his volunteer. He had no idea who she was or what her life was like. All he knew about her was that she was in the right place when they needed someone and an easy target walking alone in the dark.

He was supposed to use members of the hapless One Front for the People, but the Chechen grew tired of tracking them down after the second volunteer. The first two were easy enough, but how to convince more actual volunteers when they knew what was coming. He didn't bother trying to convince anyone anymore. He'd use whoever was at hand; had done so for the last nine volunteers and no one was the wiser. The police were still chasing OFP all over the city.

Other than where he found his volunteers, he'd done everything according to plan. He had made his calls to the police. He had written and recorded the messages for the media. He and his men had remained unseen by the police. Even with the drooling mishap and the subsequent remote detonation, he still felt confident the police had no idea what was going on.

He wondered what the cops were getting from those people. Would one of them take credit for being part of it all? That would take some of the heat off his team. If some half-wit wannabe terrorist claimed to take credit for it all for a moment of glory… he caught himself. There is no heat, he thought. No one knew where they were or who they were. Moreover, no one knew Anatoli Rubinski was in the country… or alive. The world thought he was dead, which was the way he had wanted it to be.

How many more attacks would there be before the job was done?

Much like he did on all of his jobs, he grew bored; it was beginning to lose the luster of a challenge. He was anxious to move onto the next thing, whatever that was. Retirement was not out of the question; he had retired once before. Prison may not be most people's idea of retirement, but to him it wasn't so bad. Three hot meals a day, a private room, and a reputation that made it so he got whatever he wanted, whenever he wanted. The bars and walls kept his enemies outside and the enemies inside with him were kept under control by the guards on his payroll.

Ultimately, however, he grew bored there too. That was years ago, and he wouldn't mind going back to prison, just not in America. He'd have to go overseas to some backwater country where people were more susceptible to corruption.

"Boss," said a man from the hall behind him in a thick, eastern European accent. "Ze west is ready. Should ve geet her suited op?"

"Yes." The Chechen stood. To the volunteer he said, "Stand up." The volunteer stood. "Follow me." The volunteer fell into step behind them as the two men walked toward a bedroom down the main hallway of the apartment.

A crash through the front door piqued every nerve in the Chechen's body. He spun toward the sound whilst dashing to find cover. He saw Lev getting to his feet in the door's threshold. The man panted and his feet slipped on the hard floor; he made several attempts to right himself, finally holding himself upright on the kitchen counter.

The Chechen took two quick strides toward Lev and, with iron hands, steadied him. Lev's eyes bulged. He continued to pant.

"What the hell is going on?" The Chechen had the man by the shoulders, holding him inches from his own nose. "What has happened?"

"Zey are coming," Lev said in a desperate whisper. "Zey have found us. Comink here. Now. Right now."

21

The Second Raid

Forty-five minutes after leaving the station, the six police officers and Martin Aubrey arrived in separate cars to a location several blocks from the building Lee showed them. Police vans required special permission to use; this left them with one option for transportation: personal vehicles. Aubrey, Lee, Grant, and Reynolds traveled in one vehicle while Lewis, Winger, and another officer who was introduced to Aubrey as Detective Tony Baxter rode in the other. Baxter was a freshly minted detective, having served as a beat cop for years before his promotion eight months ago, and had been added to the Task Force earlier that week.

On the way, Aubrey and Lewis had decided not to exit the vehicles. Congregating on the street would attract attention and they were only there to observe, log their findings, and head back to the station to share their report. Communicating through the cars' comm links, Lewis's voice could be heard on the speakers.

"Lee, deploy your drones. Stream the feed to both vehicles."

Lee fished around in her duffel bag for a moment, then

pulled out four softball-sized spheres. She held one in her hand and began peeling back sections, opening up the ball until it resembled some type of large, round beetle. She gingerly held it out the window and tapped a command on the tablet resting in her lap. A small propeller in the drone came to life, sending the bot into the air several feet where it stayed while she activated and deployed the other three. She tapped a few more commands on her tablet to create a live feed to the cars' console monitors and her tablet. Each screen was divided into quarters. The top row showed the street outside and the surrounding buildings. The bottom row was covered in gray tones with harsh lines and random blotches of red, orange, and white. Aubrey recognized these to be three-dimensional renderings of the structures next to them and the bio-signatures of the people within.

"OK. Top row is live video, bottom row is basically a building X-ray with biologics and thermal readout overlays."

"Why are we only seeing two feeds here? I thought you had four drones," Reynolds asked. From the sounds coming from the other car, they were wondering the same thing.

"Screens are too small in these cars. If I had all of them on there you wouldn't be able to see anything, but I can toggle back and forth pretty quickly."

"Got it." Lewis's voice boomed over the speakers. "OK Lee, let's get a look at the target building and make sure you're recording everything."

"Alright, alright. Jesus, here we go." Lee took a deep breath and began manipulating the tablet. Aubrey heard the four tiny drones whir away over the car. On the car's monitor he watched the scene change as the bots raced along ten feet above the ground, across the street, then up and over the buildings next to them. Had he been a bystander, Aubrey thought the scene could have been mistaken for some kids drone racing and not seven people trying to foil a terrorist attack.

"Are you manually piloting these guys?" Aubrey asked.

"No." Lee was watching the screen like everyone else. She had stopped manipulating her bots by hand. "I just tell them where to go. AI does the rest."

The drones flew at dizzying speeds buzzing over building ledges, down facades, around water towers. Glancing in his rear-view mirror, Aubrey saw Grant turning a shade of yellowish green. Aubrey too began to feel a little queasy just as the drones suddenly stopped.

The target building was not very large and quite old. Seeing it up close and in high-definition, it looked like it had been built prior to the turn of the century and went into a state of neglect not long after. Almost every window had been boarded up, graffiti covered every reachable surface, litter was everywhere, almost pouring out of the structure like pus from a wound. It stood in stark contrast to the adjacent buildings. They were not luxury apartments by any stretch of the imagination, but being about the same age and size, they appeared to have been kept in good shape over the years. The facades were clean, no busted windows, and one even had a roof top garden which was occupied by a small family at that moment. Their target building stood out like a dead tooth in an otherwise healthy, bright white mouthful of teeth.

"The tiny scanners on the drones will only penetrate so deep so I have to split them up," Lee said from the back seat.

As commanded, the four drones split up with two stationed in front of the building and two behind. They all stared at the images on the bottom row of the screen. They were looking for signs of life, red body temperature signatures signifying human presence somewhere in the building.

"OK. Let's see what our two little guys out front show us." Lee was manipulating the controls on her tablet. On the screen, the others could see the view tighten to show two floors at a time. She worked the drones' scanners from the bottom of the building to the top. Aubrey saw nothing. The live video feeds showed the exterior of the building. Up close it was just as derelict and disused as it was from afar.

The interior 3D scans showed an empty skeleton. Cold brick, steel, and plaster left to fend for itself against the slow natural decay of time. The building looked deserted. Tiny bright white specks appeared here and there, but Lee explained that they were anything from loose wires to hot water pipes. Glancing at the structures to the left and right of their building showed bright red blobs everywhere. This neighborhood was densely occupied, except for their building.

"Anybody seeing anything?" Lewis asked.

"No. Nothing here," Aubrey replied. "Wait. What's that on the fifth floor, bottom right corner?" Aubrey was pointing to a cluster of several small red circles running parallel to the exterior.

"Just rats or mice. They're clustered together so the scanners pick them up. I have the sensitivity dialed down so it doesn't catch every living organism in there. The ones you're seeing are so close together that the readout thinks it's something larger. OK. Let's see what our guys around back can see." Lee tapped her tablet and the view on the car's console changed to one showing the rear of the building. Lee began the same slow scan on the rear of the building. Aubrey watched as she zoomed in, moved upward.

"Stop." Aubrey bent close to the screen and pointed with a shaking finger. "There... I think I saw something. What is that, the fourth or fifth floor." Everyone craned to see the small monitor in the car's console better. The body signatures would have been hard to miss. On a grayish rectangle sat three bright red shapes, unmistakable for anything other than human bodies.

"We see it too. Fifth floor," said Lewis's voice again. "Lee, what are we looking at?"

"By the looks of it, three people sitting on a couch. And it looks like they're leaning against each other. Bio readouts show heart rates are low, breathing is slow. I think... I think they're sleeping."

"Scan the rest of the building."

Lee completed her scan. "Nothing else in there."

"Perfect." Lewis opened his car door and stepped out. Aubrey did the same, striding to face Lewis.

"I thought we weren't going inside?"

"Three people sleeping isn't enough to convince the chief inspector to launch a raid." Lewis walked around Aubrey and opened the trunk. Inside were protective vests and tactical rifles. Lewis, Winger, and Baxter began suiting up. Aubrey was reaching for the fourth vest when Lewis grabbed his arm. "There isn't anyone I'd rather have with me, but you can't come. The thing that makes this legal is my badge. You go up there and you'll end up in jail. I can't have that on my conscience." Lewis let go of Aubrey's arm. "Besides, it's just three guys sleeping on a couch."

Aubrey nodded and watched the three officers jog across

the street and around the corner.

"They're going in?" Grant asked as Aubrey returned to his car. "I thought we weren't going in."

Aubrey knew better than to believe Lewis never intended to go inside. "We were never going to stay put. You think he brought six people with him to be witnesses?" Reynolds's look told him she had caught on too.

"Lee, can you move in on that floor? Show me multiple angles." Aubrey had turned his attention back to the car's monitor. The scenes changed as the drones moved down to be eye level with the fifth floor. The red shapes were framed in both windows on the monitor.

A few minutes passed as they stared at the unmoving red blobs on the translucent gray couch.

"I'm patching his ear-piece comm unit through to the vehicle." Lee was busy tapping commands on her tablet. Then, Lewis's voice came through on the car's speakers again.

"Everyone hear me OK?" Lewis asked, panting. "We're entering the building."

"Lima charlie," Aubrey replied, unable to avoid the military phonetic code for loud and clear.

"Where are we going, Lee?"

"Rear of the building. Looks like last apartment on your left." Lee was panning the angles of the drones' cameras and scanners to ensure her directions were correct.

"Movement?"

"None." Aubrey replied this time. The tension in his voice made his throat growl as he spoke.

Down the shadowy hallway of the fifth floor, the occupants of the car could see three more red shapes coming to life.

"On the fifth. Moving to last apartment."

"Roger that. We can see you coming. Still no movement from the three on the couch," Aubrey said.

"OK. Going in." Lewis's voice came through as a whisper.

On screen, Aubrey and the others in the car saw the grayish outline of the apartment door fly open as one of the officers gave it a powerful kick. Simultaneously over the comm link came their cries.

"POLICE. POLICE." They repeated the warning as they moved into the front room of the apartment, then they stopped.

On screen, the four watched the three red bodies of the officers stand and stare at the suspects. Two of the officers then began moving through the apartment.

"Jesus," Lewis's voice came across frustrated. "These are definitely not our guys. They're just junkies passed out on each other. We're searching the rest of the place, but I don't think there's anything here."

Those in the car let out a collective breath.

"Lee, are you sure there is nothing else in this building?" Lewis asked.

"Checking again, but I didn't see anything else." Lee repeated the scans of both the front and back sides of the building. "No, nothing."

"You're sure it's the right building?" Aubrey asked.

"Yes. Positive." Aubrey could see Lee begin checking the maps on her tablet. "Yes, this is the building. I don't get it. I checked all the surveillance footage on the way here. They have to be in there somewhere."

"Hey," Grant said. "You said those things can't penetrate very deep into the building, right?"

"Yeah, but…"

"Can they see underground?"

"No, they can't see through solid earth very far, only a few feet."

"He's right." Aubrey turned in his seat. "Under ground."

"Under what?"

"Basement." Reynolds followed their lead.

"Lewis, they could be in the basement. But you can't search the entire basement on your own. Let us come meet you." Aubrey opened his car door and began to step out.

"Just Grant and Reynolds," Lewis said before Aubrey's feet touched the ground. "You and Lee hang back."

Reynolds gave him a sympathetic look, then with a nod she and Grant grabbed their gear and left the car.

"And Lee, send a drone inside to go ahead of us. Make sure we aren't about to step into a hornet's nest." Lewis sounded tense, ready for action.

Lee sent a drone in through an open window. Seconds later, Aubrey and Lee watched the live images of Lewis, Winger, and Baxter come to life in a dark hallway, the only available light from small windows at each end of the long hall. The air was full of dust kicked up by these new arrivals. Moments later, Reynolds and Grant joined them.

"We found the stairwell. Let's head down."

Lee piloted the drone down into a pitch-black stairwell, scanning the entire way. One of the officers switched on a flashlight.

"Nothing so far." Lee searched her small screen. "There are two levels down here, I think." She moved the hovering robot into the first level, floating from room to room in concentric circles from the centralized staircase. "Nothing. I don't see anything on this level." The live feed was pitch black, but the scanner feed showed the same gray-ish outline of the walls with random white spots scattered around.

"Roger that. Move on to the lowest level and we'll do a quick manual search." Lewis was breathing heavily over the comm link.

"OK, but there is no way an eight-man bomb making team could hide from these scanners." Lee looked at Aubrey, her forehead creased. He looked back with equal disbelief.

Lee continued to the lowest level of the basement and made the same scanning pattern with the drone.

"Nothing on the lowest level. Damn it." Lee slammed a fist on the seat of the car. "I don't get it. This has to be the place."

"Alright. We'll just manually search the whole building. Maybe your scanners are on the fritz." Lewis sounded resigned.

"No way that's true but go ahead."

Aubrey sighed and turned back to face the front of the car. How could we have missed them, he wondered. He began considering all the possibilities of a terrorist cell picking up shop and moving all of a sudden when he glanced at his car's monitor. The screen had not changed like Lee's tablet. It was still on the rear shot of the building. He stared at it, willing it to show him something. He saw nothing but the gray, three-dimensional shell of the building and its interior with occasional white specks.

Everywhere, he saw the white specks. Everywhere except the seventh floor. Every floor had the random white hot-spots, except the seventh floor. He looked closer. Part of the seventh floor appeared entirely uniform, just one large gray rectangle across the screen.

He also realized that the interior walls that he thought were part of the seventh floor were from the eighth and sixth floors. The drone's 3D rendering with its X-ray scan caused a great deal of overlap when viewed at an angle. It was difficult to distinguish one floor from another.

"Lee?" Aubrey leaned even closer to the car's screen.

"They're moving up to the second floor now. They just swept the first. I'm telling you they're not going to find anything. Nothing gets past these scanners." Lee continued shaking her head in exasperation.

"Lee?" Aubrey reached behind him and grabbed Lee's wrist to get her attention. "Look at the seventh floor." He pointed at his screen.

"What? There's nothing there. The building is empty. I fucked up, OK? I don't know how, but I did. We can't be at the wrong building, but somehow no one is..."

"Look at it again. I don't think you fucked up."

Lee leaned over the front seat to look at the car's larger screen. "What? I don't see anything."

"Exactly. Turn up the body signature sensitivity on the exterior drones."

"The what..."

"Just do it, please."

She sat back in her seat and after a few taps, red spots began to appear on the screen. The spots grew in number as she dialed up the sensitivity.

"See, I told you if you bring it up too high you'll see every damn critter in there. They're everywhere in a building like that."

"Not everywhere."

On the screen, the entire building was lit up like a Christmas tree. Red dots appeared all over the building, in some cases making it difficult to discern one dot from the next. The red dots scampered and wriggled, on every wall, on every floor. Everywhere except a large portion of the seventh floor; that section of the building was still a blank gray rectangle standing alone in a sea of red specks.

"Oh shit," Lee screamed. "They must have it screened with some kind of sensor blocking material. Holy shit, that has to be them."

"What?" Lewis demanded. "What has to be them? Talk to me."

"Seventh floor, Aaron. The entire back half of the seventh floor is totally blank on the scanners. They must have it screened from the inside, blocking the scanners. That has to be them."

"We're on our way." The digitized forms of Lewis and the other four cops began zig-zagging up the column of stairs as they made their way to the seventh floor. Panting and short of breath, Lewis said, "OK, we're at the door onto the seventh floor. Lee, send up the drone to scan ahead of us."

"Roger that." Lee bent over her tablet, tapped and swiped spots on the screen to maneuver the drone into position. Aubrey watched from the drone's point of view as it spiraled up the stairs over the heads of the others and stopped dead at the door next to Detective Lewis. Aubrey caught a glimpse of all the officers gathered in the stairwell. Faces were tense and steadfast; white-knuckled hands gripped pistols and rifles.

The door opened a crack as Lewis pushed it slowly and quietly. The drone crept through the opening and into the hallway. It spun in mid-air from left to right. Aubrey watched the hallway go by. A window at the left end of the hall let in some light showing him several doors, some off their hinges, peeling floors, and graffiti on every surface. He could almost smell the place through the drone—the dampness, the dust, the stagnant air.

The drone spun to allow Lee to scan the entire floor. As it neared its spin, Aubrey and Lee caught site of the opposite end of the hallway. The window on this end had been boarded up, there was no light to show them what they were seeing, but the shape of the man was obvious enough even in the dark. Tall and thin, he was holding some type of duffel bag in one hand. Even in the dark they knew he saw them. He stared at the drone. The drone, Lee, and Aubrey stared back.

"Shit." Aubrey attempted to maintain a calmness in his voice as if the man in the seventh-floor hallway could hear him through the drone. "Lewis?"

"Yeah," Lewis replied in a harsh whisper.

"There's someone in the hallway. Tall guy. Holding a bag... Shit. He's bolting." The man on the screen dropped his bag, turned and bolted. "He's going back inside the apartment."

"On me, let's go." Lewis flung open the door to the hallway. Aubrey watched as the neat, orderly line of officers followed him, weapons at the ready, each sweeping the hallway left to right out of pure instinct. They watched Lewis and the others stack up on either side of the apartment door, now shut again. Lewis gave silent hand-gestured instructions to each of them, commanding them where to go upon entry. Baxter moved to kick the door from its frame when Aubrey yelled, "Wait."

"What? They know we're here. We have to move." Lewis was still using the half-whisper, half-shout.

"You have air cover, let us use it." Aubrey turned back to Lee. "Put one of your drones through that window." He was pointing at the screen to a window on the seventh floor.

It was in the far corner of the building, but still within the grayed-out area.

"It's boarded up." Lee looked up in confusion.

"Here." Aubrey pointed to a small jagged section in the corner of the window that had gone missing. "It's rotted away or something."

She piloted the drone toward the hole. It buzzed in the air two feet from the window as Lee positioned just so.

"Aubrey?" Lewis hailed him in a sharp whisper.

"One second and we can give you a good sit rep." The tiny drone moved forward. The hole in the boarded window was a tight squeeze but they now saw the interior space clearly on their screen as the little flyer began to hover around inside the room. It was empty. Scanning the room, they could see a dirty mattress, some magazines, and an ashtray full of butts. Now inside the screens, the sensors showed unadulterated signs of life in the apartment. Scanning right to left, the body signature scanner began to pick up bio-signatures in adjacent rooms.

"OK, Lewis. We're inside now, in an empty room." Aubrey was in the backseat now, nudging Lee this way and that to move the drone for a better look. "Looks like there are at least six suspects inside, maybe eight. Hard to tell. Some of them are clustered together." He nudged Lee again and pointed his finger to tell her to rotate the camera to the right, then back to the left. "They're in the far back rooms, down a hallway. Looks like the front room is empty. Might be a kitchen up there. They're in two groups in rooms opposite each other in the hallway."

"Weapons?"

"No idea. Can't tell with these sensors." Aubrey pointed in

the direction of the room's exit. "Lee, let's go into the hallway and take a peek."

"OK, we're going to breach," Lewis said in a hurried whisper. Lee stopped the drone before it reached the hallway. "Baxter, get up here."

"Wait," said Aubrey. "Let us check it out first. You have no idea what you're dealing with up there."

Either Lewis didn't hear Aubrey or ignored him outright. On the second drone, still in the main hallway with the group, they saw Lewis give Baxter a nod. With a powerful forward kick, the door burst from its frame.

"POLICE. POLICE. Come out now with hands up." The shouts blasted over the car's speakers. Aubrey and Lee were still watching the feed from the drone in the main hallway. She moved it further into the apartment and they saw the crew of cops spread out in the front room and kitchen taking cover behind furniture, counters, and behind walls. Not one of the suspects revealed themselves. For a moment, the cops crouched and panted. "We know you're in here. Come out now."

Aubrey pulled the tablet from Lee's grip. She didn't protest. He toggled back to the feed from the drone still in the backroom of the apartment. He tapped and dragged to controls to move the robot. Under the control of unpracticed hands, the drone jolted each time Aubrey touched the controls. It bucked like a feral beast released from a cage. The view on the screen bounced back and forth in a blur. Finally, he lifted his hands away and the view was steady. The drone was just outside the room, staring straight ahead at a blank wall. He carefully rotated to the left. Slowly, the wall ahead moved away and another scene materialized before him. He was now looking straight down the middle of the hallway toward the front room by the main entrance. He could see the heads of his compatriots poking out from behind their respective hiding spots.

Ahead of the drone, to the left and right were two open doors. The angle wasn't quite right to get a good view, so Aubrey moved the drone ahead, taking great care not to make sudden movements. He decided to check the room on the left first. As the drone came abreast of the door, he rotated to the left.

He couldn't believe what he was seeing. A squat, dark-haired man in a dark blue track suit stood holding a large caliber pistol. Aubrey wasn't looking at the man in tracksuit, though. He was looking behind the man and what he saw made his breath catch short in his chest. It sent cold waves of panic down his back and legs. There was a woman there; she stood in the middle of the room with a faraway look in her eyes. She was wearing a vest. Wires in the vest wound their way around thick, rectangular blocks. Two men flanked the woman, adjusting the wires in the vest and attaching more small devices.

The squat man now had his gun pointed at the heart of the drone. He cocked his head to the right and with his free hand, he waved at the tiny camera. He pulled the trigger on his gun and the screen went black.

* * *

Martin Aubrey threw the car door open with such force that the hinges groaned in protest as they strained backward. In a few long, determined strides he was at the trunk of Lewis's car. He threw it open, dug out the extra protective vest and donned it. From an interior hard, black case he withdrew a short assault rifle and every magazine of ammunition he could carry. After performing a quick function check on the rifle, he turned, about to take off toward the mayhem now ensuing when he caught site of something else in the trunk. It was a blue and yellow crumpled mass. He recognized the jacket at once and without hesitation threw it on over his vest.

Stunned, Lee watched Aubrey run across the street away from the car. He was running flat out toward the sound of torrential gunfire in the near distance. His rifle was slung and made ready; his jacket was stretched tight over the ammunition pouches and bullet proof vest. Tall yellow letters stenciled across his back read POLICE.

* * *

Lewis and the rest of the team crouched silently for a moment. They waited. They breathed. Every eye focused on Lee's tiny drone making its way toward them. They watched as a hand broke the threshold of a bedroom door. The hand held a large silver and black pistol. Before any of the officers in the apartment could utter a word, the pistol fired. The large caliber bullet shredded the tiny plastic robot like a pillow caught in a boat motor.

Every weapon in the front room of the apartment erupted in unison. Around the doorway, no longer occupied by the hand or the gun, craters materialized as plaster, paint, and wood separated from the wall in dusty chunks. The fire was well ordered chaos, each officer firing a handful of rounds, then as if it had been planned, the guns ceased fire.

Silence, smoke, and dust filled the air. The collective breath of the officers held in their lungs, waiting.

"Lee," Lewis called. He was panting. "Suspect opened fire. We returned fire. Call it in. Tell them we need back up. Get some heavy guns down here. We'll hold it down here until they arrive."

"Lewis," Lee said in near panic, "Aubrey is on his way. Before they shot the drone, we saw something… they've got…"

"What? They've got what?"

"A bomber… they've got a vest on her. I don't… I don't know what they plan on doing, but… but they were wiring her up. There's people in the next building… families."

Every eye in the front room of the apartment was on Lewis. The understanding passed between them without any one of them uttering a word.

"Roger that." Lewis pressed the magazine release on his rifle and inserted a fresh one. The half full magazine hit the ground with a thud. "That simplifies things a little bit. We can't let them detonate."

With hand signals he directed his team to their places. Baxter and Winger planted their backs against the walls around the entrance into the hallway, rifles poised to swing inward. Grant and Reynolds were moved to be in a better position to cover the doors of the occupied rooms.

"Stay low, you two," Lewis whispered into his mic, pointing at Baxter and Winger. "You two," he said, pointing at Reynolds and Grant, "aim high at the doors if anyone shows themselves. Remember, aim high." Lewis squeezed the pistol grip on his rifle and took a deep breath. Everyone was waiting for his signal.

The rooms occupied by their targets were directly across

the hall from each other, making assaulting and clearing each in turn impossible. They'd have to hit them at the same time and he'd back up whoever needed it the most. The butcher's bill would be high, he knew, but how much higher would it be if they did nothing?

Lewis raised his left hand. All eyes were on him. Baxter and Winger steeled themselves for the go order. Reynolds and Grant took careful aim at their respective doors. Lewis exhaled. His hand began cutting the air in a downward motion, but before the hand reached its termination point, a body tumbled out of the room on the right.

Gunfire blasted all around them in every direction. The body was that of a woman holding two large caliber pistols, one in each hand. She stood in the middle of the hallway and fired in a slow, steady rhythm, wildly sometimes into the floor or ceiling, but sometimes directly at them. Her arms seemed to have a mind of their own while her face was blank. Lewis couldn't see any emotion whatsoever in her expression or any thoughts behind her eyes. She just blasted and blasted away at them. When one weapon emptied, she dropped it and clumsily pulled another out of her belt.

Ducking behind a cabinet, Lewis looked around and saw Grant on his back. He had his hand pressed to his belly, just below the navel. Dark red blood soaked his shirt and pants.

"Fuck. Reynolds, get him out of here." With no response from Reynolds, Lewis looked around and saw her crouching behind the kitchen counter. She was holding her shoulder. Blood poured down her shirt sleeve. "Reynolds. Can you get him out of here? Reynolds." She looked up, her face pale and her arm immobilized, but she nodded. "Wait until she reloads." Reynolds nodded again. "Baxter, Winger, when she reloads take her down."

"She's drugged, Aaron. Just like the last bomber." Winger shouted over the gunfire. "We can't just kill her."

"Legs then," Lewis shouted back without looking over his cover.

At last, both pistols clicked empty. The woman fumbled for her next weapon. Baxter and Winger swung their rifles around and took well placed shots in the woman's lower legs. She began teetering on the spot but did not fall to the floor; her expression was unchanged.

"Go." Lewis pointed at Reynolds who grimaced as she reached for Grant, gripping him in the armpit with her working arm. Still in a semi-sitting position she shimmied him to the front door, one painful push with her legs at a time.

The shooter was still standing, but her shots went into the floor now. One leg buckled, forcing her to lean against the wall with her pistols pointing downward. Lewis was about to issue new orders when several things happened at once.

The front door flew open and, half expecting a new combatant joining the fight, Lewis swung his weapon toward the intruder. What he saw was a stone-faced Martin Aubrey, weapon in hand, ready for a firefight.

Seeing Reynolds and Grant, Aubrey bent low to help as shots exploded from the hallway. Lewis turned to see the woman falling forward; her chest blossomed into a red mist. She was no longer firing. The firing was coming from behind her. As she fell with a thump, Lewis saw them. Four men, stacked two low and two high, firing over the body of the woman they just eviscerated. Their fire was more rapid, more sustained, and much more deadly than the woman's.

Lewis felt something dull hit his side, below the ribs. It

felt like being hit with a ball-peen hammer. The sensation traveled through his side into his abdomen. Looking down he saw a gaping hole in the wooden cabinet, and a bloody stain in the bottom fringe of his protective vest.

* * *

Aubrey ran hard. He took the front stairs of the building two at a time. With lungs panting in the dark hallway on the main floor, he found the stairwell. He pounded the stairs like he had a vendetta against each one, his steps echoing in the tight space. Winding his way further and further up, willing his body to move faster and faster, he found the door marked "7".

In the main hallway on the seventh floor, he followed the sound of the strangely slow gunfire to the apartment door. He threw it open and the scene unfolded before Aubrey. Lewis was ducked low behind a small cabinet. Baxter and Winger were in kneeling positions, poised at the mouth of the hallway. Almost at his feet, Reynolds was dragging Grant's body with one hand toward the door where Aubrey stood. He reached down to help Reynolds. As he did, the hallway released a torrent of lead and smoke; it spewed rounds into the front room of the apartment like a dragon breathing fire on a lowly knight.

In quick time, Aubrey managed to get Reynolds and Grant to the relative safety of the hallway. Dashing back inside he found the situation unraveling. Lewis was still crouched in the lee of the cabinet, which was being turned into matchsticks. Baxter and Winger were returning fire but doing so blindly. Based on the rate of fire and sounds coming from the hallway, Aubrey assumed they must have killed or wounded at least one of the enemy combatants. Four long strides brought him to Baxter's side at the mouth of the hallway. Baxter looked up and gave him a nod.

"You go high, I'll go low." Aubrey pushed the butt stock of the rifle into his shoulder and made sure the safety was set to SEMI.

Aubrey nodded, and as one they swung their rifles around to breach the hallway, firing at whatever moved. Three men were there, shooting back. One of them staggered back in the quick exchange. Three quick heartbeats and he and Baxter were back against the wall. Chunks of the corner were blasted away as they did so. Aubrey replayed the scene he just saw in the hallway: the original bomber with her vest now removed lay face down in a puddle of red pulp, one man lay next to her on his back, another was propped against the wall.

"At least two down," Aubrey shouted. "The other two are covering for the others retreating into the rear of the apartment."

"Fire escape?" Winger asked.

"Probably. Can't let them get there. All together." Aubrey began his quick turn.

Baxter was faster, though; his head and rifle moved beyond the protective cover of the wall. As he did, before Baxter had a chance to squeeze his trigger, his head jerked back. A fountain of red shot from the rear of his skull and he slowly fell, his blank eyes staring at the ceiling.

Aubrey paused for the shortest of moments to register that this man was dead. This man who he barely knew. The shooter, recognizing that his shot had landed, shifted fire toward Winger. This gave Aubrey his chance. He stepped over Baxter's corpse to stand fully in the hallway's opening and fired two shots. Both met their mark—center mass of the two shooters. The hallway went quiet.

With his weapon trained down the hallway; Aubrey assessed the situation. Baxter was dead. Lewis, Reynolds, and Grant were wounded. He and Winger were good to go. On the floor in front of him lay five bodies: four gunmen and the drugged bomber. No one was moving. Lee reported there was likely eight men holed up here. Not including the bomber, that left at least four more combatants somewhere.

Without looking back, Aubrey took a step forward. "Winger? You coming?" Before he could finish the last syllable, Winger was by his side. Shoulder to shoulder they moved ahead as one unit.

Stepping over the carnage at their feet, they made their way. They came to the two rooms originally occupied by their assailants. Aubrey on the left spun into the room nearest him. Empty. Wasting no time, he bounced back to the hall. Winger had done the same with the room on the right. A nod and they continued. A movement at his feet and with lightning quickness, Aubrey fired into it. The movement stopped. A new stain adorned the wall.

This end of the hallway was clear of bodies. They approached a T intersection where their hallway met two more. A figure darted into view, both men fired, and he tumbled out of sight into the hallway on the left. A quick peek around the corner and Aubrey confirmed he was down for good.

Winger motioned to the hallway on the right. Aubrey nodded and turned into the one on the left. Ahead of Aubrey were two rooms, both to his right. He reached the nearest one and leaned close to listen. He heard nothing. The door was already open a crack. A breath and he was inside, arcing his rifle around the room. It was an empty bathroom.

Back in the hallway, he moved to the last doorway in this hall. The door was closed. Leaning in close again, he heard something—thuds, then metal on metal. No time, he thought. He steadied himself in front of the door, lifted his right leg, and hurled it forward.

The flimsy door flew in as if it were hit by a truck. In a flash, Aubrey's weapon was up, he stopped. A man stood at the end of a bed, unarmed. They stared at one another. A pistol lay nearby on top of a dresser, within arm's reach. Aubrey shook his head at the man who didn't move. Aubrey pointed at the ground, pointed at the man, then the ground again. The man's arm moved. Aubrey was expecting it; he pulled his trigger two times and the man crumpled sideways to the floor.

On the bed were metal boxes of ammunition, large duffel bags full of electronics equipment, pill bottles in small bags, and medical equipment—IV tubes, syringes, and small glass bottles full of white liquid. Three shots from Winger's direction and Aubrey was back in the hallway moving toward the commotion.

The hallway was dark, but he could see that one room occupied that end; the last room in the apartment. A scuffling sound, someone cursing, and Aubrey was running.

Five steps from the last room and two bodies burst from it. A tall blond man in cut-off jeans had his hands around Winger's rifle, using it like a bulldozer to throw Winger into the wall opposite the doorway. They both maintained a powerful grip, Winger holding his own as they wrestled side to side with the weapon in a desperate game of tug-of-war. Winger kicked low. The blond man headbutted, catching Winger's orbital socket.

Aubrey took careful aim as the barrel of Winger's rifle came down, pointed in his direction. A flash from the barrel and a punch in Aubrey's thigh. The shot took out his leg, forcing him to kneel. Winger and the blond man fell toward him. Winger landed on his back and let out a shocked groan. The blond man lifted his head, Aubrey fired and it fell forward.

Rolling the body off of Winger, he could see the cause of his friend's pain. As the two of them hit the floor, the blond man had plunged a knife into Winger's side. The dead man's hand still gripped the hilt.

Winger moaned and squirmed. He wanted to say something, but Aubrey could tell the knife made it difficult.

"How many left?" Aubrey thought he knew what Winger wanted to say. His friend held up one finger and pointed toward the door. Aubrey nodded and got to his feet.

His right leg was shaky, the bullet lodged deep within it. Two breaths and he made for the room. Entering the room, he stopped cold. White, rectangular blocks lay in the middle of the floor in a pile as high as his waist and just as wide. Wires ran from several parts of the heap to a small plastic box on the floor.

He estimated there was enough polysemtex-D there to take down this entire building and the next one over. Maybe more.

Movement to his right. There was another door inside the room he had somehow missed. He fired, his bullets going astray into the far wall. A man dove from the other door to the floor behind the mound of explosives. Aubrey stopped firing. He knew the likelihood of setting off an explosion with a bullet was low, but there was enough polysemtex-D there to give him pause.

An arm raised from behind the pile. The thick, meaty hand

held a small green box. It was a transmitter with four raised buttons. "Drop it or I detonate." The voice was accented but clear. The arm was muscular with dark, wiry hair. "Looks like vee are in showdown, no? Like von of your cowboy movies? Only… my boom-stick is much, much bigger, you see."

Aubrey recognized the switch. He knew it required a code, a code that would be at least four digits. This, he knew, gave him time if he missed his shot. He aimed carefully, ready to blow the man's wrist apart.

"You put down your veapon. I valk avay, everyone lives. Or… or ve all die. Your choice, cowboy." Aubrey applied slow pressure to the trigger. A sound at the doorway made him turn, but Aubrey never found out what made the sound. Turning back toward the man with the accent, he barely had time to duck as a red toolbox flew through the air and caught him on the crown of the head.

On his back, blackness filled his line of sight. A heavy weight on top of him forced the air from his lungs. The weight pushed down on him, but also pulled at him, pulled at his weapon. Reflexively, he held tight. Light flickered back into his vision. Flashes came to him. Musty, sweaty odors in his nose. The scene materialized before him.

The thick man had his knee in Aubrey's chest, pulling at his weapon. The man let up to reach for something. Aubrey looked; the toolbox was open. The man grabbed something long and dangerous looking.

Aubrey brought his knee up hard, dislodging the man somewhat. He brought his other leg up and around, throwing it over the man's outstretched arm, pinning him. Aubrey sat up, bringing his rifle to bear when a powerful leg connected with his head.

Dazed and vision blurred, his grip on the man wavered. The two of them twisted on the floor, fighting for dominant position. They wrestled and grappled in close quarters across the room. Bodies too close, grips too tight for Aubrey to bring his weapon into play.

They rolled into the pile of explosives, blocks tumbling onto them. Another blow to the head and stars appeared. His rifle flew from his hands. The man was strong, powerfully built, and a skilled hand to hand fighter. Aubrey was out of practice, his reaction time too slow.

The stout man wriggled free. On his feet now, he lunged for the next room. With head still spinning from the last hit, Aubrey dove at the man as he reached for an object. He slammed his full weight into him, and they crashed into a cold, tiled wall. He twisted and threw the man into a nearby bathtub, leaping on top of him in the process. Then, Aubrey saw his hand. The man had managed to grab what he was reaching for: a large silver and black pistol. The pistol swung toward Aubrey's face, he deflected it with one hand and with the other pressed the man's head hard into the bottom of the tub, grinding his scalp against the cast iron.

A hand found Aubrey's throat; he twisted away and for the first time saw the rest of the bathroom. Tools, spare wires, fuses, and silver blasting caps lay scattered around the room. Lying on top of the toilet, two feet away, was a coil of detonation cord. Six to ten feet of it, he guessed. Attached to one end of it was a silver tube. Hanging from the end of the silver tube was a small ring.

The hand and its iron grip found Aubrey's throat again. This time it would not let go so easily. The hand clenched. Aubrey felt woozy. His vision narrowed. His strength failed him and his hold on the pistol hand slipped. The pistol came down with a blinding crash against the side of his head. Aubrey tottered back. The pistol leveled on him, but with a flailing leg Aubrey knocked it away skittering the gun across the tile floor.

With strength gone and endurance at its end, Aubrey fell forward onto the man. Hands closed on his throat once more. With his left hand he reached out, searching. Seconds passed as his hand felt empty space, swinging wildly in the air. At last, he felt the cold porcelain of the toilet. Blackness descended in his eyes. The rim of the toilet seat. Stars in front of his eyes. The thick cord, in a neat coil, his fingers wrapped around it. His head grew heavy. Now, he had both hands again to push back. Push back he did, against the man's head, neck, and arms.

The world came back into color, his breath freshened in his chest. The man sat up, trying to push Aubrey off balance and gain leverage, but with his head lifted off the bottom of the tub, Aubrey saw his chance. He forced the coil of det cord over the man's fat head, found one end and with both hands, he pulled. Thick hands released Aubrey as they scrambled and tore at the stout cord crushing into flesh, choking blood and breath.

With a stout grip on the cord, Aubrey rolled out of the tub. The big man on the other end of the cord fought like a sailfish. For a moment, Aubrey felt like Santiago from *The Old Man and the Sea.*

With one hand he felt for the silver tube. He twisted the blasting cap to arm it and saw one red light on its side. His finger found the small ring and he let go of the cord; the pin pulled free. The weight of the man fell flat into the tub like the doomed sailfish into the hull of its captor's boat.

A second passed, then the world shook with shock waves and hot wind. Aubrey was thrown across the room as heat and blackness filled the world around him.

22

Unemployed

May 1, 2043

Martin Aubrey cracked one eye open. Bright white light blinded him and he shut it tight again. He was awake for the first time in... he had no idea. How long had it been? His body was stiff and sore as if he'd been run over by a train. His head and neck were one immovable unit, his right thigh itched, and his ears buzzed with a quiet hum. At least he could hear, he thought.

Sounds filled the room—beeping, humming, shuffling of feet. Someone else was in the room with him, but he didn't care. Friend or foe, he didn't care. The air was sterile and cold in his nose. Something lay across his face. A tube. A cold plastic tube... or a cord.

He'd seen a cord not too long ago. A cord on a toilet. Then... then, around a neck. He pulled on the cord. His finger slid through a silver ring. The heat. The noise. An explosion.

Aubrey's eyes shot open. He tore at whatever was on top of him. He pushed at the hands holding him and kicked with stiff legs.

"Whoa, buddy." Aaron Lewis stood lopsided next to Aubrey, arms outstretched. "Settle down, Marty. You're OK now, buddy. We're taking care of you." He spoke in low tones, forcing himself to sound relaxed. Lewis was wearing a hospital gown. The beeping, the humming, the smell, it all made sense. A hospital. Of course, Aubrey thought.

The memories came back to him, now. Running from the car to the firefight inside the old apartment building. The shooting, the pile of explosives, the detonation cord around the man's neck.

Aubrey, calmer now, lay back down. His friend said nothing but winced as he sat in the chair next to the bed. Aubrey watched him for a moment; Lewis watched the TV on the wall with no sound on, reading the subtitles. His gown caught on the chair's arm revealing the large bandage covering the left half of his abdomen. Aubrey remembered seeing him crouched behind the cabinet.

"I'm glad you're not dead," Aubrey croaked with a wooden tongue. He was so thirsty.

"Me too, buddy." Lewis glanced back at Aubrey. With a finger he mimicked the flight of the bullet into his side. "Wound was through and through, but it nicked a couple of important items, so they wanted to observe me for bit." Lewis pulled at his gown, attempting to cover himself better.

"How long have I been in here?" Aubrey stared at the ceiling. It was blank white. That's what he wanted to be right now—just blank. He envied his former self from a few minutes ago, lost in sleep, lost in darkness. He wanted no thoughts of the real world to ink-stain his blank white mind. But he knew it would come. It must come. And it did; Aaron Lewis brought it.

"Couple of days. We found you unconscious, well the medi-drones did. Scanned you through the window and directed the team in. They didn't want to send anyone in with the mountain of explosives they had in there, so Reynolds volunteered to go in. She and a couple of other cops dragged your and Winger's happy asses out of there."

"How's she doing? And Winger... and Grant?"

"Fine. She'll be on light-duty for a few weeks with that blown shoulder, but she'll be alright. Grant and Winger are OK too. Medi-drones got them out of there lickety-split. They're still in recovery, but they'll be fine." Lewis turned to Aubrey with a look of real concern. His friend looked like he'd aged twenty years in the days since the raid. "You on the other hand, we weren't so sure about. The explosion caused you some severe trauma to the head plus the shot to the leg, which barely missed a free bleeder. You were in a medically induced coma up until now. I'm no doctor, but I'd say you were in pretty bad shape."

"I do have quite a headache. I could use one of those dirty beers from Winky's." That filthy hole of a bar felt like the place to be at that moment. "Where's the doctor? When can I get out of here?"

"Listen, I need to talk to you about something." Lewis ignored his question. On the TV, Aubrey saw a tall dark woman appear in front of a large group of reporters. It took a moment to register who he was looking at. The bar at the bottom of the screen identified her as *Acting Chief of Police Chevelle Long*.

"Turn the sound on. Let's hear what she has to say," Aubrey said. His friend groaned and hit a button on the remote control.

"...Very proud of the work of the Metro PD." Her face held a look of somber triumph. "These fine women and men brought down the deadliest network of domestic terrorists our city has ever known. Our hearts and prayers go out to the wounded officers still recovering and the family of our fallen brother, Detective Anthony Baxter."

"Is the city safe, Chief?" asked a reporter in the crowd. "Are you declaring an end to the bombings? And what about BSS?"

"I'm declaring an end to One Front for the People. I can't declare an end to violence in general, but I don't believe the people of this city have anything to fear from OFP any longer."

Lewis muted the television again.

"Why does it say Acting Chief of Police Chevelle Long?" Aubrey turned toward Lewis.

"The old Chief retired the day after the raid... our raid. I heard he had planned it for a while. Just a coincidence that he did it after all of that went down. So, they appointed her as Acting Chief."

Lewis turned his chair to face Aubrey. "Marty, I need to tell you something." Lewis paused as if waiting until he knew he had Aubrey's full attention. "You've been fired from your role as special consultant to the Metropolitan Police Department." Lewis had the look of someone bracing themselves for some verbal thrashing.

Aubrey didn't move or speak for several seconds. "Yeah, I figured."

"You figured?" Lewis leaned back with a look of mixed surprise and relief.

"Yeah, I knew this would happen. I mean it's going to be a hell of a cover up to make it look like I wasn't even in there and I didn't shoot those people or literally blow that guy's head off."

Lewis chuckled and shook his head. "I guess you would have seen this one coming."

"I knew it the moment I got out of the car to come help you. It was an inevitability. Anyway," Aubrey laughed out loud and it felt good, "I was a volunteer, so how can they fire me?"

Nodding in agreement Lewis said, "It sucks though. You directly contributed to finding those assholes and risked your life to stop them. Had you not been there and intervened when you did, there could have been a much bigger explosion than the one you set off to decapitate that piece of shit in the bathtub. We'd all be dead plus all those people in the buildings next door."

On some intellectual level, Aubrey knew all of what Lewis said was true, but he couldn't come to terms with it on an emotional level. Taking credit for his deeds was never his thing. As such, he lay there watching the TV, which now showed the scene of the raid. The raid where he killed six people as a private citizen.

"Nice touch by the way," Lewis said back to the TV again. "Bomb techs said you used det cord to blow that fucker's head off. That's some hardcore shit, man."

Aubrey didn't respond. After a moment, he said, "I guess I should feel lucky I was fired and not zip-tied and sent to the Keep."

"I wasn't going to mention it, but yeah. That's what Chief said."

The two friends, former co-workers, sat in silence watching the silent TV. Each had their own demons to face when they parted company for the night, but for now the presence of a friend made facing those demons seem a little further away and somehow less frightening. Taking life was never easy. Having your own life almost taken was never easy. Watching friends die was never easy. The mental stress that resulted filled the mind like a bucket under a slow faucet, drip by drip. It was when there was time alone with nothing but your thoughts that the sides of the bucket burst under the pressure.

Aubrey had no idea how long it had been when Lewis spoke again. "I was going to wait to tell you, but they found some good stuff at the scene of the raid."

Aubrey spun his head toward Lewis then winced from the pain.

"Yeah, we found a lot of stuff," Lewis continued. "Pins damn near everything on those guys. Bombs, BSS, everything. We're still analyzing all the chemicals they had at the scene. We have to reverse engineer how they used it all for BSS, but we think they used the same chemicals to dose their bombers." Lewis ran a hand through his hair. "They were mercenaries, by the way. Eastern European. They had done work all over the world, according to Interpol." Lewis straightened his gown, which had found the arm of the chair again. "One interesting thing we found was a phone. A burner. Pretty badly damaged in the firefight, but it had some salvageable data."

"Anything worth writing home about?"

"Actually, yeah." Lewis turned his chair to face Aubrey full on. "You know how the tips for those previous raids came from an anonymous caller on the hotline?"

Aubrey sat up in bed. "Yeah…"

"Strangest thing, Marty. The calls into the hotline came from that phone." A knowing look crossed Lewis's face.

"That is strange," Aubrey said.

"I know. I'm only telling you *because* it's so strange. And since we caught the bombers, I don't see why it would hurt to tell you even if you aren't working for us anymore."

"Anything else strange on that phone?"

"Actually, yeah." Lewis paused and fiddled with his gown some more. "The only other activity on that phone were incoming calls. Many, many calls coming in. But only those few outgoing calls, the ones to the hotline."

"And?"

"Another strange thing." Lewis raised his hands and shrugged. "We couldn't figure out where the calls came from. They covered their tracks too well through proxies and what not. So, we don't know much of anything about who was calling that phone, but we do know this: all the incoming calls came from one source. Just one person was calling our mercenaries."

"Who? Who was making those calls?" Aubrey coughed and groaned as a pain sliced through his chest.

"Don't know. They hid the trail too well for us to figure it out. Untraceable, Lee and her team told me. But now that the bombings are over, the Mayor and the new Chief don't care enough to pursue it."

Aubrey sighed as he lay back down on the soft hospital bed, wishing it would all just be over. They sat for a brief pause until Lewis turned to him once more.

"I know it's a lot to take in," Lewis said. "but I have two more things to share. First, we found something else after the raid. Or I should say we *didn't* find something."

"Tell me." Aubrey was tired and sore and didn't feel like playing a guessing game.

"Nothing about the goddamn Z pill. No manifesto, no press

releases, no diary, not a single fucking syllable of printed word or the tiniest megabit of text or anything else about the pill. Now, we're still combing their cloud drives, but, well, there you go."

"If those guys had no interest in the pill..." Aubrey said.

"Then someone else did."

"And the second thing?" Aubrey asked.

"We got word about those scientists at the Keep. The ones you interviewed."

"The Ventana scientists." Aubrey nodded. "What about them?"

"They're dead."

"Dead? Which ones? Alkorn or..."

"All four of them," Lewis said.

Aubrey couldn't believe what he was hearing. He stared at Lewis, hoping this was a joke. "Shit. How? Was it a prison brawl or an accident or what?"

Lewis shook his head. "Tapped."

"Tapped?" The image of the white-haired Tapper in the black cassock came rushing back to him. His gentle voice. His dead eyes. The black gloves covering so much death in his hands.

Aubrey had never heard of a group of financial fraudsters getting Tapped. Then again, no one knew for sure why one prisoner was tapped and another was spared. Only the Tappers themselves knew.

"When?" Aubrey asked.

"Oh, I thought you'd never ask," Lewis said with a grin. "They don't release details like that. You know those Tappers and how secretive they are. But based on what I've been able to piece together, I figure it was about a day or two after you went to see them." Lewis's eyes narrowed and he leaned forward. "Odd timing, don't you think?"

Aubrey had no response. He had no words. He laid back down and glared at the ceiling once more. After a moment, he said, "And you say the bombers were just mercenaries. And there was that caller. Which means..."

"Which means it ain't over, buddy." Lewis threw his legs onto a nearby ottoman. "You've still got a lot of work to do."

"I'm off the job, remember. I don't work for the police anymore."

"Yeah. But I don't see that stopping you," Lewis said. "There is a really bad guy out there somewhere. And I can tell you the new Chief of Police is not interested in hunting for him. Someone else is going to have to catch him."

Aubrey closed his eyes. Lewis was right, the firefight that landed him here in this hospital bed was only the beginning; the job was far from over. He didn't know what he would do next or how he would do it, just that he would. He would carry on until it was over.

But first, he needed some sleep.

Epilogue

June 10, 2043

Deborah Laverno had just finalized the guest list and seating assignments for the annual Symphony Orchestra Gala when her housekeeper Manny went upstairs to wake her son Dominic. This told her the time must be close to 7:00 a.m., which meant she had been finalizing the details of the guest list for the last three and a half hours.

Staring at her computer screen, she reviewed it one last time—dozens of tiny digital headshots with even tinier name tags arranged around two dimensional tables on her screen. With a final sigh and a nod, she was finished. Feeling satisfied with herself, she forwarded the file to her committee members, instructing them to start putting together the formal invitations. As a reward for the hard work it took over the past several weeks for her to get to this point, she decided to treat herself to a cup of Gyokuro tea—her favorite. Leaving her office, full of dark wood antiques and tapestries, she crossed the cavernous and finely appointed foyer through the more spacious and comfortable great room, her soft, bare feet silent on the hard tigerwood floors. She entered the minimalist kitchen with its shiny surfaces and white and gray tones.

In the kitchen she prepared her cup of tea, mentally fussing over the list she just sent. It was the third version of what she kept calling "Final." Again, she found herself worrying about the specific seating of certain guests. The mayor at the head table was a no-brainer, but she wondered if seating him next to the CEO James Sarazin was the best possible placement. That hero cop, an honored guest, and the new Chief of Police should sit together, she thought. Then there were the social welfare philanthropists. Was it a good idea to seat them so near the venture capitalists?

The Symphony Orchestra Gala was the most important event of the fall, bringing high profile guests and their fat wallets from every part of the city. The Gala had a minimum price per plate of twenty thousand dollars, with all proceeds going to support the Metro Children's Hospital—all but honored guests were required to pay full fare. Although the Children's Hospital was an important cause of hers, the objective for perfecting the guest list and seating assignments had little to do with the amount of money they hoped to raise for the children.

The Gala was where the power brokers of the city held court, conceived partnerships, struck deals, and sewed discord. Her husband Simon Laverno was one such broker of power and had the distinct pleasure of being married to her, the Gala's gatekeeper. She was the one person who had final say on who would be invited, at which table they would sit, and where that table was situated in relation to others.

Her role on the Gala's planning committee, although unpaid, imbued her with the kind of power people like her husband held every day. Needless to say, she took a sadistic amount of pleasure in the groveling of who wanted to be counted among the who's who of the city's elite. She also didn't mind the significant monetary benefits that came before, during, and after the groveling. It could not be compared to Simon's financial contributions to their family, but at least it was hers. All hers. The Gala and the power she wielded because of it was one of the most important things in her life, second only to her son.

Sipping her tea, she thought of him. Dominic was seven years old and the love of her life. He had inherited all of her and her husband's best traits with very few of the bad ones. Sweet, funny, and smart, he was so special. She knew every parent thought their kid was special, but in her case it was true. There was no other kid like him. She smiled.

She noticed the time on the refrigerator's clock. It was almost a quarter past seven—they would need to leave soon if Dom was to be on time for school. She glanced across the foyer toward the wide white stairs curving up to the second floor. At this point in the morning, she could usually hear Dom's whining refrain, begging to stay in bed for five more minutes and Manny refusing in his stern tone. Today, however, they were both quiet.

She reached in the pocket of her robes and fished out her mobile phone. Scanning the headlines of the day, she grew bored. Almost every headline was still talking about that ransacking of the last One Front for the People hideout over a month ago. It looked like the cops got it right this time.

The Chief of Police, whose tiny head she had just placed at a table near the speaker's podium, had been everywhere declaring the capture and eradication of OFP. Finally, she thought. She placed her phone on the counter.

She sipped her tea, savoring the rich earthy flavor and enjoying the warmth of it in her hands. She breathed in the steamy aroma, cherishing the rarity of this quiet moment.

Something cut through the quiet. Someone crying. At first, it sounded like Dominic was roused and begging to stay in bed. After several seconds, she realized the crying was not Dominic's.

"Manny?" she called toward the stairs that disappeared above her into the second-floor landing. "Everything OK?"

The crying continued. She crossed the foyer and started up the stairs. The wide marble treads were cold under her feet. As she climbed, the cries grew louder. Four steps from the top of the stairs, she could see across the landing and down the hall. Dominic's door was open and the crying was coming from his room.

The cup of tea clattered to the steps below as she broke into a run. She cursed the oversized home and the extra seconds it would take her to get to her son. She slid to a stop outside Dominic's open door and only just maintained her footing as she swung inside the room.

To her horror, she saw Manny crumpled in a desperate heap next to Dominic's bed. Manny sobbed into one hand with the other resting on Dominic's chest. Deborah rushed to the bedside, crashed to her knees, and threw Manny's hand aside.

"No," she whispered. She couldn't breathe. She felt her eyes burning. Hands shaking. "No. No. No. Not my boy! Not my little boy. Dom? Dominic!" She shouted at her son. She shook him by the shoulders. She threw the blankets off him, hoping to find some reason for the state he was in.

She held his face between her hands and shook him once more. This had no effect, so she pulled a hand away and slapped his cheek. She kept slapping harder and harder and harder. Redness bloomed in splotches where her hand struck. Still no response from the boy. Dom's face didn't flinch, his eyes didn't open.

"Please god, no," she pleaded. "Manny, what's wrong? What happened to him? Did you do something?" She asked these questions in desperation, praying it wasn't true. Praying it was something else. Praying it wasn't what she knew it to be.

"He has it, miss." Manny sobbed into both hands. "He has it. They got him. He has the syndrome."

The Adventure Continues

In...
Executioner's Lament, Book 2 of the Martin Aubrey Series,
now available at most major book retailers.

Get a free preview of *Executioner's Lament* by visiting justinrishel.com.

A Word From Justin

I hope you enjoyed *Every Dying Hour*. It was a lot of fun to write and, since it was my first full-length novel, it holds a special place in my heart. Martin Aubrey was inspired by two of my favorite literary characters—Jack Aubrey and Stephen Maturin, hence the name Martin Aubrey. These two heroes are the main characters in the *Master and Commander* series by Patrick O'Brian. If you haven't read those books, you should. Jack Aubrey is the daring, swashbuckling, master tactician of a sea captain, while Stephen Maturin is the cerebral, intellectual, man of science who serves as Jack's ship surgeon. I couldn't think of a better combination to create a badass, intelligent detective like Martin Aubrey.

Aubrey's story continues in the next book—*Executioner's Lament*. In *Book 2*, we get to further explore the world of the Tappers and the Keep. We also meet a few more characters, like the plucky Malina Maddox, who was an absolute joy to write.

The world of Martin Aubrey will continue from there as I have many adventures in mind for him and the people around him. Please join me as we navigate this exciting universe! To keep up to speed on all things Martin Aubrey and other stories I write, join my mailing list by visiting my website: www.justinrishel.com.

About the Author

Justin is an author of thrillers, science fiction, and technothrillers like the *Martin Aubrey Series*. Before becoming a writer, Justin was a U.S. Marine, a high school history teacher, a woodworker, and a corporate schmuck.

Born and raised in Long Beach, Mississippi, Justin now lives in Tennessee with his family.

You can connect with me on:

- https://www.justinrishel.com
- http://www.twitter.com/jrishelauthor
- https://www.facebook.com/justinrishelauthor

CPSIA information can be obtained
at www.ICGtesting.com
Printed in the USA
BVHW070230181221
624424BV00005B/245